Praise for W

"Angelo Cannavacciuolo ha
and this novel may be hi
ful. *When Things Happen* shows prodigious range, setting the
rich and coddled across a café table from hardscrabble slum
dwellers. It's a portrait in the round, shot through with
compassion and stirring poetry. Overall, it feels like Elena
Ferrante's entire Neapolitan Quartet wrapped up in one,
illuminating both a city unlike any other and a whole world
tormented by the rift between Haves and Have-nots."

—John Domini, author of *Earthquake I.D.*

"*When Things Happen* is a vivid story suffused by the indifferent air of Naples. Gregory Pell's translation captures the
urgency of Cannavacciuolo's prose as he reminds us of how
the unexpected encounter with innocence can draw us back
to the refuse of our own childhoods."

—Rebecca R. Falkoff, author of *Possessed:*
A Cultural History of Hoarding

"From Raffaele La Capria to Fabrizia Ramondino and to
Domenico Starnone, we now have Angelo Cannavacciuolo's view of Naples from a triple perspective that includes
and integrates class, identity, and the harsh reality of urban
life. Boldly unmitigated, *When Things Happen* offers a unique
and necessary version of Naples to the non-Italian reader."

—Anthony Julian Tamburri, author of *Re-Reading*
Italian Americana: Specificities and Generalities on
Literature and Criticism

"There is no refuge in Cannavacciuolo's captivating novel,
and yet it is so difficult to put down. You want to know

where it's going, you need to get there, and you'll do so in a story that wrenches your heart and shows you a city you might not have found in any other book before."

—Barbara Alfano, author of *The Mirage of America in Contemporary Italian Literature and Film*

"*When Things Happen* is a mesmerizing tale that explores the intricate layers of human relationships and the cost of leaving one's roots behind. An eloquent portrayal of society's stark inequalities and a poignant portrayal of a man's quest for identity, Cannavacciuolo's novel is a must-read for anyone in search of a captivating story. He reminds us of the importance of understanding our own histories and of the potential for connection and growth even in the most unexpected places."

—Diana Abu-Jaber, author of *Fencing with the King: A Novel*

Praise for the Italian Edition

"Cannavacciuolo is accomplished at vibrating the delicate string of his tired heroes—inveterate dreamers who, though vanquished, look forward to that moment when they will regain everything . . . His pages are crafted with the skill of an artisan and with the love of someone maniacally dedicated to them, because every word, every turn of phrase rewards the attentive reader with a world, a whole universe governed by the iron law of truth."

—Marco Lombardi, *La Repubblica*

"In these pages, we realize that Cannavacciuolo's narrative engine is marked by his obsession with the presence of suffering in the world and by the moral obligation to portray it—to translate it into words."

—Generoso Picone, *Il Mattino*

"An interesting, incandescent book that offers a ruthless examination of the same Neapolitan reality in which it directly participates."

—Mauro Trotta, *Il Manifesto*

"Cannavacciuolo has written a jarring novel, set in his own Naples, of which, in unexpurgated fashion, he observes and describes the most problematic aspects, such as the divide between the rich bourgeoisie and the working classes that are in perpetual difficulty."

—Roberto Carnero, *Famiglia Cristiana*

"*When Things Happen* is a touching and unconventional journey into the heart of Naples. It is a novel that reveals a great virtue: the sociological acumen to acknowledge the contemporary underclasses in Italy . . . It is a novel written about a society from the bottom up."

—Filippo La Porta, *Left*

"*When Things Happen* is a book of debris . . . because it burrows deep into everything that Michele Campo had previously expunged from his life."

—Beatrice Manetti, *L'Indice*

"This is the story of two Naples: the one of daily trafficking and crime, with no expectations of anything better; the other a deaf, indifferent world of the bourgeois, incapable of solidarity and civic commitment. Michele Campo knows both: he was born in the first; he wants to belong to the latter at all costs."

—Cinzia Tralicci, *Il Tempo*

"In his fourth novel, more than just a narrator of storylines, Angelo Cannavacciuolo confirms himself as a narrator of emotions and states of mind."

—Ermanno Paccagnini, *Il Corriere della Sera*

When Things Happen

Titles in the **Other Voices of Italy** series:

Other Voices of Italy: Italian and Transnational Texts in Translation

Editors: Alessandro Vettori, Sandra Waters, Eilis Kierans

This series presents texts in a variety of genres originally written in Italian. Much like the symbiotic relationship between the wolf and the raven, its principal aim is to introduce new or past authors—who have until now been marginalized—to an English-speaking readership. This series also highlights contemporary transnational authors, as well as writers who have never been translated or who are in need of a fresh/contemporary translation. The series further aims to increase the appreciation of translation as an art form that enhances the importance of cultural diversity.

The present novel explores the exploitation, marginalization, and poverty (both cultural and economic) that has plagued southern Italy for centuries, which not even the financial boom of the mid-1900s managed to improve, let alone erase. *When Things Happen* highlights the haphazard nature of human destiny when the protagonist Michele Campo comes into contact with a foster child named Martina. Suddenly confronted with the past he believed to have left behind thanks to a professional career and a comfortable middle-class life he painstakingly built for himself, Michele will come to the realization that the proletarian roots he sought to eradicate are still alive in all their force and fury. He has no choice but to relive painful memories and to try to find a place in a family he never knew he had. An artful, existential investigation of the complex relationship between past and present, the novel explores sociological, cultural, and anthropological issues while highlighting the brutal and uncompromising beauty of Neapolitan life.

When Things Happen

A Novel

ANGELO CANNAVACCIUOLO

Translated by Gregory Pell

Foreword by Jay Parini

Rutgers University Press

New Brunswick, Camden, and Newark, New Jersey

London and Oxford

Rutgers University Press is a department of Rutgers, The State University of
New Jersey, one of the leading public research universities in the nation. By
publishing worldwide, it furthers the University's mission of dedication to
excellence in teaching, scholarship, research, and clinical care.

Library of Congress Cataloging-in-Publication Data

Names: Cannavacciuolo, Angelo, author. | Pell, Gregory M.
(Gregory Michael), translator. | Parini, Jay, writer of foreword.
Title: When things happen : a novel / Angelo Cannavacciuolo ;
translated by Gregory Pell ; foreword by Jay Parini.
Other titles: Cose accadono. English
Description: New Brunswick : Rutgers University Press, 2023. | Series:
Other voices of Italy | Includes bibliographical references and index.
Identifiers: LCCN 2023007460 | ISBN 9781978837102 (paperback ; alk. paper) |
ISBN 9781978837119 (hardcover ; alk. paper) | ISBN 9781978837126 (epub) |
ISBN 9781978837133 (pdf)
Subjects: LCGFT: Novels.
Classification: LCC PQ4903.A56 C6713 2023 | DDC 853/.92—dc23/
eng/20230224
LC record available at https://lccn.loc.gov/2023007460

References to internet websites (URLs) were accurate at the time of writing.
Neither the author nor Rutgers University Press is responsible for URLs that
may have expired or changed since the manuscript was prepared.

rutgersuniversitypress.org

For Martina and Enzo, whoever you are.
For my mother and my father.

May your cradle be as swaying as the sea so that you, nurtured by
the lullaby that urges you to journey, might turn your gaze to us
without reproach.... We have had to explore the boundaries of
what divided us, what weighed down upon us. But you, as a poet
from around my parts used to say, should never know
exasperation, yearning, or resentment.... May no tragedy
befall you and may you have an easy life.
—Francesco Biamonti

Contents

Foreword

Although widely known and admired in Italy, Angelo Cannavacciuolo has not yet been translated into English, and this novel—his fourth, published in 2008 to considerable acclaim—marks a beginning. It heralds the introduction of an important voice, one that should have resonance with American readers, as it deals with issues that have become so crucial in recent years, including the clash of social classes and the desperate search for identity in a bewildering time, our contemporary postmodern world, where all certainties—religious, familial, political, and ethical—have apparently been swept away.

This is also a novel of place. *When Things Happen* offers readers familiar with Naples only through the ultrapopular novels of Elena Ferrante a wholly new take on life in this ancient and important city, with its complex and teeming life. Naples, for Cannavacciuolo, is very much a real, living place—anyone who reads a few pages of this book will see what I mean; but it is also a place that, like Faulkner's Mississippi, has universal appeal, as it is a playground for every class of society, a place where history meets contemporary life at every turn, where everything and nothing is sacred.

The narrator here, Michele Campo, mentions in passing the novels of Philip Roth, drawing attention in particular to the character of Coleman Silk in *The Human Stain*, one of Roth's later books. The allusion is brief, almost incidental, but it becomes substantial, offering a subtle key to the novel's deeper meaning. Silk, in Roth's unnerving story, was a light-skinned Black man who lived a life of hiding in plain sight, "passing" in a way that is painful and real. The same might be said of Michele, who "passes" for a gentleman of the upper classes, shifting among the wealthy and sophisticated layers of Neapolitan society, with its glittering villas on Capri, its intellectual debates, its dinner parties, and social engagements. But as the reader soon discovers, Michele does not come from this environment, which is really the world of his partner, Costanza, who has lived her life as part of an elite bourgeois world. Far from it, he's the child of the countryside, a world of goatherds and hardscrabble living, where sophisticated conversation and elegant dinners are unimaginable.

Michele's father got a job in a posh building in Naples, as a doorman, creating dissonance in his family. In moving (however awkwardly) into a wider world, he opens a figurative door for his son, who gets a glimpse of life in the higher echelons, where, indeed, he develops a taste for this life, which, ironically, becomes a source of dissatisfaction as he moves into middle age. Having become a speech pathologist with a gift for working with children as well as those who come from less fortunate backgrounds, he cannot but help encountering his past, however obliquely. This work reflects the inner turmoil that burns at the center of his character, and his restlessness reminds me of so many characters in Roth or Saul Bellow: dangling men who are out of sorts with their environments, living on the edge of quiet despair as they attempt to reconcile aspects of their lives that finally defy the act of reconciliation.

Oftentimes, an unexpected encounter leads a "hero" or protagonist into a fresh consideration of his or her life, and here, that encounter happens when Michele meets Martina, a child of five, whose plight begins to tug at his heart. He comes upon her by chance while visiting a foster home called Little Rabbit House, which is just outside the city. Michele already had been filled with a strange premonition, believing that the day he met Martina was not like other days in his life. He was drowning (unbeknownst to himself) in a metaphorical swamp. He needed to be rescued, though he is scarcely able to imagine that this rescue might come from "an awkward little girl with a bony, emaciated face." The child, indeed, reminded me not so much of any children in Roth but, in fact, the poor children who inhabit a shelf of novels by Charles Dickens.

And just as Dickens is a novelist of London, with a special gift for seeing its overpopulated and gritty aspects, Cannavacciuolo is a novelist of Naples, drawn to its harsher sides without needing to condemn them wholesale. His novel reveals the underside of this teeming Italian city in a way reminiscent of such writers as Roberto Saviano, Valeria Parrella, or Domenico Starnone. We see many sides of Naples in this novel, too: the glittering life of the Vomero neighborhood stands, for instance, in direct contrast to the cement jungles—those rundown, dangerous, and filthy suburbs where the Neapolitan poor wander in clouds of poverty, violence, and alienation.

As with any good novel of this kind, there are family secrets in *When Things Happen*, and these plague our narrator, Michele, who, through the encounter with Martina, is afforded the chance to unpack these mysteries. The novel becomes, in the end, an elaborate psychodrama, deeply self-revelatory, and riveting as well. In the sharp, succinct, and intelligent prose of translator Gregory Pell, this novel comes alive on the page in English, opening a door to American readers that, I hope, many will choose to walk through.

Jay Parini
Middlebury College

When Things Happen

Prologue

There had always been a lot of people betting on me. Word had it that I had the right stuff—that is, if I had wanted to, my attributes could have taken me anywhere. So, that excessive confidence in my abilities led me to believe that if I worked hard and had fortune on my side—perhaps also aided by a certain optimism, which I had—in one way or another, I would have succeeded. I would have made it, despite the many obstacles to contend with around these parts and notwithstanding the fact that I had not started off—how shall I say?—with a rosy future ahead of me.

So, comforted by the hopes of others and by my own wishful thinking, I steered my boat toward the safe harbor of a peaceful life, a stable job, a roof over my head, and God willing, a wife and kids. After all, I wasn't asking for the moon, though in the shadow of Vesuvius, even a reasonable goal might be a pipe dream. And I knew it. Yet what I couldn't have known was that, in order to realize my ambitions, throughout my whole life, I would have to find a place in which to take shelter from those things that just happen. In other words, a place that didn't exist—or, rather, an imaginary place where I would always hear the sad yet cheerful music of life as though it were background noise. For quite some time, it was like being there and not being there at the same time. I mean, I was there because my destiny was to be there, but I wasn't there because I always avoided any sort of developments by hiding behind my many masks of nonchalance. However directly or indirectly certain facts related to me, they barely touched me. But if someone were to ask me the reason why I remember what happened—around the time I was turning forty—I would simply reply that one fine day, in the process of trying to make sense of the voices bombarding me from every direction, the whole world collapsed around me, thereby reawakening me from a long hibernation.

Michele Campo

~ 1 ~

The same thing would happen to Martina. The awareness of it seemed to be plotting with fate against me. At a highway rest stop, my eyes glanced at a newspaper left on one of the little tables in the café, and then, straining to see into the future, I saw the horizon blurred by large, dark clouds of misery. A drum started beating inside my head, and my heart felt as though it wanted to rip through my chest and flee.

Since that morning there had been some signs—the kind of details that often slip away from our attention and that we think about only in retrospect after realizing their ominous significance. I paid no mind to Costanza's words when she spoke about the sky portending sadness, nor the look she shot me as she greeted me by the front door, and I certainly thought nothing of the rainstorm that started to pour down right after. They were just details and I didn't give them a second thought.

"Hello, Counselor Serra? This is Michele Campo. Unfortunately, I've run into trouble. I'm on the highway . . . yes, with this rain . . . and my Vespa broke down. . . . How did I do it? I had to push it myself. . . . To tell you the truth, I don't feel well. It could be a fever. . . . Okay. . . . Yes, next Tuesday at five. Have the girl's grandmother and her husband arrived yet? . . . Oh, so can you tell them that I won't be able to make it? . . .'kay, see you Tuesday."

For an instant I felt relieved, almost freed of the burden of those responsibilities that had loomed over my miserable condition for quite some time. Then something rather nondescript had intervened. Maybe it was that feeling of oppression that had been with me for a while; perhaps it was the fever that was threatening to burn up my thoughts as well. One thing for sure, though: that newspaper opened up on that table tethered me to its dark premonitions. The more I read that article, the more I was overtaken by chills. I was shaking from head to toe.

Meanwhile the rain beat down loudly from the sky with dense, cutting bursts, which would come and go as the wind changed direction. With headlights on, cars sprayed sheets of water onto the shoulders of the road. On an electoral poster a young candidate from our region, paying no mind to the weather, raised a fist, indicating the upright determination that a faint smile on his face wasn't able to convey. With his good-guy demeanor, he seemed to be provoking a challenge with the man on the poster next to him; the other guy's sideways glance seemed to suggest that he would have swallowed the first guy in one bite.

The atmosphere on the highway was gray. Barely illuminating it on either side were rows of yellow streetlights, one after the other, like frozen little souls watching over a new day that was determined to die.

The old gas station attendant, bundled up in his yellow plastic rain gear, trudged from the pumps to the cars with the pained expression of someone likely plagued by arthritis.

The percentage of children removed from their original families through precautionary injunctions issued by the juvenile court is on the rise; many, in fact, will never return home. They are destined for a long pilgrimage involving shelters, group homes, or short-term care centers; temporary custody with relatives or available foster families; even adoptions. When these measures fail, they are reunited. Upon turning eighteen, if they have not found a nuclear family to take them in or are forced to leave the program, they find themselves free, alone, and with a body full of rage. So they look around with scared, suspicious eyes and see a potential ambush lying around every corner. They will never see a single honest face that they can trust. Behind every promise or helping hand, they will see betrayal forever lurking. These children's stories are a jumble of painful events. There is sixteen-year-old Manuela. Her mother died of AIDS. Her father found another woman. With two foster care stints behind her, she says she loves no one. She prefers to stay at the group home, where she has been living for three months, because there, no one will ask her to reciprocate the affection they claim they feel for her. Luca, on the other hand, has spent the last three of his short nine years in a group home; in the beginning he would eat the dirt from the garden. Then there is eleven-year-old Matteo, who extracted one of his teeth with a screwdriver. And Maria, thirteen, who started cutting herself with a razor blade.

The article ended with some testimonials by some professional social workers and a series of numbers, statistics, and percentages about methods of abandonment, short-term care options, as well as permanent ones.

My head sank between my shoulders. I was floundering in a sea of despair. I had never given much credence to coincidences, or at least, each time that I had experienced one, I could never take too much stock in their prophesizing powers. When things happen, they just happen, and that's that, I thought. It's just a simple matter of cause and effect.

And the results of that investigative report, reinforcing my earlier convictions, amounted to what could be—as sad as it might sound—an apt conclusion to Martina's whole story: an accurate reflection of her future.

One day, she will end up joining the ranks of lost children. Having become the children of no one, those kids will cut their flesh to alleviate the pain; they will be passed around from one home to the next; they will fall asleep in the semi-darkness of cold rooms adorned by a few tawdry icons of happiness. They will reawaken, crying over the disappearance of their own shadow, as it dissolves away in the morning, along with their dreams. So they'll rack their brains to make sense of things. They'll wander through the streets, fuming with anger and resentment until the end of their days, and eventually they'll fizzle out.

It will happen to Martina, too.

But does being born like her necessarily mean ending up like that? And was her brief life truly at risk? Had threats gathered like storm clouds on her horizon to the point that they would change the dimensions of her existence? These were questions for which I could not hazard even a shred of an answer. I only knew that one day, someone whom she had never met before, whose voice she had never heard, the existence of whom she could not even imagine, had decided that the lot she'd received from life was not worthy of her. Who knows who had decided that her being born from her particular mother meant being suspended in limbo? It was a world in which, though you might be alive, you didn't truly exist. Sort of like being only half-born.

~ 2 ~

The winter during which fate threatened to commandeer her future and mine was so bitterly cold that for quite a long time Vesuvius took on the look of one of those perennially snow-capped Japanese mountains; and then came the torrential rains and cloudbursts. It was the winter—in soccer terms—of Napoli's tragic descent, after the splendor of "El Pibe de Oro" (aka Maradona), into the circle of hell known as Serie C; and in the country at large, the winter was a colossal orgy of reality shows like *The Farm*, *Celebrity Island*, and *Big Brother*, which was airing in who knows which season by then. It was also the winter in which the imminent regional elections promised salvation, if only we embraced Berlusconi's *way of life*. It was March 2005.

I had met Martina roughly a year earlier, in a foster home, called "Little Rabbit House," just outside the city where I had gone to help a seven-year-old boy with a speech issue. Initially I paid little attention to the somber hues that shrouded his world, even though I had been familiar with such cases for some time.

It was a tepid late-April morning, and the temperate weather blossomed as if by magic. Down the street, I already had the tickling sensation that the day would not be like all the others. Not so much because of the intrusion of a strange event, but because, for an unexpected instant, I was pulled from the swamp in which I was floundering. It was like a premonition that had suddenly made a breach in my life. It was like an intuition, a mirage, a hope that came knocking on the door of my daily routine, ensuring me at least a glimmer of happiness. I had experienced it once before, and I knew how it would end. All told, I felt oddly relieved: as usual, the long-awaited event would not materialize. It would always happen that way—no big deal. Instead, what I loved was the joy of anticipation. I've always considered it a gift that resides in the brief space of a long moment: it leads you on, seduces you, and deceives you. And it bestows you with a smidgen of happiness.

"Doctor, Enzino is a bit nervous, but he's actually a sweet, quiet child. He was so excited that last night he didn't sleep. Just think: I found him in the kitchen at six, already washed and dressed. After breakfast he sat down here and started waiting for you." Miss Clara, the director of the group foster home, didn't skimp on words. "Enzino, say 'hello.' . . . Come on, look up, say 'hello' to the doctor," she added, turning to the child.

She welcomed me into the kitchen, fidgeting as though she were dancing on hot coals. She seemed to be about fifty, and her most obvious trait was her rapid-fire, impulsive, and anxious talkativeness, likely owing to a mild form of neurosis commonly called tachylalia. Stout and sturdy on her muscular legs, that woman appeared well equipped to look after a brood of little children who were rather disinclined to follow rules but brimming with energy.

"That's fine. There's no rush. We will get to know each other gradually."

Miss Clara poured some espresso in a cup and offered it to me, as she sang the praises of the facility. She told me about the business that she ran along with her husband, about the myriad problems, and above all, about the "devotion" with which she dedicated herself to "less fortunate children."

"But you probably have no idea what I go through. . . . I spend my life between baby food and diapers, between lullabies and fairy tales . . . and holding tiny hands before the youngest ones fall asleep. And then there is the tutoring . . . and the after-school programs for the older ones. And breakfast and lunch and dinner. You know, sometimes they show up here crying in the arms of a police officer, after an ugly separation from their mother, or directly from the hospital where they've been abandoned just after birth. You see, then my heart skips a beat. Definitely! Because I know every aspect of these things. I can't just think about their physical needs. No, sir! But also about winning over their trust, making them feel that someone in this world cares about them. It means becoming their guide. I am the person whom they meet in their new situation, and when they see me, they almost seem happy. The ones who are a little older, they know what's going on around them; they're ready to deal with anything . . . not just from me and from my husband but also from my colleagues. . . . Yup, because we have a couple of professionals working alongside us—a couple of really good guys. The children grow attached right away. They like it here . . ."

I had made a futile attempt to interrupt Miss Clara's monologue with signs of a question, but she seemed entirely immune to dialogue.

"Anyway, we are not equipped for when they are older. We accept children up to ten years old. This is just a transitional place. Then they have to move on. They either go back to their homes or they go to a new family. Of course, when they leave, it hurts, but when I imagine them in the future, I'm sure that they'll remember me."

With downcast eyes, little Enzino was tracing the red and green checks on the tablecloth, his arms leaning on the table as if to guard the coffee cup in front of him. He sat motionless with a subdued exhaustion in his eyes. Maybe he was pursuing that terrible dream he'd just had: men dressed in black were rummaging through everything and yelling; a woman was throwing herself from a balcony into the unknown; mice and cockroaches were roaming through the house fixing their wicked eyes on him. He'd spent too many days alone staring into space. Or maybe he had absorbed too much darkness during those nights spent looking up at the black ceiling.

Suddenly, with a twitch of his arm, he knocked over the coffee cup.

"Enzino, what are you doing?" said Miss Clara, jumping up. "The morning's off to a great start!" she added, busying herself with a dishcloth.

Raising his head with vacuous eyes, the child stared at the woman and then at me.

Was it a ploy for demanding our overdue attention? A sample of the fear he carried inside of him? A call for help? Perhaps none of those things; just a scared child and a knocked-over coffee cup. At any rate, his action had proven providential in pulling me from the endless flow of chatter emanating from that woman so intent on impressing me.

"I-I-I w-w-wan-t to g-go ovv-ver th-there," said Enzino, lifting his skinny arm.

A sharp and playful voice was coming from the next room. Two children were chasing after a ball.

"There, you see? You wanna tell me it doesn't take patience?" the woman grumbled, slapping herself on the thighs.

Noticing that it was time to begin therapy, I motioned Enzino to the hallway. With his hand clasped in mine, I happened to think of one of the most overused maxims over the course of my training as a speech-language pathologist: every action corresponds to an equal but opposite reaction. I speculated that the more Miss Clara gushed forth in her fast-paced, incomprehensible babble, the more tongue-tied that boy became. Could it be that the child with the sad smile was spiting her? I was barely able to contain the laughter in my throat. If only it had been that easy. Unfortunately, Enzino was affected by a considerable alteration in his discourse fluency. In other words, he was a stutterer. And no mother, now or ever, would have had the power to heal him.

He was seven, and his problems had manifested themselves right after the tragic event that would scar him forever. I knew that sort of impediment: most of the time, it originated from traumas experienced in early childhood, and recovery could be slow and laborious. At times impossible, even.

Just one day earlier, on the phone, Miss Clara had told me his whole story.

Enzino lived with his mother in one of those cement beehives that everyone around here calls the *Vele*, the Sails, in the residential community of Secondigliano, where people surf the short wave of survival. One day the police burst into his apartment and carried off his mother, a young drug addict without a husband who was selling heroin out of her house. Trained to sniff out moments of danger and to carry out to the letter what she had taught him, Enzino had sought refuge in an attic crawl space as soon as the sudden uproar at the door and his mother's screams had unleashed all hell. He had stayed there until the dark of night, perfectly still, his heart in his throat, almost without breathing, so as not to give away his location. In the following two weeks he had remained hidden, shuddering at the slightest sound. However, as evening came, he would walk around the house on his tippy-toes, feeding on whatever leftovers he could find.

Then, someone had remembered him. They had found him skin and bones, terrorized by human voices.

I would not call Enzino a quiet child. Quietness is peacefulness. Tranquility. When you lower life's volume. But when you press the button to turn off life completely, all that's left is silence. Enzino's was the silence of someone who had chosen to take shelter in a dark corner and didn't want anything to do with the world outside.

We had gone off into a more discreet corner of the dining room: the large room was inundated by light, children were playing and running noisily all around us, but the cheerfulness didn't affect him. Sitting before me in silence, with his head up and his arms folded across his chest, he appeared absorbed in some thought much greater than he. Like a person who, used to deprivation, subjects himself to someone much stronger in hopes of garnering himself goodwill. His face was that of a child forced to mature; he had a nervous smile, and he led me to believe that the burden of sacrifice was nothing new to him. He stared at me, overwhelmed, and just waited, with those big pleading eyes. But maybe that's just what I wanted to see in him. Maybe it was just a child before me.

I began the therapy by delineating the problem in order to assess a plan of immediate action and to verify the degree of response to precise stimuli.

"Give me your hands."

He would give me his hands.

"Squeeze my hands."

He would squeeze my hands.

"Close your eyes."

And he would close them.

"Open your mouth."

And he would do it.

"Now close it."

And he got it.

"Again."

And he would keep going.

"Now stick out your tongue."

And there was his tongue.

"Again. Again. Now breathe deep."

He would breathe deep.

I lit a candle to observe an emission of air. I placed it in front of him and told him to blow without putting it out. He started to choke.

"Don't be afraid. I'm right here. Repeat . . . 'Mama.'"

"Mmm-amm-mma . . ."

"Papa."

"Ppp-ap-ppa"

"House."

"H-h-hou-s-se."

His face turned red.

"Breathe, breathe . . . It's nothing. . . . Again . . . 'Mama.'"

"Mmm-amm . . . ahahaha . . ."

He let out a heart-wrenching scream. And his eyes were begging for mercy. I held him in my arms.

"Don't be afraid. I'm right here. Don't be afraid."

Out of carelessness or distraction, I happened to look up toward Martina. I couldn't help thinking that the environment and the experiences that we had in our early childhood and then in our adolescence leave a permanent mark on us. What I could never have suspected, though, is that that awkward little girl with a bony, emaciated face might use a proverbial sledgehammer to wake me from a long sleep into which I had let myself fall.

I hadn't realized right away that via a reflection in the large mirror fixed to the wall in front of me, that strange little animal, terrified and benumbed, with such a paltry frame that she seemed to be swimming in her tiny clothes, was taking pleasure in shooting me a look that was quite unusual for a five-year-old girl. It was a look full of hatred that could turn the blood in your veins to ice. Yet, the toughness in that look stunned me no less than the words that came out of her mouth soon after, when one of the little girls, tired from playing, invaded her territory.

"Don't break my balls, you slut. . . . Ya hear? You make my head hurt!"

And in an instant she placed her hands on her throat.

A young teacher, not far away and in the middle of a "Ring around the Rosie" with some children, got there just in time. He lifted her up and released the other girl from her clutches.

"*Lasseme stà, omme 'e merda . . . lasseme stà!* Lemme go, ya piece a shit . . . lemme go!"

With arms thrashing about, she got loose by kicking, screaming and spitting venom. Having slinked into a corner, between the credenza and the sofa, she started to stare blankly beyond the porch lit up by sunlight, just for a moment before she went back to peeking at me through the mirror's reflection with her dark pupils.

The festive environment that had welcomed me a few hours earlier had suddenly changed. Everything went silent, including the laughter and the tantrums. I sensed the sudden disappearance of the pleasant aroma of cookies that children dunk in their morning milk; same thing for the smell of soap that they would use for washing. Even the warmth of little Enzino squeezing my hand eluded me.

Miss Clara sprung furiously out of the kitchen.

"Martina, how many times must I tell you that you can't behave that way?! We don't say bad words, and we don't put our hands on our foster siblings. Now apologize, otherwise I'll punish you."

"Go fuck ya'self!" she mumbled, crouched down like a wounded beast.

The woman moved like a shot. With a hip check, she moved the sofa out of the way and, harpooning her forcefully with one arm, she pulled her away. Martina didn't say a word. All she could do, while that woman dragged her out dangling in the air, was make sure she hurled that hateful glance my way one more time.

From the other end of the house you could hear, "Now you'll stay in your room until you apologize to your little sister."

Then a door slammed.

The time for our therapy session ended amid chaos, Enzino's sweating, and a few choruses of teasing that froze him up even more:

"*Cacagliooo, Enzino è nu cacagliooo*. . . . A stutter! Enzino's got a stutter. . . ."

In my attempt to get familiarized with him, I decided to stay a bit longer. The situation was getting difficult: to obtain some sort of acceptable result would have taken at least a year, but I would have done very little without a good psychologist intervening at each step to heal the other wounds he had. Had Miss Clara taken that into account? Would any time be set aside for that? More than once, right in the middle of a course of therapy, I had seen a patient slip out of my hands, transferred to another facility or placed in custody of a new father or mother, without being able to enjoy even slight progress or knowing he was on the right path.

In the doorway, taking my leave from the long-winded Miss Clara, who kept on unperturbed in her small talk, I glimpsed Martina's face peeping out into the half light of the hallway. Her eyes seemed different. There was no trace of the prior anger.

"So, Doctor, we'll see you in three days. . . ."

"Good-bye!" I said and headed out. But before I could take one step, I turned abruptly. "Listen, that little girl . . ."

"Martina?" she replied, reopening the door.

"Yes!"

"Did you hear those vulgar things come out of her mouth? How long has she been with you here?"

"A couple of months. When she got here, she was . . . what can I say . . . a little animal. All in all, from a hygienic standpoint, not well kept. Her genital regions were all red, and she complained of constant headaches. Seriously, it's only been a short time since those stopped. Even now, it's touch and go: at times uninhibited, other times she's quite sad. You know how she answered when one of my colleagues discovered that she would put objects in her vagina? She said that her grandfather used to touch her there. And when we tried to investigate further, she replied, 'Go ask them. Granpa and granma know, go ahead, go. . . . I won't tell you a thing.'"

"I felt she was quite aggressive. . . ."

"If you only knew what her family was like. And let's not even discuss the grandmother. . . . Since Martina has been here, it's been hell. This woman, if we can call her that, doesn't observe visitation days or the schedules, and it's a major undertaking to get rid of her. She insists on staying with the girl more than her allotted time. Not only does she want to take her out, unaccompanied, but she constantly whispers in her ear, and when our workers intervene, she resists. And that's when the abusive language and insults start to fly. . . . You can imagine what might come out of her mouth. Just think, it was the grandmother who told the little girl to not let the others push her around and that if anyone hurt her, she should react. That woman can't get it through her head that this is not an after-school program. She calls me nonstop to know whether Martina has had the medical visits ordered by the judge. For Martina, meeting up with her grandmother and her aunt, who does nothing but chew her nails when she comes over, is quite unpleasant. The girl's mother, on the other hand, has never shown up once at these visits. All I know is that she is a young woman with serious problems. Anyway, these two women spend all their time inveighing against me and the caseworkers present at the visits, making threats, and screaming. And when Martina starts to cry, they give her false hope, saying that they know what to do to get her back home. . . . Again, a living hell."

Below, in the street, while I was getting into my car, my gaze wandered up and over the fence railing, made way through the bushes in the yard, and met with Martina's, up above me. She just stood there fixated on me, her hands clinging to the rail, barely a shadow behind the balcony's ironwork. I smiled. She did not.

Overhead, in the enormity of the sky, a cluster of wild clouds played tag in a vast expanse of blue. The sun had become warmer and its light more dazzling. The scent of cyclamens mixed with the salty air that was coming from the nearby coast.

It had to have been Enzino's eyes that were pleading for mercy, or Martina's that offered nothing but hate—or maybe even that springlike warmth that was luring me into happiness—that sent me all aflutter. Or, more simply, the call of the sea, which I reached by car in a few minutes. The fact is that I found myself walking on the deserted beach counting each and every sparkle of sunlight shimmering among the waves.

The apparent state of grace that had coddled me since the morning had dissipated just as quickly as it had come, leaving behind it the faded tracks of my footfalls on the sand. In the glimmer of those hours, seated on the hollowed-out trunk of driftwood with a bad taste in my mouth, I prayed for it to return. Meanwhile, along the water's edge, a meager colony of little crabs, scampering through the foam, would disappear and reappear in the ebb and flow of the tide.

~ 3 ~

The intense downpour that had been unleashed over the city was showing no signs of stopping, much less of diminishing in intensity. It just refused to let up. The streets were swept over by a cold wind, and the rain seemed to be flooding everything.

Upon returning home, I had quickly left a message for Costanza on the kitchen table. I let her know my state of health and of my intention to stay in bed and sleep. Taking care to not make much noise—by then, an hour or so must have passed—she entered the room amid the folds of darkness to check in on my condition.

"So? How do you feel?" she said, leaning over the bed.

As I turned, I made out her profile against the faint light of the candle that she had brought up to my face. And for a moment, an alarming sense of precariousness overtook me, as though she too, like a dream, might vanish from one moment to the next.

"I think you've got a touch of fever," she observed, touching my forehead. "It's better that we stay home this evening. . . ."

"Nahhh, I can do it. Don't worry."

"Where do you think you're going? . . . Can't you see that you're burning up?"

"And the concert? You've been looking forward to it for a month," I replied while planting my feet on the floor and resting my face in my hands. "Why don't you turn on the light?" I added.

"There's no power. When I arrived, it was already out. The street was dark. With this rain, all the power must be out," said Costanza, momentarily preceding some rumbling from the sky.

I stood up and made my way to the window with hopes that the whole afternoon spent at the rest stop off the highway was just the product of a recent dream. I struggled to believe that just a few hours earlier I was going to see Counselor Serra; that my Vespa really had broken down on the road; that I had pushed it all the way to the service area under that downpour; and above all that I might have even hazarded a prediction about Martina's future. Outside, in the meantime, the sheer darkness made me think of a gigantic black hole that was about to gather every last trace of life in its gaping maw: people, roads, buildings, and that strip of sea that could be seen from the window, including Capri on the horizon. Only the caterwauling of car alarms, which kept coming on and going off one after the other, gave any signs of hope.

"You know that stand of orange trees down in the piazza?" Costanza asked. "The one right above the supermarket . . ."

"The hanging garden!" I added, without facing her.

"Yes! The very one. It's gone. It collapsed onto the street with the entire embankment. What a disaster. While I was coming home, I saw the firemen working tirelessly to free the cars from a sinkhole. It seems that someone might still be down there. But the incredible thing is that the palm tree . . . you know the palm tree? It's still standing. How can it be? A retaining wall crumbles, an entire garden with a greenhouse full of flowers falls down, and a palm tree nearly forty feet tall is the lone one standing, there, in the middle of the cement."

All of a sudden, even the room plummeted into darkness. Costanza had moved away from me, bringing with her that bit of dim light from before, and she kept talking from the kitchen. But her words seemed far away, like a plaintive chanting.

The roots. Of course, the palm tree's roots. They must have been enormous to have sustained it that way. I paused to consider how, in order to resist any sort of bad weather, a tree had better have solid roots. Sure, if you've got good roots, there is no misfortune that can beat you, I surmised. And if that palm tree had been me? Would I have had the necessary force to withstand such an adverse fate, or would I have woefully crumbled, never to rise again? Of course, compared to what was happening all around me, the sense of disorientation that overtook me on the highway and the resulting state of exhaustion into which I had succumbed shouldn't have seemed like a big deal.

The sudden restoration of the power and lights mercilessly revealed all the damage caused by the flood. Down in the street a river of yellowish water ran downstream flooding the doorways of stores, dragging along some scooters, trash bags, and even a couple of dumpsters, while some electric business signs sizzled, giving off sparkling colors. I opened the window and leaned out over the railing hoping to see the palm tree still standing straight against the sky, but the corner of the building blocked my view.

Only one hour later we were making our way onto the grounds of the Mostra d'Oltremare, our exhibition center in Naples. The underground parking lot must have been flooded because a uniformed worker, stopped in front of our car, invited us to continue along the boulevard to park right in front of the Teatro Mediterraneo. The rain had stopped falling, and strong winds easily bent the line of willow and eucalyptus trees on the wide plaza, while the frigid air stung our lungs.

In the semi-deserted foyer, hostesses packed into their blue dress suits were distributing the concert programs with manufactured smiles painted on their faces. We headed toward the still-empty hall, but we were soon forced to pause to exchange pleasantries with the scant audience bundled up from head to toe. Some women quite on in years donned wizened smiles and socialized while commenting on the season's playbill. Some men of the same age, who had outlived themselves, spoke intensely about the order of the day: business and politics. All of the people in the empty expanse of that hall brought to mind some scattered castaways adrift on the sea, grateful to have been propelled, floating on the wave of music, far away from the great flood that the Almighty had unleashed on the earth, exonerated from that divine punishment because of their class privilege.

Seated on a sofa, at the periphery of the chitter-chatter that was mixing with the shrill cacophony of musicians tuning their instruments, I felt that we were all going off together to who knows what remote location, when in reality all we were doing was getting ready to listen to Holst and Rimsky-Korsakov, Barber and Janáček.

While we headed to our seats—far away, I hoped, from that human race among which I felt out of place—I thought about myself and the audience around me, as though we were a tribe in danger of extinction, swept away, delusions and all, by the sea of water that had beaten down over the city, and transported us through the streets and squares all the way to that theater for a final farewell.

But if the fever was making me linger in a dream state, the thought of Martina and her future and the concern for the abrupt about-face that destiny had dealt to the course of my life were weighing on my soul and in turn anchoring me to my seat. Costanza's presence at my side, while I watched the musicians take the stage, convinced me that I had not sunk into some dark place but was just at the theater.

When the music finally began, Barber's *Adagio for Strings* proved to be a melodious cascade of violins, violas, and cellos, which the audience found irresistibly sweet. On the spectators' faces, the venue reflected the glow of peace, beauty, grace, and harmony. It was a place that no one would ever want to leave.

However, when the music diminished, fading with the tired sound of a pianissimo, I could finally go back to dwelling on my obsession: the fate that awaited Martina and me. And so I was overtaken with sadness, my body turned to ice, and I thought I could detect a tear rolling down my cheek. Without drawing any attention to myself, I deviated the tear's course with my fingers, and with a startled head movement I turned to look at Costanza's face, which was facing the stage, the players, and the conductor, who was dripping with sweat. And whatever life was left in me had turned to the cold marble of a grave marker.

Superficially, the decisions made on Martina's behalf appeared to be awfully clear and straightforward. Yet I deemed them to be wrapped in an imperceptible shroud of mystery. It was not a question of something incomprehensible but unresolvable: hers was one of those situations that lead us to mistrust our sense of human justice and the weights and measures that the law employs to balance it.

Martina's short life was entirely reduced to a few cryptic lines found in the juvenile court's sentencing, in its decrees, in its judges' opinions, and among lawyers' documents, appellate court letters, and bureaucratic paperwork about "behavioral interactions." Now and then, in search of some mortal wound, fragments of life would resurface even among the cold diagnoses of psychologists who had probed her mind during clinical interviews, Rorschach tests, and personality tests.

Those institutional workings had taken hold of her on a cold morning at the end of January 2004, when they had carried her off right in front of her grandmother.

That day in Volla, a small municipality in the northeastern suburbs of Naples, the sky was gray and heavy like a slab of lead. And that day Martina would turn five: she certainly couldn't have imagined that she would spend her birthday that way.

Naturally I was not there; I didn't even know her. But based on the collected letters and the various accounts, I reconstructed how those events played out, minute by minute.

On its way back from Good Shepherd House, the nursery school bus is quite late. As always, the central artery of the city is choked with traffic. And, as always, the driver has to put up with a solid half hour of hell before getting off the roundabout. To slow him down even more, there is an accident that causes a heavy traffic jam in the span of a few blocks.

There are no bad thoughts in Martina's head, nor any sinking feeling threatening her. On the contrary, she seems amused by the deafening uproar of car horns, by the rumbling of the engines, and by the excesses of the drivers ranting and raging at each other's cars. She is happy. She sniffles in her own way, wrinkling up her nose, while her chin forms a little dimple.

Curled up on the seat, she must have done what she did every day since she started attending nursery school: sit there with her eyes enchanted by the bustling life on the streets. With her forehead glued to the window, surely she must have lingered over the spectacle of African hotties decked out in their multicolored Lycra pants, on display around a makeshift bonfire. And she had to have checked out the street vendors, the Christmas lights strung up and down the streets, and the various Santa Clauses leaning up against the store fronts and the walls of apartment buildings. Adjusting her little white-and-red checkered school smock, perhaps she even smiled with pride at the girl seated next to her, or maybe she just sat there motionless, her thoughts turned to the birthday gift that her grandmother Geppina must have promised to give her when she came home. Her apartment is located in one of the many working-class tenements in the outskirts, the ones surrounded by uncultivated fields and crisscrossed by the giant cement pylons of the highway overpasses, otherwise known as Il Parco degli Oleandri, Oleander Park.

At this point it's possible that her eyes fondly took in that regular spectacle: a burned-out Gypsy camp beneath the overpass; old, wrecked cars left one on top of the other; some garbage bins torched in the night, still sending off plumes of black smoke and a nauseating stench of melted plastic.

No doubt, her heart must have started to beat stronger as she imagined Geppina, dressed in black, her straw-like blond hair and that ever-present cigarette between her lips, coming toward her as she stepped off the school bus. And, as always, for her it would have been like coming back to paradise.

That late morning Geppina's face seemed more weathered than usual, with creases like wide gashes running all the way to her mouth. For quite some time she's been keeping an eye on the police squad car parked across from the park, but she seems unfazed by it. The people from around there are used to such a presence by now; all too often people see them pop out of nowhere, cruise quietly and slowly over the asphalt, up and down the neighborhood, or lying in wait behind a row of hedges.

However, after the gunfire a few days prior, when a stray bullet lodged itself in the head of a young boy playing soccer on the little field across from the park, squad cars have become part of their landscape, morning, noon, and night. But more than the police officers, it's a very determined-looking female figure roaming around in their midst that worries Geppina. She knows quite well who she is, and it's not difficult to guess the scope of danger that looms over them. The district social worker will carry off Martina as soon as the girl sets foot on the ground. And in doing so, she will drive another thorn into Geppina's heart. So, she will shed blood and scream until her throat is raw. First she'll curse God for persecuting her, and then Martina's mother and father for bringing her into that kind of life. She'll even curse her own womb for having produced children that she would sooner have killed off in her belly than to watch them drown in their own hardships.

And so, with one arm on her waist, she lights up a cigarette and starts pacing back and forth along the seed-bare flower bed, her eyes glued one minute to the social worker, the next on the entrance to the park where the yellow school bus starts to stand out against the gray of the apartment buildings, the gray of the sky, the gray of the day itself.

~ 4 ~

The fact is that the whole story begins with that social worker. Although relegated to a marginal figure, this woman appears to play a fundamental role in Martina's life. In Geppina's eyes, she is, with her inexplicable tenacity, the true cause of all her pain and tears.

But is that how it really played out? Is it possible to credit this second-tier character with a leading role? Was it the ruthlessness of her reports that set in motion an irreversible process? If she had not gotten involved with her excessive zeal, her oversized sense of duty, would the matter have developed in a different way? Or else would it have ended up, despite everything, exactly the way it did? As exaggerated as Geppina's and her family's theory appears, it is an intriguing one. Just as exaggerated and intriguing as the theory according to which judge Giuliana Conti is acting under the influence of social indoctrination with regard to a world that inhibits any hope of civil coexistence and any aspirations toward dignity.

Despite not being very young, the social worker was a perky woman who never gave in to anyone. She had materialized on their horizon even before Geppina's granddaughter Martina was born, and even then Geppina was unable to see her entry onto the scene as anything less than a divine punishment, the price to pay for what she deemed to be, in the beginning, all her fault.

At the time the woman was in charge of social services at Loreto Mare, the hospital on Via Marina, where it came to light that Geppina's daughter, Maddalena—clinging to life in the surgery wing with a cranial trauma—was three months pregnant. She was the one who, with all her strength, did whatever she could so that the little speck of life pulsing in the young woman's womb, "despite her disastrous condition," might come forth into the world. What made her persevere was the ironclad belief that abortion was a genuine crime—a belief that was the product of an unwavering, almost fanatical, faith that from time to time she would advertise, if the occasion presented itself.

At that time, Maddalena was a great big seventeen-year-old who suffered from epilepsy and who walked with a limp caused by some partial paralysis that had impaired the whole left side of her body many years earlier. She had an arm that dangled off her like a deadweight. It was purplish from her continuously banging it against sharp corners on doors, tables, and chairs. Meanwhile, her clubbed foot, which slowed her down, forced her to walk sideways and with short hops. Her mouth, twisted into a grimace, evoked a poorly treated facial scar, and once she opened it, you could see a rotten set of teeth. Their yellowness, just like her continuous fits of coughing, was attributable to the cigarettes that she put out and lit, one after the other.

When she was no more than a little girl, the doctors from that very same hospital, after a twelve-hour operation, had removed from her brain a tumor the size of a walnut, and if that wasn't enough, some months later, following complications from the wound that wouldn't close and became regularly infected, they had to operate again. On the right side of her cranium, they had applied a metal skullcap that for her family won her the nickname of "Capa 'e fierro," or "Ironhead." Sometime later, though, that same encasement wasn't enough to protect her from the brutality of a delinquent who, after having easily convinced her to sleep with him, had beaten her to a pulp while she slept, just to rob her of a few bucks. It had happened on a balmy spring night, amid the fetid air of an abandoned freight car on a dead stretch of track, far from the commotion of the station.

After saving her, when they realized she was pregnant, a few doctors had recommended abortion. The intransigence of the law, however, had obligated them to stay out of the matter, passing the torch to the social worker, who, in turn, with a resolute manner, had had an easy time of removing all hesitation. The law, after all, was quite clear on the matter. Maddalena, impregnated by an unidentified man, aside from being a minor, had been declared of diminished capacity and, thus, could not give consent to interrupt the pregnancy. And anyway, under the protective wing of the social worker—who never let her miss any of Don Gennarino's sermons at the Loreto Mare chapel—the girl was prepared to live her new role eagerly and conscientiously. She had stepped so well into her new role as the underage single mother that she had quit smoking in the hospital; she had resumed grooming herself, brushing the few teeth left in her mouth, and arranging her thinning hair with dozens of clips. Squeaky clean and made up, she would walk through the wards greeting anyone who crossed her path. She would engage in conversations with the sick patients from the second floor as well as the third floor; she would even run errands for them, not, of course, before stopping off for a half hour in the café—either for an espresso, which she would never refuse, or to jabber on the phone, in the end almost always wearing out Geppina with her requests for the latter to bring her fresh, clean clothes. In the afternoon, though, she would switch to the maternity ward, lingering there with her eyes glued to the bellies of expectant mothers or staring wide-eyed at the fleshy pink skin and the wrinkled little faces of some newborns latched on to their mothers' breasts. Meanwhile, the social worker never failed to fill her head with good intentions and high hopes for a better life, being that, according to her, children were God's blessing and they could sort everything out.

For some time, Maddalena and the social worker had lost touch with each other. But soon, after Martina was born, their paths had crossed again. Reacting to what she termed a "compelling need to test the secular aspect of my belief system," the woman had in fact asked to be transferred to one of the outlying neighborhoods, which, in her opinion, served as the front line of Christian compassion. It was precisely in Volla, amid piles of administrative paperwork on the desk of her predecessor, that she had discovered Maddalena's file. And it was not by chance that two days later, she had shown up at her house. Surprisingly, though, early on she had stuck to just following her case—which she regarded as high risk—in compliance with the sentence handed down by the juvenile authorities and made no display of either agitation or passion.

Yet she had not failed to show a good measure of satisfaction at the sight of Martina, relishing that, perhaps deep down, she had been largely responsible for her birth. She showed only occasional interest in the baby girl, the young mother, and her family, just as she had done with the other cases on her docket since she had so many of them. And when she was forced to take note of Maddalena's being away from home for days, she found it expedient to turn a blind eye to the false excuses that she tried to palm off. During the first two years Geppina and the social worker barely saw each other four times.

Yet, to better understand that pious woman's meddling and influence on the story, first we need to go back to the time when Martina had first come into the world. When, in the custody of the juvenile court, she had been officially given a brand-new life and the unusual surname of Tirli, instead of her mother's, which was Piccolo, or even her grand-mother's, which was De Nicola, much less the surname of the father, for no one even knew what he looked like.

In fact, since Maddalena was not permitted to acknowl-edge her daughter, by law there were no bonds of kinship between her relatives and Martina, and the child, a ward of the state, was therefore adoptable.

Despite all that, this was the decision of the court: "Based on the completed investigation, it is our opinion that young Martina, born from the union between a legally incapaci-tated minor, the aforementioned Maddalena Piccolo, and her sometime partner, be entrusted by the juvenile court to a Mrs. Concetta Piccolo, sister of Maddalena. Such custody appears suitable in consideration of the fact that the biologi-cal mother, though ruled incompetent, appears to be 'capable of emotional bonding,' and given the fact that the maternal (biological) aunt remains available to accommodate the minor and her own sister, and to guarantee an appropriate mother-daughter relationship." The decision came through the person of the court president, Anna Parlato, at the time so highly regarded for her advocacy in favor of minors, that she earned the nickname of Our Lady of the Innocents. Always in the whirlwind of controversy—so goes the rumor—she was known for her humanity and for her tendency to interpret cryptic legal proceedings to her liking.

Thereafter, the colleague who took over for her, Giuliana Conti, of whom I happened to be an old friend, told me that what swayed Our Lady of the Innocents toward that solution had been Geppina's desperation. Anguished by Maddalena's fragile disposition, Geppina feared that the young girl might commit suicide if the custody request had not been accepted. And if that's how it had to be, she asked the judge to arrange for her to be immediately institutionalized.

"Because with all the issues I have, Judge, I can't look after her, too. Ever since I was born, I've been thirsty, but each time I ask for water, I get vinegar," Geppina had told her, with exhaustion in her eyes.

~ 5 ~

So, Martina was going home from the hospital under the tutelage of her aunt Concetta, who had declared herself willing, with her husband's approval, to bear the burden of Maddalena as well. Aware of the difficulties in tearing her sister away from a life of dereliction, she clung to a modest hope in converting her to an emotional stability that might keep her safely sheltered within the four walls of domestic space. Concetta made it clear she was open to regular home inspections to ensure compliance of the proscriptions of the juvenile court, investing Our Lady of the Innocents—in the event that the investigations revealed Martina to not be receiving appropriate care—with the authority to take the necessary measures. Maddalena, for her part, hastily swore an unequivocal oath.

"Your honor, I swear to you, *me ne sto a casa e Cuncetta cu Martina . . . quant'è ver' a Maroonn*! I'll stay at Concetta's house with Martina. I swear on the holy mother of Jesus!"

As for Maddalena ducking out of the house, in the decree of the appeals courts for minors, which responded to the umpteenth claim by Geppina's lawyers, the judges ruled her tendency to fly the coop thus: "Incompetent by mental defect, increasingly afflicted by her pathology and prompted by her uncontrollable sexual appetites, she regularly leaves the home for days at a time, frequenting people of ill repute, placing her daughter at risk of contracting infectious diseases." And so, in the course of a couple of years, Maddalena had been transformed from a "subject incapable of emotional ties" to a sort of bitch in heat.

"Judge, where there's room for four people, there's room for six. Don't worry," Concetta had assured Judge Parlato. "And there's also Maddalena's welfare checks," she added with a furtive glance at the young mother by her side.

In the months that followed all went back to how it was before. Geppina had continued her struggle with poverty, with her other children and with her live-in partner. Martina was actively growing, and Maddalena was wreaking havoc each time she ran away. From the moment they would open their eyes in the morning until they placed their heads on their pillows in the evening, they dug in their heels to make ends meet.

But Geppina's decision to keep Maddalena and Martina with her, now that the storm seemed to have subsided and the judges and courts were a distant memory, had fomented such resentment in Concetta that she came to loggerheads with her mother.

"If they come for an inspection in my house and don't find them, *nun ne voglio sapè niente, è capito? . . . Comme chi addà venì? . . . Ma ti si scurdata che la giudice ci ha fatto tenere a Martina solo pecché stava cu me, assieme a Matalena? E tu invece, te la prendi! Come? . . . E po' come faccio a campà si tu te tiene tutta* 'a pensione? Non dico tutti i soldi, ma dammi qualcosa pure a me. . . . Pecché chella miseria che mi dai nun 'e può chiammà sorde. . . .* I don't want any trouble. You got it? . . . What you mean? Who might come? . . . Have you forgotten that the judge let us keep Martina because she's staying with me, along with Maddalena? But you want to take her! How? . . . And how will I make ends meet if you keep her whole welfare check? I'm not talking about all the money, but at least leave me something. . . . Because I wouldn't call that pittance you give me 'money.'"

Concetta could no longer get by. And her house was becoming a living hell: her husband did nothing but set her against her mother each time that he needed money. *"Si piglia tutt' 'e sorde 'e Matalena, e noi facimme 'a famme.* She takes all the money from Maddalena's disability benefits, and we're starving."

Cohabitating with Tonino wasn't exactly the sweet life, but at least he was the father of her daughters, and Concetta thanked God because he continued to stick by her, even if he never stopped threatening to leave her: *"Ma che sto a fa' dint'a 'sta casa assieme a te!* What am I doing stuck in this house with you!"

Her husband's favorite activity was coming from and going to jail, and the last time he had done a year stint was for stealing a tractor trailer on the highway. But a few months earlier he had promised to go on the straight and narrow, making ends meet by relying on his wits. He made do. One time, unloading fruit at the central market; another time, as a laborer under the table; and yet another time, stocking shelves at a cash-and-carry store. He made do, but he didn't work very hard. And he rather preferred the betting office over going to work. Most of the time, then, he would return home empty handed. Whatever he managed to earn he would squander on smoking weed, on a line of coke, or on video-poker machines. And every once in a while, he couldn't help making a foray over to the main intersection in Arzano to sample some fresh meat from Nigeria.

Concetta would keep quiet. "If he goes to the joint one more time, how will I manage? . . . And if he leaves me for another?" She had no way out. She anticipated being abandoned, whether because her husband would end up in jail or because he went on the lam trying to put together another life with a new woman whom she imagined in her worst nightmares as attractive and very young. She had no options.

From the numerous encounters with Geppina and with Concetta, however, one clear fact emerged: they both held great affection for Maddalena. It was easy to believe that her mother could feel that way, but few would have suspected it from her sister. Yet, though she didn't show it, Concetta truly cared about "Ironhead" and she was definitely not after her welfare money, even if she struggled against the squalid temptation lurking in her mind. Waking up every morning with the nightmare of having to balance their budget, and bending over backward to put warm food on the table could not have been easy. And then there's the daily need for diapers, powdered milk, and the medications that her two little girls needed.

Geppina was the incarnation of the adage according to which one mother is capable of looking after one hundred children, but one hundred children can't look after one mother, and so, she considered the matter in a different light. Paying no heed to her husband's complaint, "When you divvy up wealth, you get poverty," with Maddalena's disability benefits she managed to put food in everyone's mouth. She kept one part of the money for the household expenses; the rest she distributed to her seven children, according to their needs. She considered that money like manna descended from the heavens to alleviate, at least in part, her suffering—a sort of compensation for all the pain caused by an ill-fated daughter. All the same, deep down Geppina and Concetta knew that it was actually Maddalena keeping them solvent, and because of this dependency they detested themselves as much as they detested the poverty that tainted their love.

But that fire, which to all appearances seemed extinguished, just needed a little poking to rage again. And it raged, in fact, at the first sign of wind, the night during which Concetta was startled awake by the phone ringing just after she had fallen asleep.

Her husband, cursing next to her, turned over in bed. Her heart aflutter, Concetta didn't even get to say "hello" before the gloomy voice of a police officer chilled her to the bone. Her sister had been found in Piazza Garibaldi in the company of two Albanian men with criminal records. She had no ID and seemed to be in poor health.

"No, don't bring her to the police station. I'll be right there," she said. "*Marescià, chella è malata.* Officer, she's a sick girl."

Seated on the edge of the bed, she was left numb for a moment. Then, turning to look at her husband, who hadn't even moved a muscle, she had timidly asked him to drive her there.

"*So' cazzi tuoi, tanto chella domani stà n'ata volta miez'a via.* That's your fucking problem since tomorrow she'll be back out on the streets anyway," was his reply.

Then the abrupt ringing of doorbells and voices on the landing kept getting louder and closer. The ruckus had even awoken her daughters, who started to cry. Then Concetta had rushed to the door to find Geppina on the threshold, haphazardly dressed. Held tightly in her arms was Martina, still asleep and bundled up in a bunting onesie.

"Mammà? . . ."

"M'ha chiamato 'a polizia . . . dice che hanno truvato Matalena a stazione. The police called me saying that they found Maddalena near the train station."

"Hanno chiammato pure a me. . . . Mo' me vesto e corro. . . . Ma perché è portato a Martina? They called me, too. . . . I'll get dressed and get going. . . . But why'd you bring Martina?"

"È meglio accussí, se la vede se ne torna senza fa' storie. . . . It's better this way. If she sees her, she'll come along without making trouble. . . ."

~ 6 ~

Outside the police station, Concetta decides to wait in the shadows, away from the dangers of the piazza. The car isn't insured, and up ahead she can make out a police checkpoint. She parks on a side street, the grille jutting over the sidewalk, and convinces her mother to stay in the car. Then she heads into the labyrinth of dark streets, holding Martina in her arms. She passes two prostitutes scuffling in the lobby of a building, right in front of the amused stares of four creeps who were camped out around a car with the music blaring. On Corso Novara the rumbling of a solitary vehicle cuts through the silence, while a gust of chilly wind slaps her face. Concetta crosses the street and continues along the sidewalk, flanking the unlit storefront of the McDonald's. From under a pile of cardboard boxes the sudden groaning of a homeless man takes her breath away for a moment. The atrium of the train station at that hour, dark and desolate as a cemetery, is barely lit up by milky white neon lights. Behind a column, two dark silhouettes take shelter from the cold by disappearing under a fortification of rags, while a woman on in years tiredly tows a baby carriage full of items that must be the remnants of some life. Blurred shadows in the distance wander down a solitary train track. Murmuring voices echo from who knows where. Without her even realizing it, some officers making their evening rounds had come up behind her.

"The police phoned me . . . they stopped my sister . . . her name's Maddalena, Maddalena Piccolo."

This is what Concetta remembers from that night. What happened from there—all of the waiting at the precinct and even her return home—is all rather vague. What might have been said to "Ironhead" and to the police officers—and how she justified bringing a little girl not even two years old along with her at that hour—seems to be wrapped in an impenetrable fog bank. Afterward, assessing the episode, she revealed that she hadn't given it too much thought. All in all, she thought she had gotten off light with being awoken in the middle of the night and with the hassle of a trip to downtown Naples. A sacrifice that seemed acceptable; right on par with the other times that she had rushed out to rescue her sister.

Geppina, on the other hand, while awaiting her daughters' return to the car, noticed some whining close by that moved further away—grousing, subdued voices that would suddenly grow quiet only to rise up again furiously. She recalled feeling frozen to her seat when she seemed to make out some frightening but invisible wingbeats, the fate of yet another account to settle looming over her. She quickly understood that bringing Martina with her had been a big mistake, a mistake for which she would pay dearly. And she did. Once they took down all the child's information and confirmed that she belonged to Maddalena, the police referred the matter to the municipal authorities and the juvenile court, which dusted off Martina's case and opened an investigation, sanctioning a more constant and effective intervention by the social worker.

The decision to bring Martina with her that night, as Geppina tells it, ended up further aggravating a sense of guilt that already gnawed at her. She was inconsolable about having set in motion a relentless machine that, along with the meddling of that social worker, would bring everything tumbling down. But was it possible to view that decision as yet another random, albeit ominous, event tied to fate's vendetta against that family? If Geppina, in order to bring her fugitive daughter back home, had not attempted to play on Maddalena's affection for her child, would that woman have ever come back into their lives with such vehemence?

In fact, once that social worker had been solicited by the judicial authorities, she barged into Geppina's life, wreaking havoc on her. Convinced she'd been too charitable in the previous two years and had erred on the side of kindness, at the top of her list of tasks she made a point of conducting a more thorough investigation. She had thus made a pledge to plumb the depths of Geppina's past, snooping into her children's lives and accounting for every last cent of money circulating in that house. She exposed the true nature of the man living with her and ultimately assessed the dangers that were looming over that child.

"My dear Ms. De Nicola, we mustn't forget that Martina has no legal guardian and no one else to exert parental authority," she would repeat with a lisp that sounded like the sloshing of an overflowing river.

After making her obligatory conclusions, she reported everything to Giuliana Conti, the judge from the juvenile court, who, in the meantime, had taken up the case and who would later nullify Concetta's custody of Martina, which had been ordered by her colleague, Anna Parlato.

And the deeper she would dig, the more disturbing things she would find in Geppina's life; nothing in keeping with her moral vision.

Geppina and her family began to feel like victims of an overreach that, in their eyes, was unfounded as well as a form of harassment.

"I'm sorry, but I am more and more convinced that there is no basis for Martina to stay in this house," was the social worker's litany during each visit. And during each visit Geppina would be strangled by a fear that prevented her from even thinking straight. At the beginning she thought that it might be beneficial for her to come across as accommodating, kind, almost submissive. And to get in the good graces of that woman, she started by offering her espresso with sugar or cartons of the American cigarettes that Lino would smuggle off the ships the moment they anchored in port. One Easter, she left that woman astounded with a food basket and half a baby goat that she had won at the supermarket raffle below her house. They were all presents that the social worker would refuse in an overblown manner and by inviting them to pray to the good Lord to guide them down the righteous path. Meanwhile, Geppina felt ever more on the edge of a sharp, slippery razor, constantly on the borderline between the impulse to act and the fear of screwing up. Deep down, however, her life had always been that way: some obstacle would always pop up to impede her from doing things in the way she wanted to. Always half measures and ambiguous situations; always someone to tell her that she had bungled something. But she had never been able to see where she had gone wrong, until that morning on which she concluded—after Maddalena unexpectedly returned home from one of her escapades—that it was her whole life itself that was wrong.

It's not quite lunchtime. Only the grandchildren are playing and running around the house screaming through all the rooms: Martina, Concetta's kids, and the children of both Susetta and Monica, Geppina's other two daughters.

Suddenly the bell rings. It's a high-pitched insistent sound like a siren. Geppina leaves the pots burning on the stove and runs to the door. Before she can even open it, Maddalena comes bursting through in a fury. She's filthy and bleeding from her head. As she screams, she turns the house upside town. "*Mannaggia a Maronn'* . . . *damme 'e sold, damme 'e sold . . .'e capito o no? Bucchin'* . . . *damme 'e sold mieje, se no t'accide.* Holy mother of god . . . gimme the money, gimme the money . . . you hear me? Fuck . . . Gimme my money, or I'll kill you."

She rifles through drawers and rummages through closets. She even goes through Martina's crib. But not finding what she's looking for, right in front of the children's terrified eyes, she lunges at her mother, pummeling her with kicks and punches before collapsing to the floor.

Just like the other times when her daughter was in the throes of convulsions, Geppina holds her tightly and takes her head in her hands. She caresses her forehead, her gaunt face, and whispers the usual reassuring words in her ear; the words begin to release Maddalena from the grip of fear that shackles her during these seizures. And when she sees her on the verge of losing consciousness, though Geppina is a slight woman, she heaves her up and carries her to the bedroom, where she eases her down on the bed like a lifeless doll. She slips off her shoes and clothes, then carefully washes her arms and legs, wipes the spittle from her mouth, slowly removes the encrusted blood from her head and chest, and hopes that sleep overtakes her. She keeps vigil over her daughter until late in the evening, when she's certain she is sleeping deeply and her breathing is calm. Then she drags herself to the kitchen and flops onto a chair, repeating to herself a thousand times that she has to bear that cross until the end since it's too late to change things. There's no choice but to let her hellish life burn out to the end. That's how it has to be. To dull her pain, she spends the rest of the night by hitting the bottle, waking with the first light of dawn, her head down on the kitchen table. And that is exactly how the social worker would find Geppina that morning: with alcohol on her breath and still oppressed by her dark thoughts from the night before.

From that moment on, nothing seemed capable of mollifying that woman's interventionist fervor. Among the many reports she sent to the juvenile court, which seemed to weigh down the scales toward the notion of separating Martina from Geppina, one in particular makes references to the "rather disturbing" components of her nuclear family. But what did she find so alarming about Geppina and her partner Michele Esposito, aka Lino?

"During their more than twenty-five years of cohabitation, the couple has had four children, combined with the four from Ms. De Nicola's previous marriage to Giuseppe Piccolo. Mr. Esposito, for his part, had two children from a previous marriage."

Afterward, when I was in possession of the complete file, I had the opportunity to verify some of the holes in these statements—inaccuracies that, in and of themselves, amounted to little but, if placed along with the others, heavily influenced the judges' decisions. They were facts that, for some unknown reason, no one had bothered to verify. Michele Esposito had never been married before, nor did he have children when he met Geppina. He was of a mild temperament, and when it came to his wife he demonstrated an uncommon devotion for a man of such low birth. Lino had inherited not only a house in which he was living with his mother and sister but also a permanent disability that undermined his ability to work, even as a boy. While playing as a child, he had lost an eye, which was replaced by a glass one; and on top of that, his good eye was extremely nearsighted. It was a defect that forced him to scrunch up his face behind thick lenses.

Combined with each other, these two people, categorized as "dysfunctional" by the social worker, can become, according to the latter, a source of immorality and distress. But what makes them so dangerous? Perhaps the fact that Michele does not have any stable work or that his job as a peddler down at the port might be considered nothing more than a shady operation? Who knows, maybe it was Geppina's attitude, but she would have done anything for her seven children and brood of grandchildren—even nail Christ himself to the cross.

On the other hand, I feel confident in saying, without fear of being refuted, that the couple's immorality is in the very air that they breathe, in the very place in which they live. It's a cement jungle where any hope of a better future is just a television commercial, a place where children can die from a stray bullet, just like that. It is a place where you don't choose lawlessness; you live it with the ferocity and indifference of those who know no other form of survival.

But credit is due the social worker for her intuition: taking a pup away from a ravenous she-wolf, especially one at war with the pack, means increasing the likelihood of that pup's survival. And this coincided with what was, for my friend Giuliana Conti, the cornerstone of juvenile law. She did nothing but repeat it: her priority consists in safeguarding

the interests of the child, in spite of everything and everyone else.

Though, in my take of the social worker's report, what
struck the court council as particularly relevant was not so
much the reference to Geppina's nuclear family as it was the
general conclusion: "A number of incidents leads me to believe
that Martina's grandmother has a drinking problem."

On that cold January morning, Geppina was writhing in
a web of terrible thoughts.

Conflicting thoughts and feelings crisscrossed her mind
and her heart in those never-ending moments that kept her
from Martina. She paced back and forth on the sidewalk,
with her arms folded over her chest and an uncontrollable
anxiousness, not knowing what to do.

The little school bus appeared on the church square, making way among the rings of smoke that rose up to the ashen
sky. A row of smoldering dumpsters oozed streams of green-
ish plastic onto the asphalt and released an acrid smell into
the air that was harsh on the throat. The driver went around
them, avoiding a scooter going the wrong way against traffic, and stopped on the edge of the park, in front of the bus
shelter, which was the usual spot. Right away a small congregation of mothers and fathers gathered and huddled
before the unopened door to the bus.

Geppina, who, until that moment, kept to the margins
of the group, rushed toward the school bus, thinking she
would grab her granddaughter and take off. But the social
worker, showing an unusual amount of sympathy on her face,
advanced at the same time as Geppina, with two police officers in tow. They got the best of Geppina, surpassing her
before Martina set foot on the ground.

Geppina screamed and thrashed about, trying to free
herself from the officers' grip. She launched into a tirade of

swearing and cursing as she reached desperately toward Martina, who ended up arm in arm with the social worker.

"Ma'am, I'm sorry, but you cannot take the child. . . ."

"No! No! . . . *Lassatemi stà, lassatemi stà.* . . . Lemme go, lemme go! . . . Martiiiiiinaaa!"

Among the women gathered around her, there arose cries of protest. One of them cursed up a storm.

"*Ma tu vide che maniere.* . . . Look at that behavior. . . ."

"Where are you taking her?"

"*Chesta è 'na vergogna . . . povera creatura.* This is shameful . . . poor little child."

Another one even tried to get Martina back but was soon held back by the police.

From the mob that had gathered around the little school bus, you could hear a threatening clamor. Geppina screamed as she slapped and scratched her own face, while Martina, drowning in tears, was quickly taken out of her sight. It was as though they had cut off one of Geppina's arms—or a leg. When the squad car took off with its sirens wailing, she slumped down to the ground and succumbed to her grief. Then, a woman tried to console her, whispering that everything would work out. Another one leaned over her, trying to embrace her. For a moment she interrupted her sobbing to reply to the others' concerns; then she lost all ability to speak and entrusted her heartache to silence.

~ 7 ~

Perhaps it was all that rain that drenched me on the highway. Perhaps it was the wind or the humidity during that evening concert. Either way, a high fever kept me in a regimen of forced bedrest for a few days—days that passed in what felt to me like a slow, liquid death.

Had Costanza not intervened with her usual stubbornness, I would have attempted to get out of the house the following day, hustling from one side of the city to the other. According to her, I only had to stay in bed for a bit longer: my patients weren't going anywhere and the world would not have missed me. After a few years of living together, she appeared all too familiar with my inability to stay shut in the house. So she thought she'd better jump into the front line of defense, skipping precious moments of time at her job in order to fight the bronchitis that I'd contracted. She nursed me with various broths and herbal infusions; she would remind me when to take the antibiotics; she administered the syrup and, most of all, she tolerated me. When she was absolutely fed up with my infantile refusal to take care of myself, she would strike at my weak points. She would point out what a mess I had become because of my tendency toward self-neglect: that was her very personal way of goading me into getting better. She meant well, she would add pleasantly, even if she would almost always end up hurting my pride with that subtle sarcasm of hers. Then again, with my run-down appearance, a gut that had been growing over the past few years, and hair that was prematurely reduced to a faint crown around my head, I couldn't blame her. In essence I had undergone a metamorphosis, and the incontestability of the facts irritated me more than Costanza's stinging irony.

Oh, well, at least I had my height, which, in the collective imagination, was half the measure of a man's good looks. I also had wide shoulders and muscular legs—qualities that made me still an attractive guy in some people's eyes, even though I was already past forty. And anyway, two other things that contributed to my, let's say, residual charm, were my cheerful personality and my tendency to smile. Nevertheless, reflecting on my earlier shape, of which I retained only a vague vestige, I was more inclined to believe that the indignities of time were exceeding people's praise. And anyway, with regard to objectivity, the only person in whom I had complete faith was the woman with whom I shared a bed, which, beyond never becoming officially marital, struggled from time to time under the weight of a tense relationship.

Wearily lying between the sheets after who knows how many personal assessments of my physical condition, I could not help thinking about the athlete that I should have been and that I never became; about the good looks of bygone days, faded over the years like a sketch traced onto carbon paper; and about how naively confident I used to be when contemplating my future.

One thing that used to occupy my time as a boy was running. Running just to run. In the beginning I wasn't aware of doing it and perhaps I didn't even like running. But it was what came to me most easily. To go to school, I would run; to meet up with my friends, I would run; to take care of errands for my mother, I would run. I had a natural propensity for devouring asphalt, spinning my legs one stride after the other. I couldn't go without it. It was impossible to resist. From the moment I woke up in the morning, I would be running. It was around that time that I learned to listen to my inner voice. There was me, the road, and my voice that would pose questions. Eyes looking downward, I would see the cobblestones disappear under my feet and having gotten my second wind after a bit, I felt as though I were flying in those old shoes, one size too large, which I was forced to overtighten so that they wouldn't fall off my feet. To this day, if I close my eyes, I can still hear my mother say, "Don't run. Take it slow or you'll get sweaty."

I can't recall when or how—maybe at school—but someone noticed what I was doing and dragged me off to a track. They would bring me there every afternoon in a rickety van, along with many other kids, crammed one on top of the other. Following the instruction of a coach, I would circle the track with my long legs lap after lap, paying attention to his tips about breathing, posture, and counting steps to clear the hurdles and whatever else might have come in handy in my training as a future 400-meter specialist. I always came in first. I was the fastest. They signed me up for the youth races and I won. There was no coach, regional champ, or federation director who doubted my talent. Everyone predicted that I would have a bright future in track and field, a road paved with success, with trophies and medals.

And there you have it: my dream was to run.

Then, one day, that inner voice went silent and something took me on a turn for the worse: a pain in my groin that never healed, my legs that stopped working as they used to, my friends, and many other distractions. Who knows what it was, but anyway, I ended up losing my way on a road that I never should have taken. And, after high school, as a way of staying in that environment, I enrolled in ISEF, the college of physical education, so that, I decided, I could at least coach track. But at times life doesn't even allow you to realize a meager portion of your dreams. One application after another, certification courses, and various stints as a substitute teacher weren't enough to get me enough leverage to become a full-time teacher. I gave up. It was then that I was presented with what would become my current career. Specialized training and an associate's degree helped me, at already more than thirty years old, to become what I am today: a speech pathologist. Once I heard someone say that at that age, people become what they will be forever. Maybe that person was right. They used to call me *professò*, prof. Now, exaggerating a bit, they call me *dottò*, doc. I'm not used to it, and it makes me feel uneasy. But my parents, who never even finished middle school, swell with pride when they hear that title.

Given the dreadful state I was in for those few days, my main concern was not so much the fate of my patients—whom I had passed on to one of my colleagues—as much as the fate of Martina, over which I had no control. Costanza knew this quite well. She too, like me, had let herself get mixed up in the web of mystery that surrounded that little girl, and now she was entangled, though for different reasons. Yet what she would not reveal even to herself concerned her coming to terms with being a woman on the verge of forty, with no kids, and with the prospect of spending the rest of her life by my side. But apparently she faced the issue head-on, allowing her pronounced rationality and her own professional competence to carry the day. She was a child psychiatrist who worked in an *Azienda Sanitaria Locale*, or a local health-care agency, with high-risk children from one of the many high-risk neighborhoods in our city. So she had her finger on the pulse of the situation. At least it seemed that way because in reality, Martina became an obsession for her as well as for me. We would spend entire days and sleepless nights talking about her.

"If you were forced to give up your dream, what would you do?"

"You still have a high fever, huh?" asked Costanza, placing the tray with tea on the nightstand next to me.

"I think so, but why do you ask?"

She let a few moments pass as she made her way around the bed, straightening up the sheets and the blankets.

"So?"

"Uh . . . I don't think people should ever give up on their dreams."

"Of course, but what if you were forced to?"

"Well, I don't know," she replied, a bit annoyed, unrealistically trying to restore some order to the chaos that I had created in the bedroom.

"I used to have one."

"Oh, yeah? Which one?"

"To be a runner."

"I thought you had forgotten about that."

"Hmm . . . Why won't you answer me?"

"I told you . . . I don't know. Maybe I would invent another one."

"And if you don't have another one?"

"Listen . . . Real dreams are the ones that you can never realize. It's a question of proportions, of maturity."

"What are you talking about? Dreams are dreams and that's that."

"It's personal need that brings about dreams. I mean that your dream might not have any significance for someone else, while someone else's dream might not be what you would call a dream. It's a question of necessity. . . ."

"What's yours?" I asked, not relenting.

She didn't answer. Busying herself with the wardrobe, she took her time carefully organizing the clothes that she had picked up here and there. Then she turned slowly and, staring right at me, replied, her words welling up in her throat, "A child!"

I could see her blushing intensely. Then she quickly threw herself headlong into some pointless task in an attempt to hide her face. That emotional embarrassment was not caused by a revelation—since I already knew her desire quite well—but by something that touched a raw nerve within our relationship. Regretful for having poured salt on what she thought was still a fresh wound, she shrugged her shoulders and, before disappearing into the safe space of the study, she muttered under her breath, "Sorry, I didn't mean to . . ."

Yes, that was one of the few unresolved aspects of our relationship. And it weighed down on us like a boulder. Not that I was against the idea of having a child. On the contrary. Although it wasn't exactly the first on my hit parade of dreams, I had begun to readily accept the idea. At that point in our lives, after having broken up and gotten back together so many times, a child seemed like the crowning achievement of our history as a couple since we were by now fully committed to each other.

One time, when I was a child, I heard my grandmother, with a particularly bright expression on her face, say, "*I figli si cacano*. Having children is easy as taking a shit." For us, though, who were at risk of choking on our own foul air, it wasn't a walk in the park. Having discovered an occlusion of my seminal duct the year before, which had rendered any attempts to expand the family futile, I had undergone an operation that had not achieved the desired results. On the contrary, it had revealed that the real problem was a low count of very lazy sperm found in my seminal fluid. So Costanza, without losing heart but playing the same old song about her age and her tyrannical biological clock, had convinced me to forget about my tired sperm that, not wanting anything to do with climbing up into her, "just needed a little push." Encouraging me not to bow my head down before nature's stinginess, she had then flipped through all the possible scenarios involving the techniques of artificial insemination.

"Today, in this field, science has made huge strides. And I'm sure we have a few friends who can give us some advice on the matter."

Hers was a meticulous and zealous plan, which would see us sacrificed on the altar of procreation to become, despite Mother Nature's designs, happy parents of a happy family. It was an endeavor in which I hardly recognized the free-spirited, anti-conformist woman with whom I had fallen in love.

The first months were hell. In the specialized clinic that she had carefully chosen, we subjected ourselves to treatments that—it would not be an exaggeration to say—were pretty close to torture. Naturally, the larger share of discomfort pertained to her, who, to start with, underwent a hormonal therapy with shots in her arm every other day and painful injections in her stomach every morning. My seemingly pleasant task was assigned to me a bit later on: I was to shut myself in a room and improvise an unspoken dialogue with a couple of sexual acrobats, who, in the pages of a porno mag, were demonstrating in great detail what the imagination often attributes to depravity.

And while Costanza was having her most intimate areas violated by a tube searching for some nice buxom ova ready to be fertilized, I was in my little cubbyhole next door, beneath the white fluorescent lights, one hand struggling to raise my old glory stuck at half-mast, while the other one held up a container for my dear lackadaisical little flagella, which, in short time, after a leisurely trip into some of Costanza's ova, would be frolicking to their heart's desire as they attempted to carry out their duty under the watchful eyes of God only knows who.

We subjected ourselves to that regimented rigmarole twice, and twice Costanza cared for that little miracle in the warmth of her belly. And twice it was all in vain. But these failed attempts didn't keep her from clinging to her dream; she hunkered down and tried again, no matter what she had to sacrifice. As for me, even with wavering doubts, I felt flattered to be a part of that plan, to be involved in a project of mutual inclusion, the purpose of which was creating the flesh of one's flesh. The notion of becoming a father, then, had taken hold of me to the point of becoming an indispensable expectation.

Our bedroom plunged into silence. Wrapped in dimness I tried to lose myself in studying for one of the many refresher certifications on rehabilitating vocal disturbance. I would read and reread without comprehending a single concept, lost as I was in my thoughts. What would my child's face look like, provided I had one? I was certain about one thing: it would never have a groveling expression. In this world there is nothing more cruel than a child's eyes asking for sympathy.

They cut right through you. No, my child, you will never have those eyes. I have a memory from my childhood that reviles me every time I run into that look, and it hurts.

My family had recently moved to the city, and I was in the third grade. I can see myself now, running furiously through the schoolyard and pouncing on one of my classmates, who, in order to get to the exit before the others, when the bell rang, had tripped me. Ready to pummel him, I had been disarmed by the frightened look of a little girl next to him begging for mercy.

"Please, don't hurt my brother. He didn't do it on purpose."

She was lying. But it was actually her lying that made her eyes that much more terrified. And she had that look. If you've seen it once, you've seen it a million times. The same one that I would encounter so many times afterward on the faces of children escaping the squalid streets of their neighborhoods, in the hallways of juvenile detention centers, in orphanages, in group homes, and in foster homes. It was Enzino's and Martina's look. And maybe even mine, too. No, my child would not be scared. He won't plead, nor beg for tenderness; he won't tremble at the sound of a voice, nor live in the fear of falling asleep, nor will he experience dread upon awakening. As a child he will not be a little man as I was forced to be. He will be my son.

I had already learned in the early years of my life that no one gives you anything for free and that there are no half measures. To get in the good graces of men—that is, the ones who really count—you have to be willing to do what is necessary, at any cost. And whoever obsequiously bows his head once will do it over and over. I still have my mother's words etched in my mind: "*Se porti le mazzate a casa, ti prendi il resto. You need to give as good as you get.*" That's how it was.

Raging through the streets of my town, I was forging myself for survival, an art for which I discovered I was particularly predisposed. And if someone dared to cross me, even in the slightest, he would risk being buried by a hail of rocks or, if he got the better of me, by an avalanche of curses and insults. By the time I was six, I had taken aim at the windows of houses, run over innocent pedestrians with my bike, torched the tunic of a priest who wouldn't let me in the church, burned dozens of lizards at the stake in the middle of the courtyard if only for the pleasure of seeing them roast in the flames. And naturally I had learned not to fear anything or anyone and to get the first shot in on anyone who crossed my path.

At the café, all the playboys who would spend all their time way over their head chasing skirts would have fun with me. And they would taunt me for the sheer joy of seeing me pissed off and ready to come to blows. I would deliver their love letters—and, perhaps without knowing it, also their death letters. I would make cigarette runs and bring them carafes of wine that they'd gulp down while sitting at the café in the piazza playing hands of tressette and rummy. I got comfortable dealing with ex-convicts at just four years old, when my mother—who broke her back on the sewing machine to single-handedly support the household and two other small children—would plop me down next to my father, who for some time had been on vacation in the Acerra prison. Members of the Camorra and murderers vied to win over my affection: they would carve little wooden soldiers and seahorses for me, they would play soccer with me in the penitentiary courtyard, and they would lavish me in their own way, with stories about betrayals and settling scores. And behind those bars I also saw for the first time someone getting a tattoo, by hand with a needle and ink: it was the holy face of Jesus illuminated by rays of light, and it covered my father's entire back. One of his cellmates had carved it into him. Later, my father told me it had taken the guy a month. Anyway, I've always been disgusted by tattoos—and by the people who sport them.

Thinking back, more than being a little man, in my early childhood I was closer to a little animal.

We moved to the city when I was about seven. And it did not take me long to figure out where I stood: if I didn't want to give in, I would have to adapt to the rules required by that new world. Rules that did not take into account some primitive instinct that I had developed elsewhere. Bitter about what I had left behind and shocked by what I would find there, I had landed in a situation that would slowly bend me to its will, break my legs, and straighten my spine, making me ashamed of what I was. Then, once I had gotten over the unshakable certainty that my new life would unfurl before me like a soft skein of yarn, I never misbehaved again. I became a good son, a diligent student, a well-mannered boy, and a tireless worker. Qualities that would also make me a devoted husband, an affectionate family man, and if luck favored me, the owner of a house in the Vomero district of Naples, saddled with a nice twenty-year mortgage. I would never break the law, I would never appear before a court, and I would go to church every Sunday morning. And the rather ferocious eyes that I had as a child would one day become solicitous and see things in a different light. My son would never have eyes like that.

For the rest of the evening Costanza did not set foot in the bedroom. If it had not been for some muffled noises that would come from the study now and then, I would have thought she was out of the house. Before surrendering to sleep, I slipped into a flight of fancy as though I were dreaming. And I found myself with Martina in her foster home. I imagined her first few nights in that still unfamiliar space.

Falling asleep became difficult for her. Continuous flashes of light streaked across the underside of her shut lids: details enlarge, almost exploding inside of her. Hour after hour, frozen on the bed trying to let it all go, to forget, to shut out those sharp pains behind her eyes. Then sleep overcomes her. It comes suddenly and it seems as though the mattress is opening up, splitting in half and dropping her into a silent place where her body floats weightlessly, wrapped in a sheet. A long fall without a landing. That's when she gets scared. It's better to be awake. The night is full of holes. Everything in the room seems to fall on top of her, springing from the darkness. In the dark, though, memories take form. The cavernous voice of her mother, the cranky voice of Concetta, and the festive voices of her cousins. Their altercations. The wrinkle etched into Grandpa Lino's face, and his gigantic eyes behind his Coke-bottle lenses. The gray sky of that morning on the little school bus. Geppina's heart-wrenching screams while they carry her away. It's as though all of the misery of the people who live in that place had landed on her and continued to climb over her with a thousand hands and a thousand feet. As though it were her fault, or as though she had to be the one to pay for her loved ones. She thinks about doing something. But she's only five years old, and what can a five-year-old do?

~ 8 ~

When I met her, Costanza was an open-minded woman. And that's what struck me about her: her free thinking, along with a pragmatism that allowed her to see things for what they were. In pruning her life's garden, she preferred the clean cut of lopping shears to bring everything into clearly defined, solid focus.

I met her at the house of a common friend, Gianluca Grassi, who was celebrating his birthday that evening. She was seated there on a sofa, her legs crossed with perfect posture, expounding, with seraphic conviction, on the destruction of one of the most sacred totems: the family. To heal the many sufferings of the human psyche, it's necessary to go to the very origin of them, she went on, because the moment these problems are born, they encapsulate themselves like cysts and proliferate right within the family. The most reasonable action is, thus, liberating oneself of everything, amputating, in no uncertain terms, any ties with blood relations. And I felt that her speech, which went on for quite a while, seemed to proceed fast and linear, like a bullet toward its target.

Some pretended to listen to her; others didn't even bother to listen. Meanwhile, a young woman seated across from me interrupted the awkward moment. With a shrill voice, she ferried our attention toward more frivolous topics that were more in keeping with the time and place. So Costanza, grasping the lack of widespread support for her, put on an amused smile, left us, and consigned herself to the chitter-chatter and laughter of a group of friends who welcomed her arrival with gratitude and deference, like worshippers before a vestal virgin.

Closer to forty than to thirty, my future partner had a certain youthfulness about her. And the soft tone of her voice betrayed her robust yet well-proportioned physique. She had a narrow, oval face framed by a wonderful head of untamed copper-blond hair, which she tied up in a makeshift pony-tail, and a heart-shaped mouth. Later on, I would learn at my own expense how the sweetness of her features and her big blue eyes clashed with the icy determination of her personality.

I caught up with her in the garden, where I handed her a glass of the same Brunello that I had been slowly sipping all evening long, and sat down on a lounge chair next to her. A pleasant evening breeze had finally picked up—an unex-pected break in that torrid July—and carried fresh air along with an intense fragrance from the jasmine vines that climbed in lush, white clusters up the cast-iron arbor on the patio. The scenery was perfect, the ambience, too. From the living room, the warm, unmistakable voice of Frank Sinatra singing "Stormy Weather" reached our ears. (Old Frank, along with Sammy Davis Jr. and Dean Martin, was part of a Rat Pack CD box set that Costanza had given the guest of honor for his birthday.) The only thing missing from our scene was a nice dialogue, like the ones in an intellectual salon: banally intelligent, agreeably up to date, superficially deep.

We broke the ice by joking about our reactions to those who had tried, however coyly, to lead us into each other's arms. And though our friends were keeping themselves at a distance, we laughed each time we intercepted one of their hypocritically furtive glances coming our way. Only the birthday boy, with a keen eye and the discretion of a good waiter, dared to get close enough to fill our glasses and then disappear with an air of approval. At that point, we broke into a sophisticated conversation on cinema, art, and literature. In truth she was the one who held court. I just followed along, both flattered and intimidated, as I usually did in situations involving social promotion. Costanza talked at length about Woody Allen's latest film and the latest Renaissance painting exhibit at the Capodimonte Museum—being sure to point out that her real passion was contemporary art. She even let me in on her interest in photography. Then she went on at great length talking about Philip Roth and his *American Pastoral*, even if the book that touched her the most was *The Human Stain*. That is how I came to know about Coleman Silk: that evening I felt that the secret about his identity and his roots was all too similar to mine.

But precisely that painful thought, along with the Rat Pack, the Brunello di Montalcino that I was still nursing, and Costanza going on and on about Kieślowski and Basquiat, convinced me that that woman was utterly captivating me with her charm because the world that she evoked was her world, and just the idea of being part of it thrilled me more than any other desire. That evening, among those people, I felt certain I had finally reached the destination I had always dreamed about. And even though I had always struggled to keep up, nobody would ever discover where I came from and who I really was.

As for Costanza, then, her anti-conformism and her complete absence of bias, which she had continued to display during the early days of our relationship, made me hopeful that I would not hold out any surprises for her or, worse, disappoint her. I was hopeful that she would always appreciate me, even knowing about my past, for what I had become—for that which, with a little help from her, I could still become.

Although those sick days had really taken their toll on me, they were no match for the sheer boredom of being forced to stay in the house, not to mention being exposed to Costanza's gloomy face. My cloistering had weakened me, but I was a new man. I decided it was time to sneak out of the house. On the doorstep, before she let me go and without even saying a word, Costanza renewed her request to make another sacrifice in exchange for a solemn promise: it would be the third and final attempt at having a child. Then the two of us would resign ourselves to the long, cold winter of our lives.

That afternoon the streets of Naples were swept by a cold wind. The dazzling light of dusk lit up the ocher-colored facades of the tenements over in Poggioreale. Far off, past the highway toll booths at Corso Malta, the Centro Direzionale, our business district, gleamed like a forest of glass and concrete with its sparkling skyscrapers that stood out against a red-streaked sky. A maze of overpasses hovering above the wide valley branched off in various directions, while below, among the run-down buildings, you could make out the turreted walls of the prison snaking through blocks of apartments. Despite the traffic on the exit ramp, which led right into a copse of skyscrapers, I arrived well ahead of schedule. After the fateful morning in that café in the highway rest

area, which culminated in having to postpone my appointment, no one had seen hide nor hair of those two. For that whole week I had spent in bed, not one single phone call, which was rather unusual, given their urgent insistence of late. At any rate, I was counting on the lawyer to exhibit extreme tact in convincing them of my good faith and of the difficulty I was having in breaking through the barriers to satisfy their hopes.

In the mind of Kenzō Tange, the Centro Direzionale was to represent a harmonious epitome of contradictions. The two building styles were to also symbolize the two souls of the companies residing there: one was dynamic and solid; the other propelled skyward and yet was firmly anchored. But both were capable of inspiring enthusiasm and confidence. For this reason they had erected cement towers at the entrance with glass viewing elevators and skyscrapers with mirrored facades and sharp angles. On the avenues there would be ample space for different works of contemporary art, not only for the aesthetics of urban design but also for the symbolic common denominator: the image of a man who is aware of the means at his disposal, and master of them, in the new technological society—a rather ambitious and daring idea in a city like this. It was a project that was supposed to launch Naples into the new millennium, unleashing a renaissance and instilling self-awareness in its citizenry (at least that was the wishful thinking of the governing class at the time, in the second half of the 1980s), which wanted no part in assuming any personal responsibility, despite all good intentions and the numerous injections of government monies, which invariably were lost in the trickle down of myriad private interests. Anyway, what came out of all this was a cathedral of illusions falling to pieces in a desert of ruins that has nothing to do whatsoever with the spirit of the city.

The inner workings of the district are a labyrinth of abandoned streets and parking structures inhabited by darkness. The only thing providing illumination for these structures were the flashes coming down from the lampposts on the overpasses through the skylights. Occasionally the lamps spotlighted a network of lanes on the highway that are choked by exhaust fumes and by garbage of every variety known to humankind. Here and there, a series of exits lead you to the surface by way of forsaken escalators that reek with the persistent odor of urine. After a single day of rain, these dark chasms flood with puddles that are too wide to step over and remain stagnant for days on end.

After parking on the sidewalk, entering the belly of what seemed like a big, agonizing iron serpent, I headed into the semidarkness of the underground lot, glancing at the rusted signs that indicated a way to the outside. On the landing of the last staircase, a shadowy figure blocked my path. A scrawny guy in a long black overcoat with a scarf on his head was crouched down in a corner with a hodgepodge of his junk around him, taking shelter behind some cardboard boxes.

As I passed him, I was overtaken by an unbearably pungent odor. Without even looking at me, the guy held out his hand and asked me for a cigarette. His fingers were stained yellow from nicotine.

"Sorry. I don't smoke."

I rummaged through my pockets and handed him one of the menthol candies that Costanza had given to me before I went out.

"You eat it!" he grumbled resentfully, creeping back among his boxes.

With a hint of a smile, I went on, wondering how it was possible to inhabit a body like that.

With my coat collar turned up and hands in my pockets, I braved a gust of icy wind that suddenly blew, whipping down the main avenue. There wasn't a soul in sight. The purplish glow was spectacular. The sky streaked with red, orange, indigo, and black, reflected onto the mirrored facades of the office buildings. Under the porticoed walkways, the bright signs from the cafés and bistros packed with people were flashing. From time to time, a solitary figure, briefcase in hand, would duck into some entryway. On the pedestrian mall, despite the police patrols, a throng of youngsters played soccer, while on a park bench in the withered flower bed, two lovebirds were warming themselves with passionate kisses, oblivious to the cold.

Across the avenue, on Island F, I found Building 5, which was wedged between the Banco di Napoli offices and a clothing store, in the window of which three mannequins were showing off the pretentious though inexpensive apparel, which was in keeping with the clientele. In the dark lobby near the store window was an abandoned reception desk, and a little further past that, waiting at the only functioning elevator were two guys who, at first glimpse, seemed like rookie lawyers. The two were engaged in small talk with a young woman in a miniskirt and a top with a generous neckline.

Meanwhile, I was scanning a plastic directory that was mounted on a central column near the foyer. It bore a long list of offices and their related floors. In small characters, I read:

Law Firm of
Castaldi and Serra, Attys at Law
15th Floor, Suite 56

According to the clock, I still had about a half hour before the appointment, and I had no intention of being kept waiting.

The prospect of staying in that chilly grotto was not very tempting but certainly more so than the prospect of wandering the maze of the windswept porticoes. Although I had recovered from that terrible flu, my throat still felt raw; each time I coughed, it was like eating glass. Right in front of me, there was a café in the covered portico. Its lights, along with the heat I imagined coming from the swirls of steam inside, came to my rescue. I walked in and sat down at a table on the opposite end, far from the doorway but close to the windows that overlooked the main entrance of Building 5, which was suddenly bustling with people who would have been unthinkable a few moments earlier. And just as quickly, the café, for its part, began to empty. Two customers seated at a small table next to mine, engrossed in their documents, case files, sandwiches, and coffee, suddenly stood up and slipped out, the echo of one of their voices dominating the café. "The pope is dead!" said one man, while the television showed images of Saint Peter's Square brimming with crowds of tear-soaked people who had been camped out for days and nights, keeping vigil and praying. Everything went quiet. The barista stopped making coffee, the cashier left his post, and two cold and shivering ladies stood petrified at the counter. The waitress, who stopped in her tracks a few feet away from me with her tray in hand, stepped backward and glued her eyes to the TV screen. In the by now religious silence, all you could hear was the jingle from the slot machine that was chiming nonstop. It was revealed to be untrue. It was one of the many rumors going around hour after hour, keeping millions of worshippers on edge. In reality, the newscaster, with a sad voice, was referring to another clergyman who, at the pope's bedside, had said, "This evening, or perhaps this very night, Christ will open up the gates of heaven to our Holy Father, and waiting there to embrace him will surely be Mary, to whom the pontiff has already said, 'I am all yours.'"

I was savoring some boiling hot tea when, casting my eyes at Building 5, the slight figure of a man hunched over from the cold caught my attention. It was Michele Esposito, or Lino, as his wife, Geppina, called him. He was on the covered portico, motionless and shivering, with the frightened expression of someone who, feeling out of place, extends a shy smile to anyone who passes by, almost apologizing for his mere presence. Now and then, behind the thick glasses that would slip down his nose, he would shoot me a subtle glance and then go back to looking elsewhere as though awaiting a sign. When one did appear, it almost seemed like charity to him. So, performing a half bow, he turned to chat with someone behind him, hidden from sight by the billboard advertising the bar. And one moment later Geppina appeared, arms crossed tightly over her waist to keep warm. She was wearing dark clothing and a wool scarf, which revealed a few locks of the yellowish hair that covered her head; she stared silently at me with her pale, haggard face. Like Lino, she too directed a supplicating look at me—the same unbearable look that I detest in children. And seeing it on their faces was just as pathetic.

Seeing her there, hunched over from the cold wind, was like feeling your heart break in two, as though, in that precise instant, a part of me were falling to pieces with her. That woman had only appeared on my horizon just a few months earlier, and for a number of reasons I forced myself to keep my distance from her. Yet she had unleashed a war with my very sense of rationality, which, though pressing for some necessary distance, would succumb to a senseless feeling of affinity. For some inexplicable reason, I took a liking to her expression—including that certain something in her stare.

I gestured for them to come inside. Only Lino, after some insistence, finally accepted an espresso. Geppina, instead, took the black scarf off her head and granted me a melancholy smile, which elicited an inopportune feeling of guilt on my part.

"This is for your mother," she said, handing me a plastic bag that was sitting at her feet. "It's nothing much. Just sugar and coffee. And do me a favor: tell her that it was nice to see her. . . ."

The man, on the other hand, letting his cup rattle on the saucer, rummaged through his pockets and handed me some golden-colored packs of cigarettes of some unknown brand—perhaps American.

"Thank you, but I don't smoke. . . ."

"So give them to someone . . . your father, a friend. . . ."

My insistence was of little avail. Although I was uncomfortable doing it, with a reluctant grimace of gratitude, I was forced to accept their offerings. I bundled them into a single package and placed it on the little table in front of me, with the determined intent of getting right to the heart of the matter so I could dispense with the awkward pleasantries.

When it came to Geppina and her husband, just as with their entire family, I experienced a strange contradiction of feelings. On the one hand I felt caught up, invested in their lives, even responsible for their destiny. Yet, on the other hand, I rejected them for who they were, for the way they came across, detesting them almost because of the ignoble destiny to which they were bound. More than once I had found myself thinking that their misfortunes would never come to an end; that, sooner or later, all of them, in one way or another—by drinking from life's bitter chalice—would have been poisoned to death. They weren't like me. They weren't part of my world and this put me in an uncomfortable position. Although I struggled to erect barriers between us, because this whole process was beyond their comprehension, they had no choice but to hang on my every word about decisions concerning Martina and about the day-to-day things in which they forced me to participate, even against my own will. Nevertheless, the more I tried to extricate myself from the sticky swamp of their misfortunes, the more they pulled me down to the mucky bottom of an affiliation I wanted no part of. And this hidden hostility of mine contradicted my good intentions of shedding light on Martina's situation. For, even as I struggled to protect the tenuous flame of their hopes—a flame destined to be snuffed out by the inevitable fury of a fierce wind—I was more and more convinced that for Martina, any other path open to her would have been better, all things considered. This tormented me day in and day out. And even though I was ashamed of it, out of love for my mother and because of that sense of guilt she carried around, I gave in to the torment. Often my bending over backward became a right and proper act of devotion, a sacrifice that shed the vital lymph necessary to narcotize my very rationality.

"I'm sorry about last week . . . just that I had the flu, and . . ."

"*Pe' carità.* . . . Don't even mention it. . . . When you called, we were in the waiting room. Then the lawyer came over and told us, and he said that it was better for us to meet today. . . ." replied the man.

"I don't understand. . . . He sent you away?"

"Yes, uh, I mean, no. . . . He just said that it was better for you to be there and he moved our appointment to today."

"And that's it?"

"It's about the money!" Geppina added, hanging her head.

"What do you mean 'about the money'?"

"You see, Doc, the lawyer even called us this morning," Lino cut in timidly.

"Listen, do me a favor: you can both call me Michele," I replied, trying to disguise my annoyance.

"No, no, please, I could never," he said and then paused. "Your name is Michele? Like me," he added with a hint of surprise, looking at Geppina.

Geppina, for her part, seemed to suddenly liven up.

"No . . . Just like my father," she said, embracing me with her eyes. Then she turned toward her husband. "On his birth certificate, papa's name was Angelo, but they always called him Michele. . . . In my family everyone named after papa is called Michele."

Then turning toward me, she added, "All my sisters have sons named Michele."

"So what did the lawyer tell you?" I asked, trying with all my might to nip that conversation in the bud.

"He said that there's been a complication. He said that the judge won't even see him. And then he talked about money, too. He says that he has bureaucratic expenses. But we . . ."

"How much have you given him up until now?"

"Since he's been on our case, we've given him three hundred euros a month, but we've missed two months' worth of payments. You know how it is," said the man hiding behind a veil of embarrassment.

"I've pawned every bit of gold that I had to pay the lawyer," added Geppina despondently.

"The necklace and the bracelet that I had given to Geppina and our wedding rings," her husband chimed in.

"Now it's getting tougher," his wife added.

"How much have you given him up until now?" I asked. Geppina couldn't recall.

"Around three thousand euros," Lino replied, fixing his glasses that had slid down to the tip of his nose.

Some irksome prattle took over the café once more; from where we were sitting, you could hear not only the laughter of some customers at the counter and the whirring of the espresso machine going full tilt but also a raucous metallic clanging followed by obnoxious music and intermittent beeping sounds. It was the video-poker machine. And the guy playing it was the same one who hadn't even lifted his head from the screen when they announced the pope had died.

"How is Martina? Have you seen her? . . . Have you talked to her?" Geppina asked.

"Yes, I see her each time I go to the foster home. She's well. She's eating and she's healthy. She isn't my patient, so I can't see her for too long, but last week I brought her a chocolate Easter egg and I talked with her a bit. She told me that 'mommy' had brought her an 'egg with chocolate in it.' I figured she was referring to Maddalena and so I asked her how she was. Martina replied that 'she's not good. She falls down when she gets shaky, and she runs away so no one can see her like that.'"

"Yeah, that's what I would always tell Martina when *Matalena*, Maddalena, would suddenly leave."

"And now how is Maddalena?"

"It's been two months since we've seen her," Lino informed me.

"We even went to the police. We checked all the hospitals. Nothing. No one's seen her," Geppina added, not taking her eyes off me.

When she would talk about Maddalena's escapades, that woman's blue eyes would flame up with anger, but in that instant I saw the light in those same eyes go out forever. One day she had confided to me her perennial desire for time itself to roll over her without leaving a trace, like water over glass.

~ 9 ~

The last time that they let her see Martina was a sunny late-September day redolent of summer's warmth, with the fragrance of wet grass. As she had done for quite some time, in the middle of each month, when she would come see her granddaughter, she awoke at dawn. That morning Geppina had a long face and swollen eyes from a sleepless night; yet her spirits were unusually high. While she brushed her hair in front of the mirror in the bedroom, she detected the aroma of fresh-made espresso, mixed with the scent of aftershave. Lino was waiting for her in the kitchen, sitting at the table with a cup in his hands and his eyes glued to the window, staring at a solitary streak of whitish clouds in the otherwise blue sky. After the violent thunderstorm the previous night, everything seemed to come into clear focus. Geppina walked down the hallway as the rest of the household slept. In the dim light she paused for a moment to look at the photo on the wall: it was a portrait of her son Salvatore, condemned to an eternal smile, to eternal youth.

He had died in the simplest way in the world, without any fuss, amid the sunshine and dazzling reds of a brisk, beautiful autumn day, still reminiscent of summer. It happened in an instant: a misstep, the fear on his face, a five-story drop from the scaffolding, an interminable scream, and then nothing more. So much time had already passed since he met his demise while working as a black-market laborer, instead of at the barrel of a gun waiting in ambush or in a crazy car chase trying to outrun the cops after a robbery.

A few months later, Geppina had been seized by a crippling pain and was overwhelmed with desperation. She could not have ever imagined surviving her son, much less being able to take a single breath after his death. She was in the clutches of a terrible torment, a monstrous being that revealed itself in all its horror. Each of her eight children were like eight thorns planted into her side, but Salvatore's drew more blood than the others. Staring at that young man's smiling face, she caught herself thinking that if on the one hand death had cut him down in the blossom of his youth, on the other hand it had preserved him for all time and in her eyes he would always be the same. He would never age or show pain and suffering, nor would he be gunned down in the street. Although it could not permanently console her, this thought had allowed her to wake up in a good mood that day.

Parco degli Oleandri was shrouded in a dead silence, and the side streets were still deserted. Stepping around a pile of garbage that blocked the main entrance to their building, Geppina and her husband headed down the long avenue flanked by rows of scrawny saplings that seemed to suffocate under the heavy apartment complexes, staggered one on top of the other. Through an open window came the sound of quarreling voices, cursing, and inhuman screams. The couple skirted around the parish of the Redentore, the Holy

Redeemer in Arzano, a building made of gray concrete that more closely resembled a ship's bow than a church, and to them it must have seemed as though the Lord, crushed under the load of so many sins around those parts, had decided that very morning to set sail for more pleasant surroundings.

The concrete median on the highway blocked their way, forcing them along the shoulder of the roadway where cars sped by, spraying water from the puddles in the chewed-up asphalt. After a dozen or so yards, they crossed the round-about, which by now was like a swamp, and made their way along the sidewalk to the bus stop, where a crowd was jostling to get on. Despite the fresh air that late-summer morning, the heat was quite bothersome.

They took one bus and then another along the ring road without saying a word. They passed through one small municipality after another, as the sun moved higher from the horizon. In Marano, the bus stopped next to the town hall. The square was brimming with people. There was a market and they walked right through it. She was still not talking, but she was smiling at him as a gap opened up in the crowd. They advanced along the only clear path, clinging to each other, pushed ahead by a sea of human flesh, until Geppina cast her eye among the baskets chock-full of shoes and piled up in a jumbled array. What caught her attention was a pair of white-and-blue-striped canvas close-toed sandals with a rubber sole. She examined them, ran her hand along the length of them, asked the size and the price, and had them placed in a shopping bag. Finally, she got underway, her husband in tow, in the clear morning light down the unpopulated street that led to the public gardens.

As they walked under a fierce sun that was baking the town, it seemed that anything was possible—that even the dusty streets and the deafening traffic and the hostile heat could release a sweet scent of hope. Now and then, when they happened to look at each other, they could see an unusual serenity and uncharacteristic calm on each other's face. It was like a cease-fire in their many daily battles. There was no apprehension in their expressions, nor worry, and their hearts were beating normally. Each time the tenth of the month came along and their visit with Martina got closer, it was as though, for no apparent reason, they would experience inordinate faith in life and in the infinite possibilities it held in store.

In front of the park gate, dogs feasting on some garbage would growl as they rummaged from one thing to another. Beyond the fence at the end of a tree-lined path, between the swing and the orange plastic slide, Geppina and Lino could barely recognize Martina in the child seated on a park bench with her head down. Close by, two young assistants from the foster home—a young man and a young woman—were smoking and casually conversing. Geppina immediately recognized them and winced. All around her everything changed. Suddenly the world revealed itself in more somber hues and in absolute uncertainty. Everything went back to being as revolting as before. Each thing reminded her of the life that she so detested. At the sight of Martina, she felt sucked to the bottom of an endless pit of misery, drowned in her own adversities and in her children's, too. So, staring at her husband, she shooed away the dogs that barked as they retreated, and she headed straight for her granddaughter. Meanwhile, Lino, who had been denied any legal contact whatsoever with the child, hid behind the fence grating, popping his head out to make sure he didn't lose sight of her.

Geppina stopped a few steps from Martina, just enough time for a quick glance before she felt something bladelike pass through her heart. Her granddaughter just stood there, frozen, gawking at her with a vacant stare. Unlike the last time, when the moment she greeted Geppina she had broken into uncontrollable tears, now she was showing little emotion, her feet planted firmly on the ground, while the young female assistant nudged her toward Geppina. Martina's brush-cut hair made her oval face seem more gaunt than usual. Her little flowered dress, two sizes too large and down to her knee, gave her the appearance of a twig about to snap.

"*Signora*, please don't make a scene. . . . No yelling or arguments. . . . Otherwise, we'll have to take her away," said the male assistant resolutely.

"But what have you done to her hair?"

"We had to fix it. . . . Yesterday we found her with scissors in her hand. . . . She had clipped all of her hair. . . . But she looks good like this, don't you think?" the young woman added, patting Martina on her head. Martina seemed like a frightened sparrow.

"Martina? Come on. . . . Go to your grandmother. Come on. Go!" she added, pushing her forward by her scrawny shoulders.

With the plastic shopping bag in her hand, Geppina shot a scared look at them and kept her eyes on her granddaughter who advanced toward her dragging one foot with a pout on her face. When she was right in front of her, in her granddaughter's eyes she could see flashes of a thousand memories burn out in the cruel shadows of acquiescence. Geppina was unable to speak. Such was the fear gripping her that she would have screamed, but she was paralyzed by terror. So she crouched down, took the girl in her arms, and held her to her chest. She shed a few silent tears that she quickly dried with her hand so that no one would notice.

"*Nun te preoccupà bella da nonna, ancora nu poco e te porto 'a casa . . . nun te preoccupà*. Don't worry, grandma's little cutie. Just a bit more time and I'll take you home. . . . Don't worry," she whispered in her ear.

Then she sat down on the park bench and held her tightly, while all around them the happy voices of children running on the grass and going up and down the slide got louder.

Martina didn't speak the whole time. She didn't utter a peep. She just kept her head resting on Geppina's shoulder, staring at who knows what, with no sign of a smile. Upon seeing the blue-and-white sandals, she just said that her foot ached. So her grandmother took off her little shoe and discovered that she had a cut on her heel. From the raw wound a little trickle of blood ran down to the sole of her foot. She looked over toward the two assistants, but they were engrossed in their conversation, so she looked for Lino but didn't see him either. She got up, washed Martina's foot in the fountain and dried it with a tissue. She took the socks that she had brought from home and slipped them on her grand-daughter; then she slipped on the new sandals. Martina let her do it without saying a word. The rest of the time they just sat in silence, one next to the other, hand in hand, feeling like nervous passengers waiting for the last train.

~ 10 ~

All of a sudden, the café door opened and a man bundled in a stylish puffy coat took over the place with his cavernous voice.

"*Signori*, my name is Gennaro and I'm not an addict; I'm not a delinquent. I'm just a family man who has to feed his children. I'm not begging for a handout but for a little bit of help. . . . You'll be doing some good because *il Signore è tardariello ma nun è scurdariello*, the Lord might take his time, but he never forgets."

Standing in the doorway, he kept talking while he displayed a series of products stuffed into the pockets of his coat: six-in-one interchangeable screwdrivers, compact needle kits and spools of thread, the latest electric-arc lighters, battery-powered toothbrushes, microfiber dusting cloths, palm-length folding umbrellas, and other worthless knickknacks.

"Everything for two euros. What you do for me, the Lord will give you back. . . . It's better than stealing. I'm just asking for a little contribution. . . . Everything for two euros. . . . And I've even got facial tissues with a two-year warranty."

Someone yelled at him, complaining about the cold wind that was coming in through the open door; another groused about how his voice was hurting their eardrums. By contrast, a young lawyer, who seemed to be in a big hurry, in trying to slip past him and exit, seemed rather to be dancing with him in the doorway, but the vendor blocked his way, waving a pair of socks under his nose. "*Avvocà*, Counselor, these are perfect for ya. . . . Cotton lisle socks . . . Five pairs for five euros. . . ."

The two shared that tango until a waiter showed up, dumped some change into the vendor's hand, and pushed him brusquely out into the cold street. The man knelt on the sidewalk and started to slam his merchandise on the ground; despite the storefront window and the bustle inside, his expletives were distinctly audible.

"What can I do? . . . What should I? . . . If I was born in Milan, Turin, Genoa, or even in Cagliari or Palermo, someone was gonna definitely help me out, but since I was born in this shit-hole city, I'm treated like a beggar. . . . I don't want to steal. What am I supposed to tell my kids? What can I tell them? . . . *Che 'o padre è 'nu strunz? Sí, è vero, song 'nu strunz.* That their father's a loser? Yup, it's true, I'm a loser. But if I've been reduced to this, it's not my fault. If they give me a job . . . I'm not asking for no handouts. . . . *Chillu curnuto 'e Berlusconi e chill'ato cornuto 'e Bassolino pensano solo 'e cazzi loro, e po' vonne pure 'o voto.* That jerk Berlusconi and that other jerk Bassolino only think about their freakin' selves, and they have the nerve to ask for my vote."

I don't know why, but I caught myself eyeing the cigarettes, the sugar, and the coffee that I was holding in the bag on the table in front of me. And I even cracked a half smile as I recalled a newspaper article that was quoting some tax assessor, from I don't know which town in lower Padania, who had put before the council a proposal to arrest all the panhandlers and unlicensed street vendors because, in his opinion, they were defiling the city's decorum.

The office of Castaldi and Serra, attorneys at law, consisted of a single cramped little room on the fifteenth floor. They had their degrees on the wall, along with a number of fake *gouache* works that broke up the line of brown Formica shelves on which neatly arranged multicolored case files prominently stood. An L-shaped double desk made of brushed metal and glass took up just about all the space, such that to open or close the door it was necessary to get up from one of the two chairs. The well-polished desk, conscientiously uncluttered by files, was free of any objects except for two framed photographs of a young woman and a little boy, a black laptop, and a set of Spalding & Bros. pens meticulously aligned on the desktop in front of the black leather swivel chair with a high back. That minimalism led me to imagine the lawyer as being about thirty years old. Taking into account the order that dominated that room, one could surmise that there was nothing out of place in that man's life and that he cared a lot about his image. Not so much out of professional necessity but for a devotion to style that was forged by the rules of his world: one of social gatherings, of high-performance cars, of beautiful houses, and of money. In short, a rising young lawyer from the *Napoli bene*, the well-to-do Naples.

Except that it was cold in his office—really cold. So cold that all you could see of the young woman sitting at a monitor, bundled up as she was, were her fingers clacking along the keyboard, the whites of her eyes whenever she turned to take a gander at us with her vigilant look and her furrowed brows like those of a mastiff defending an impenetrable house. Once in a while, the phone would ring and she would answer in monosyllabic utterances, maybe to keep her chattering teeth quiet.

"No, anytime now, Counselor Serra will . . . no, Counselor Castaldi is not here either. Good afternoon." That's what came out of her all in one breath by the umpteenth call.

She paused to look at my wool cap lowered over my ears, which must have seemed ridiculous with its red pom-pom like a feather. Then she quickly threw herself headlong into her work with a slight wrinkle of disappointment on her mouth.

As intimidated as they were, Geppina and Lino remained glued to their seats, even focusing on their breathing, while I was intrigued by the brass plaque on the wall, right behind the desk. It bore four lines of engraved wording, and because of the arrangement of the lines in a squat pyramidal shape, it seemed to be some pronouncement from above:

Those who know
History are aware that the
Law is viewed in the streets, in factories and
in families more clearly than in the dark halls of politics.

In that aseptic, minimalist environment, the plaque was totally out of place. Stuck amid the numerous prints on the wall, it clashed with the rest of the decor. But how did it end up there? The only possible explanation is that someone, having found it already hanging and having grown attached to such noble- and solemn-sounding words, had left it there, believing it had a certain evocative quality. To me, knowing nothing about the law, it seemed to be the only thing that made sense in that office, even though it contradicted the image I had formed of Counselor Serra.

Suddenly, a voice on the other side of the door, accompanied by the loud commotion of footsteps, announced the arrival of the lawyer. Geppina and her husband, who hadn't made a peep the whole time, were now forced to stand up so that he could come inside.

Adriano Serra was a handsome young man with straight, jet-black hair like silk. Tall, lean, and athletic, he wore a dark designer suit, which seemed to be sewn right onto him, a light-blue shirt with a small checkered pattern and a high button-down collar, pulled together by a bold, wide tie knot, and not without affectation, French cuffs sans links. His attire was a clue that this young professional aspired to something greater than this broom-closet office in the Centro Direzionale. Of course the metallic fixture around his right hand seemed to be yet another indication of his studied elegance.

"Sorry for being late. . . . I just stopped off at the hospital to have them adjust my splint," he said, lifting his hand bandaged in a brace. "An accident at the gym . . . judo."

If it was even possible, his very appearance intensified Geppina and Lino's uneasiness. How they had ended up there with that particular lawyer, I simply had no clue. At any rate, confirming with his secretary that there were no urgent calls to take and telling her he wasn't taking any new ones, the young man asked her to have the café deliver a hot tea for him but not before first asking whether we wanted anything. Then, without deigning to look at us, he began to organize his things. He took off the stylish, blue three-quarter-length overcoat and, after getting comfortable in his chair, turned on the laptop in front of him. Last, from inside of a black leather bag, he took out a yellow folder, opened it, and scrutinizing two documents, finally cut to the chase.

"So, Doctor Campo . . . these are the two motions that I filed . . ." he began, handing me some papers, ". . . one at the *Carabinieri* station in Volla, the other at the court in Naples. In both, I requested injunctions against the foster home, in compliance with the provisions issued in the juvenile court's decree, but I haven't gotten any results yet. Judge Conti hasn't even responded, but her assistant assured me that she would investigate the facility to assess the veracity about Martina's absence at the monthly appointments. But this is just a minor battle, which I feel will be resolved in the end. You just need to wait and press on. Beyond that, I'm afraid, there's not much that can be done. . . . But there's more to the story: I get the impression that Judge Conti has some preconceived notions about the matter. She follows her convictions, which just happen to be supported by fact of law. Now, you have to take into consideration the home environment in which Ms. De Nicola and Mr. Esposito live: given their past and their present, no court of law will ever believe them. Unfortunately, in this world, the last things to die are prejudices. . . . In the end it was pointless to contest the decree. . . . As you know, the request was rejected because Concetta Piccolo, Martina's ex-guardian, had no legal right to even be involved in the writ. The same way we were denied the right to review the court proceedings that pertained to Martina's order of removal, and for exactly the same reason. Concetta's intervention was considered voluntary and therefore without legal rights."

Hearing him speak in that way, Lino, who had paid attention carefully, upright in his chair, could not hold back his surprise—not so much for the lawyer's uncommon courtesy as for his taking the time to provide incomprehensible and, above all, unexpected explanations. Only a few minutes earlier, down at the café, he had pegged the lawyer as being too uncharitable to give them two words of comfort. As a practice, he usually gave those two no more than five minutes: between taking one phone call and another, he would rattle off a series of laws and subsections of the civil code; then he would see them to the door, and without forgetting to leave the monthly check with his secretary, he would promise to cash it sooner or later.

Encouraged by the new situation, Lino lifted his head and asked, "Excuse me, but I don't get it. . . . What do you mean 'no legal rights'? Why don't we have any rights?"

Then he looked at Geppina sitting next to him, as she stared at him with resigned eyes.

"It means that . . . according to the law . . . Martina is no one's child, much less your granddaughter," I replied.

"No! Martina is my granddaughter. . . . *'A figlia 'e Matalena*. Maddalena's daughter . . ." Geppina butted in. "You told us that we shouldn't worry, that you knew what you were doing."

With the sort of naivete of someone who still counts on her fingers, Geppina believed that to defend herself from some abuse of power, all she had to do was turn to a lawyer, who, after combing through the big book of law, would right the wrong. If she didn't believe in divine justice, she at least believed in the sort of human justice that went hand in hand with the law, whose only raison d'être was defending the weak. I had spent days meticulously examining the court proceedings and the decrees in order to decipher the legal jargon, to piece things together, to explain the words, the legal channels, the questions and the answers. And even I, though admittedly without any expertise, was beginning to learn that whoever thirsts for justice will more often than not die of dehydration, and no lawyer can help you then. There aren't a thousand different ways of administering the law. There are only two: guilty or not guilty. One or the other. And this never takes into account the pain of the most vulnerable.

"The law is the law, my dear woman, even if it's not always just," said the lawyer. "Judges don't beat around the bush, especially when they find some hole in the system. And in this case, Judge Conti found a gaping chasm. To tell you the truth, the strange thing is that nobody dealt with it earlier. At times justice is like water: crystal clear until someone stirs it; cloudy, when something rises to the surface."

Geppina was quite impressed by his words. First, she stared at her husband right next to her, then at me, revealing a flicker of desperation as it crossed her eyes.

"Counselor, as I mentioned last week, I know Judge Giuliana Conti. We've been friends since we were kids. You think it might help if I spoke to her?" I asked, duly keeping him in the dark about already having visited her and that she, by virtue of our old friendship, had even procured for me a copy of the court's separation decree.

"Well, things are not looking up for us, but a close contact can't hurt. . . . Actually, if we succeed in creating a channel, it might be easier to mollify the judge, maybe even get her to give us a plan of conduct. . . . In short, it might be better for her to give us some direction there. In the meantime, I want to see whether there are any case precedents as a basis for appeal. You know, as I've been telling these kind folks, it's not exactly my bailiwick, but my partner, Counselor Castaldi, has a lot of experience in. . . ."

In effect, there were no loopholes, at least according to Giuliana Conti. For her, Martina's best interest was not some one-size-fits-all receptacle in which to slip a cookie-cutter decision just because it happens to coincide with a single aspect of her life. Martina's interests were a much more complex matter, which had to take into account her prospects for the future—in other words, she needed some relationship with an adult who might be able to take full responsibility for her; she needed to develop significant emotional bonds, thereby removing herself from any dangers or stressors. Unfortunately, Giuliana Conti had firmly convinced herself that the child's relatives did not have a place in her conception of the "minor's best interest." And how could you blame her? Moreover, when she asserted that no plan of action seemed to include relatives, how could you rebut her when the only plan Geppina and her daughters had was simply surviving? Of course, I could have encouraged her to have more faith in the resourcefulness of love, which existed even in that destitute and dysfunctional family. But to what avail? I would have risked coming off like some idealist floundering on a surging wave of social demagoguery.

I had turned to face Geppina and I saw her shut her eyes in a vain attempt to hide some kind of shame. It was as though, in the slow closing of her eyelids, some unbearable weight had also pulled her head and shoulders down; it was as though in that seemingly trivial gesture, the storm of pain that stirred within her was firmly entrenching itself in her psyche, driving her to madness.

"So, Counselor, what shall we do to work out the money?" I said, cutting to the chase.

The young professional looked up from the documents and stared at me with an expression that was half-surprised and half-peeved.

"I dunno, really that's not my area, I wouldn't know," he replied, trying to meet the eyes of his secretary, who reluctantly emerged from her frozen cocoon.

"So!" the young woman exclaimed, leafing through a ledger. "Ah, yes . . . Ms. De Nicola has not sent us the last three monthly payments," she added with a dry tone, sort of implying that it was better to not approach the topic.

"Okay, okay . . . I see!" said the lawyer, rising from his desk. "You see, Doctor, it's not a money problem. . . . I'm quite familiar with Ms. De Nicola and Mr. Esposito's situation; I have many clients in their circumstances, and I know all too well that they're not rolling in dough. Instead, I care about resolving what I consider an obvious injustice and about restoring their affection. . . . It's precisely for that reason I accepted this assignment, even if, to be perfectly honest, I would advise against cultivating too many hopes."

Going through his rhetorical spiel, Adriano Serra put on what he surely intended to be his "sympathy face," an expression of his profound understanding for the suffering of others. Ultimately, among his tools of the trade, filling his mouth with emotions he knew nothing about was not his strong suit. I don't want to say he was lying; it's just the song he was singing seemed a bit off key.

"Counselor, so let's consider the three thousand euros paid until now as a retainer for the work. . . . And . . . when the case is settled . . . hoping that all goes well . . . the balance will be settled . . . if there is a balance," I interjected, taking care to not demean his good intentions because deep down they were likely admirable.

Adriano Serra, Esquire, of the Law Offices of Castaldi and Serra, with a big-time office in the Centro Direzionale, a plaque on the wall and a splint on his hand. Another key figure to add to the no less important figure of the social worker and to the clearly crucial figure of Judge Giuliana Conti. But really, how relevant is the young lawyer—this amateur *judoka*—in this entire affair? Would it be wrong to assert that Martina's fate rested in his hands? If another lawyer more sensitive to the human condition and more savvy in extricating himself from legal labyrinths had manipulated the strings, would things have gone better? If he had more diligently followed the case and researched it appropriately, or if he had been more involved in creating an adequate network of connections, would things have gone differently for Geppina? To be honest, even this hypothetical—just like the one where the judge and the social worker were doggedly involved in the sad destiny of Martina—appears contrived and impressionable. Just as contrived and impressionable as the belief in destiny. At the core of the matter, when things happen, and they happen in a certain way, namely by unleashing devastating consequences, who is the party most responsible? Can anyone proclaim exemption from guilt? Or is it possible to attribute these misdeeds to the workings of a malign fate that always persecutes the weakest? Of course, it goes without saying that when things happen, if they happen to those forced to lose something, we call it *destiny*; when it's the more fortunate involved, we call it *injustice*. So what should we do? Shall we just consider this indulging in impressionable thinking? At any rate, like me, the social worker and Judge Conti, even Counselor Serra, must have found themselves, if only for a brief moment, having to face their own sense of culpability.

As the darkness began to fall over the Centro Direzionale, a sudden sense of desolation also descended with it. The storefront grates were lowered on the cafés, the offices were deserted, and the dim light from the clusters of lampposts barely gave off a whitish halo. Only a few lit-up windows on the upper floors of the skyscrapers suggested any signs of life, while all around a feeling of oppressive desertion lingered in the air. All of a sudden, a frosty wind, like an invisible, sibilant serpent, took control of everything, streaking through the main avenue, between the corners of buildings, down the side streets and across the public plazas. Under the walkway, there was a frightful whistling sound; in the flower beds, the wind bent spindly trees and batted around a cloudlike mass of paper and litter that seemed to be dancing in mid-air. Before ducking back into the bowels of the underground garage, I paused to look at Geppina and Lino who were moving off in the distance, walking side by side, with their hearts full of hatred. Right next to the stairwell, I ran into the vendor who had been chased out of the café earlier. He was hunkered down, his back against a cement planter, staring at his shoddy goods strewn on the ground. He seemed suddenly thinner, as though that treacherous wind, along with his rage from before, had desiccated him, drained him of the very blood in his veins. When our eyes happened to meet, for just a moment, I glimpsed a flash of hatred move across his pupils. I deposited the plastic bag full of sugar, coffee, and cigarettes at his feet and I went off into the darkness, thinking that just as with Geppina and her husband, that sentiment had resided inside him his entire life.

Geppina and Lino had disappeared into the evening's darkness, with the slow, lumbering shuffle of two shadowy wraiths, carrying the weight of their world upon them—a world that, for all of its noise, remains forever silent if there's no one willing to listen. It was a world in which all that takes place is invisible to other people's eyes, invisible to the world of light. Invisible to the world where Mr. Serra, Esquire, the social worker, Judge Giuliana Conti, and the people from the foster home resided. Invisible to the same world in which I thought I belonged.

In reality, since destiny had snatched me from their world, I never felt I belonged to one or the other. I felt a bit like a victim and an executioner all in one. My soul was hanging in the balance between what it should have been and what it yearned to be. My soul was neither rotten nor healthy, neither black nor white.

However, I knew then, as I still know now, that I was born into a world where, in place of saying "Good morning," they curse Christ on the cross, and for the rest of the day no one knows what time it is because the clock hands are stuck in the same position—that of poverty and resignation. I also knew then, as I still know now, that I was a hybrid resulting from an anomaly; I was an exception to the rule because, by some strange trick of destiny, I was brought into a different world, and I began to make it mine without even knowing how. It started when my father, sometime in the mid-'60s, pulled us from the shadows of Acerra and brought us to live in a place bathed in light on the Vomero hill. A place where people didn't curse; they spoke a language that sounded pleasant and wasn't vulgar. A place where you heard "Good morning" and "Good evening"; where people exchanged birthday presents, and boys like me went on class trips to places like the Catholic Association where we would clean up trash for the poor— and who even knows how I pictured those poor people in my head. It was a place where you would study at your classmate's house, and during snack time a mother would show up with a tray full of cookies. When we were older, it was parties where, at the home of one friend or another, one time, as I was cross-legged on the floor, focused on a game of spin the bottle, I was caught with holes in the bottom of my shoes and almost died from embarrassment. The kind of world that, when you're young, teaches you civil coexistence, leads you to school and to the university. And then you get bigger and you go to concerts to hear Barber and Rimsky-Korsakov, and you learn about the Renaissance; that there once lived a guy named Basquiat who expressed himself by hurling buckets of paint on canvases; that Kieślowski had probed the human condition through his film trilogy of colors. And that Coleman Silk, because of some joke of destiny—despite being a person of color, even if you couldn't tell—had been unjustly crucified for having used the word *spook* in referring to two of his students. The world I came from, though, was quite different. It was the world of Nicola, my childhood friend who at seven years of age had been crushed under a truck's wheels while he was hitching a ride into the country by hanging onto the tailgate. I wasn't playing with him that morning; I had a fever.

Nicola had gone out in a hurry, like Salvatore, Geppina's son, and like Nunzio, who slipped out of the reformatory one night and ended up impaled on a fence railing. They dropped dead just like that, without even getting to savor one of life's small joys. But they did not belong to the world of light; they belonged to the world of shadows. Only death showed them any love—enough to carry them away forever.

～ 11 ～

That cold month of April was memorable for a number of decisive events that stole the general attention away from the mass of arctic air that was continuing to assault the north.

John Paul II died on the second day of the month at nine in the evening, and never before that occasion had there been such a showing of religious fervor. Demands for birth control and struggles for the recognition of common-law families were forgotten; medically assisted procreation was put on the back burner. We witnessed scenes of honest-to-goodness fanaticism, of nauseatingly choreographed televised broadcasts involving all sorts of political hacks and Vatican correspondents. Each one offering his two cents about the man who tore down the Iron Curtain, about this or that reason for which this represented a watershed moment in today's society, and about the big shoes that a future pope would have to fill. In those hours all of Italy came to a halt and three days of official mourning were decreed. And that's what many other countries did, even some of the Islamic ones.

Legions of worshippers from all around the world converged on Rome, and the Eternal City seemed to collapse of its own weight. On the Via della Conciliazione they were packed in by the thousands; everyone lined up to see the pope's body lying in state in Saint Peter's. And those who were unable to get in camped out in the make-do shelters in front of the giant-screen televisions that showed images of the papal coffin. Then came the funeral, and all the heads of state from around the world turned up, and the representatives of all the various religions came to pay their respects to the pope who had made bringing the different faiths together one of his prime objectives. Everyone joined in a final farewell in a tribute that, in living memory, no pontiff had ever received.

In addition, the regional elections at the time, surprisingly, left the country in the midst of a political crisis. As if by magic, a few million votes switched from one side to the other, and all the regions that were solidly center right—with the exception of the strongholds in Lombardy and in the Veneto—went to the opposition, thereby unleashing serious pandemonium. The Casa delle Libertà party looked as though it would crumble, and those on the left, ipso facto, got rid of that hangdog look they had been wearing for quite some time.

Where I'm from, things hadn't changed in the least. Bassolino had taken a scorched earth approach with everyone, and he couldn't have cared less about Italo Bocchino, the young candidate sent into the fray by the right-wing Alleanza Nazionale, who swore he'd make things difficult for Bassolino, despite his drubbing at the ballot boxes.

Around the end of the month a new pope was also elected. Another foreigner. Cardinal Joseph Ratzinger, deacon of the College of Cardinals, prefect of the Congregation for the Doctrine of Faith, and the most vocal opponent of religious relativism, surprisingly became Pope Benedict XVI—quelling the minds of all those who would have wanted another Wojtyła in the pulpit of Saint Peter's.

Many things happened in that month of April, even though I, in my distracted state, saw them as nothing more than an annoying buzz whirring around me; those things kicked up quite a racket and they seemed to be banging down the door of my attention, but it was as though they had left no lasting impression on me. Those things just happened and that was that. By the time I would notice one, the next would take its place. It was as though, as they overlapped one another, these occurrences were reduced to the point of irrelevance.

And there were other things that took hold of my heart—small things that escaped me at first but that got under my skin as they intersected my path. Everything else was just so much background noise as the days that were always the same inexorably succeeded each other in my existence.

Although he loved fierce competition, that evening Professor Augusto Argentieri dreaded an escalation of the dialectical dispute among his guests. So in order to alleviate any likely tensions, he had suggested that his wife, Marisa, also invite a certain Clara Belladonna. A marine biologist as well as a journalist at a local television station where she headed a weekly segment on the Mediterranean sea bed, Ms. Belladonna was also quite fond of lounge acts—maybe even too keenly so; when an opportunity presented itself, she would perform poignant numbers from the classical Neapolitan repertoire. The "bella donna," like a haggard cabaret singer, would always travel with her son—a twenty-year-old beanpole who would accompany her on the piano, bobbing his big head around like Ray Charles—in tow, harboring hopes that Marisa, Costanza's mother, might take him under her wing and introduce him to the song world through her contacts. Not to disappoint her, then, Marisa guaranteed that Mimmo Di Francia—one of the maestros of Neapolitan song and writer of some memorable works like "Champagne," sung by Peppino di Capri—would be present that evening. And, given that woman's charm, the maestro dug deep into his repertoire of seductions, which she reciprocated, for halfway through the evening she had glommed onto him like a fly on flypaper. And the biologist-journalist-singer's date that evening was a certain Antonio Marruocco, a lawyer who had his hand in a bit of everything: the two of them had formed a business relationship that spanned from buying and selling advertising time on local television affiliates to greasing the wheels for anyone who needed protection from the bureaucracy of the various local health-care agencies of which the gentleman was a trade union representative. The motto that the couple would endlessly broadcast was, "Glad to make ourselves useful."

Meanwhile, the master of the house, comfortably encamped in the sitting room, along with some of his more devoted guests, had gotten the conversation going with a cocktail. They had lined up facing each other on the long damask-accented sofas and in armchairs, as though forming a boxing ring. And right from the first verbal skirmish, as usual, the most combative proved to be Donato De Nittis, the chief of surgery at Napoli General—an ardent activist in the right-wing Forza Italia party, not to mention Augusto Argentieri's closest friend. But unlike Costanza's father, he exhibited the air—that I had learned to recognize as a boy— of someone who tries to come off as overburdened by his own colossal responsibilities. And he would address everyone in attendance with a patronizing modesty, which seemed purposely designed to make the others feel uncomfortable.

"Look, not even the people from the coalition of L'Unione expected to win. And now what are they doing? Reading political significance into their results. The usual left . . ." he said, stroking his well-groomed mustache on a face that resembled a rodent's. "These are regional elections. National elections are something entirely different. You'll see in a year. . . . Unfortunately, Berlusconi's mistake was to under-estimate the election process, to not roll up his sleeves and take it to the people, and so the people didn't go out and vote . . . and then add to that the pope's dying, the press with their attacks . . ."

"What are you talking about? Il Cavaliere even admitted defeat. Don't you get it? Berlusconi's dazed, he's grasping at straws, and he seems to have suddenly aged. I'll grant him one thing, though: he had the courage to go on television to recognize that he'd lost," chimed in Mariano Coppola, a regional functionary and also part of the Bassolino admin-istration for a number of years.

"What defeat? What defeat are you talking about?"

"Your defeat . . . The defeat of the Casa delle Libertà! It's in shambles. Everyone from Fini to Casini is asking for a sign of discontinuity in this government's actions. . . . Look, I certainly didn't invent all this. They declared it openly. The papers and television networks have talked about this. . . . *Discontinuità*, discontinuity . . . A fancy term that means in plain language, 'Sorry. We were wrong to lead the country with this program; the people want something else.' Where I come from, that amounts to failure!"

Between one course and the next of appetizers consis-ting of whitebait fritters and stuffed zucchini flowers, the dis-cussion finally touched on a topic dear to the master of the house: politics, something that had inevitably heated up emotions. In order to defuse the tension, Costanza's mother instructed Consuelo, the Bolivian maid, to start serving at the table. But not before shooting a chiding glance at her husband who wanted no part of getting off the sofa, joyfully engrossed as he was in the rhetorical crossing of swords.

"Well, somebody's getting their nerve up. Yes, that's what you've done . . . and now you also want early elections. What arrogance!" Donato De Nittis pounced, pointing his finger at Mariano Coppola. Then, turning to his friend Augusto, he continued, "They talk about the country coming back to its senses, and they promote a plan for an alternative government, which would bring economic changes and jump-start growth. I would really like to know what they're talking about," he added in a huff, smoothing his shirt over his chest. "The sooner we get rid of these people, the better off we'll be. . . . But one day soon, it will happen. You'll see."

"You wanna know what they're talking about? . . . I'll tell you right now!" Mariano Coppola shot back with the angelic demeanor of someone who enjoys poking the fire. "They're talking . . . about you, me, all of us. They're talking about the South. About the South bogged down in its moral and material poverty, strangled by unemployment and by various criminal enterprises. Something that you folks at Forza Italia have never seriously given any thought to. Of course, with Bossi busy lecturing you guys, how could you think about the South? You and I are in agreement about one thing, though. About early elections, I mean. They're unnecessary. Berlusconi's got to lie in the bed he's made for himself."

"You want to know what's going to happen now?" Augusto Argentieri butted in. The guests got quiet for a moment, curious to know their host's opinion. "Berlusconi's already got a noose around his neck. He'll dissolve the parliament and form a new administration, which will be the same as the previous one, except for a few minor changes involving some irrelevant backbencher. In other words, he'll shuffle the deck and go back to business as usual. He'll do this for another year until the next election."

"And so the legislature will remain intact," was the ironic barb from Eugenio Castelli, a popular art critic, not to mention a long-standing family friend. Despite his widely known disillusionment with politics and despite his having for quite some time taken a vow of deathly brooding silence even in such a vivacious setting as that, his aversion toward the leftist regime, as he would call it, would eventually get the better of him. "Unfortunately, the old rock-hard faith in Il Cavaliere is starting to waver," he added half-heartedly. But since Costanza was heading straight for them, he seized the opportunity to extricate himself from that predicament, adding, "But one thing that will never waver is my admiration for such beauty. . . ."

Timing. Yet another of Costanza's numerous talents. Not by chance, her interruption contributed to defusing the tone of the argument that seemed to have gotten more heated than it should have. "Dad, will you get up now? The food's on the table. Enough of all this politics!" she said, inviting all of us to do the same with a decisive wave of her hand.

Among the guests, there was a buzz of appreciation both for her assertive intrusion and the wonderful bounty of food awaiting them.

"Politics, my girl, is the spice of life," her father added, taking his place at the head of the table.

"Dad, in this house we always use too much salt, and you know quite well that salt is bad for you," Costanza retorted with her usual sarcasm. "Now, no more jabbering. Let's eat!"

"You see, my dear, it is this sort of jabbering that separates us from the average citizen. . . . Am I right, Michele?" he asked, turning to me for no apparent reason.

"Uh . . . Well, I wouldn't know," I hesitated, being caught off guard. "However, I find it hard to disagree with the average citizen," I added, surprising both the guests and myself. "I mean, when he wonders whether in reality that jabbering is something for the privileged few."

For an instant, an awkward silence fell over the room. Costanza's father wouldn't even look me in the eye, someone gave me a distracted glance, a few others smiled, then everyone changed the subject. Fearing that I wasn't commanding much authority, I thought it better to keep my mouth shut, even though I was dying to stand up and scream. After all, as I saw it, all of us were the reflection of a mediocre era in which people subsist on duplicity and words: from the television, from newspapers, on the street, and in our homes, without anybody asking themselves what is really happening out there.

Marisa, Costanza's mother, who until that moment had been entertaining the ladies with the latest details of yet another charity gala—this time on behalf of the victims of Darfur—was now assigning places at the table. She was alternating men and women, making sure to separate couples, as well as tactically deploying the best conversationalists across from the others.

On one side of me at the table was Monia, Donato De Nittis's charming young date, who, for the entire evening had not said a word. In her eyes, I caught a glimpse—even for a fleeting moment—of the same miserable feeling of inadequacy that I had. On the other side of me, there was the hostess, who would occasionally lavish me with reassuring pats on the back. Costanza, on the other hand, who sat opposite me, seemed to be happily immersed in conversation. She had become lighthearted and playful, thanks to the animated chatter of Maestro Di Francia with Clara Belladonna, as well as to Eugenio Castelli, who was reviewing all the season's best art shows. But most of all, thanks to Consuelo, who was busy coming and going with pasta courses and a number of different fish dishes.

From the open balcony windows, past the white curtains that danced on the spring breeze, I could see the perfect architectural lines of the buildings on Via dei Mille, the finely decorated neoclassical facades with their ocher, gray, and Pompeii-red stuccos, and the chiseled balconies with their sinuous balustrades. From below on the street no voices could be heard. Just some distant notes from a pleasant-sounding piano: Shostakovich.

From what I could gather and from how she had always portrayed herself to me, Costanza Argentieri seemed to have been a stubborn young child, then an intelligent, rebellious young woman, and finally a free woman from an affluent family that was discreetly intolerant of any form of social integration—especially when it came to acquired kinships. Not that her parents were hostile toward me. Of course not. That would be beneath their class. But now and then they would launch into an impassioned but polite rehashing on the suitability of comparing peer groups. Neither Costanza nor I had ever spoken about marriage, and that's what had led them to turn a blind eye to our living together. With an ample supply of patience, I'm sure they were secretly hoping that the time would come for the chickens to come home to roost and their beloved firstborn would pledge her love to one of the many fine suitors who hovered around her.

Her father, one of the most prominent Neapolitan cardiologists, professed himself such a staunch doctrinaire Catholic that, he believed, in order to confront the fanatical militarist Islamic credo, it would be necessary to reinforce the bulwark of unflinching faith in the Church, the last bastion of the free

Western world. Moreover, he felt a sincere disdain toward those whom he regarded as hypocritical enemies of all that is just and good—that is, the petty political bureaucrats from the left and from the right, who were ready to sell out our Christian roots on the filthy wave of progressivism and multiculturalism. An extreme proponent of keeping the nuclear family whole at all costs, he had, nonetheless, been fated with two daughters, each of whom had given him a hard time. To reassert her own professional independence, Costanza—always the supreme contrarian—had chosen a difficult path in the world of child psychiatry, when she could have, if she had followed in her father's footsteps, taken advantage of a network of solid relationships and found herself, in the not-too-distant future, the heiress of an entire cardiology ward. On the other hand, Linda, the second-born, had preferred to burn bridges behind her for a number of years: right after high school, she had gone to live in Milan, where she worked as a freelance journalist and where she was able to live her lesbian lifestyle unimpeded, far away from her family's prejudices and far from the provincial mentality that would hardly have accepted the orientation that she had discreetly kept hidden. Two daughters with two different temperaments. And their father only reluctantly bent his will to them because he loved them and because he never gave up hope.

His wife often chided him for his excessive intransigence. And she continuously urged him to lay down his weapons and to sail full speed ahead into the storm of a by-now barbarous age. She would set the course and act like his compass; she would maneuver in the dark and give him the illusion that he was navigating. And she would always push her reluctant husband through the vicissitudes of his social tightrope walking. She would organize dinners and medical conferences for him, and she would maintain good relationships with those journalists who she thought might prove useful sooner or later. Each Christmas she would organize a concert for the patients in his ward and afternoon readings for the sickest of them. All of her conduct confirmed the timeworn belief that behind every successful man there is always an amazing woman.

Endowed with genuine virtue, which afforded her the capacity to keep an eye on other people's problems, she had learned to bend over backward for the sole pleasure of being useful to others. She had also learned how to ignore all the gossipmongers who depicted her as an ambitious dealmaker, a puppeteer skilled at manipulating people and relationships toward her own interests. In the past, at the height of her success, she had assembled a network of such support that one election season, she had even run as a candidate for the Christian Democrats, missing a seat in parliament by a handful of votes. Now that her golden age was veering toward the sunset along with her beauty, she had taken up a new project: keeping talented young artists from drowning in the foul waters of economic hardship. Behind the scenes she would sponsor a private exhibition of a young Nicaraguan photographer, promote the books of a stone-broke, intractable writer, secretly pay the conservatory tuition for a talented violinist, and subsidize singing lessons for a young Albanian soprano.

As Augusto Argentieri hoped, the evening finally turned back to the issue unwillingly abandoned just before coming to the table. That allowed the electoral storm of those days to blow again in full force among the dinner companions just as the delicious chocolate soufflé had been served up for dessert.

"Just look at the numbers," Mariano Coppola attested, his face showing a ruddy complexion from the wine. "I was surprised by them, too. In terms of percentages, Bassolino's victory surpassed even his previous election results, at the municipal and at the regional levels. And this left quite a few people speechless. . . . Most of all those on the left who thought his popularity had dipped . . ."

"And so, how do you explain his victory?" Costanza's father asked.

"There were no worthy adversaries from the center-right coalition," replied Donato De Nittis. "Come on, I mean, how can we send some young, inexperienced politician from Alleanza Nazionale to his demise by running him against a sly fox like that? It's unsurprising that he swallowed him in one bite. That's how you explain it," the chief physician said, standing and starting to move around the table like a caged lion.

"That is an incontrovertible truth," Mariano Coppola contended. "Though I'm happy because that way I kept my job for another five years, I think there might be another explanation. Call it a criticism, if you like. Because, you see, we on the left also know how to be critical of ourselves, unlike you guys who—"

"This is unbelievable. You are first-class liars and swindlers," Eugenio Castelli interrupted him, once again betrayed by his animosity.

At this point, the women, led by Marisa, left the table, mumbling under their breaths, and moved to the adjacent sitting room, where they started discussing charities, concerts, and church rummage sales. However, the master of the house, content to have the floor open again, started pouring Malvasia until the glasses were brimming. Then he invited Donato De Nittis to take a seat, this time harboring the serious hope that there would be some blood in the water. From a distance, Costanza motioned to her watch with an annoyed expression, suggesting it was time to leave. I gestured for her to wait and stayed glued to my chair, anticipating the swords about to come to blows. Shaking her head, Costanza joined the ladies again.

"So, if you let me talk, I'll even tell you all why, in my opinion, Bassolino won," said Mariano Coppola. "This time, what carried him to the top was not the party's hard-core supporters consisting of the usual intellectuals, artists, young people, and civil society but average citizens, who by now applaud him as yet another king of this city. Do you remember his election posters? No name, no party symbol, just his face. There, when you get to this point, it means you own the voters. He came out of his electoral victory smelling like a rose."

"Meanwhile, nothing has changed here. Our city is going off course, lawlessness is taking it over. The Camorra war cost us more than one hundred lives this past year. Not to mention health care, mountains of garbage," said Donato De Nittis, rebutting his argument as he got up from his chair again.

"Why are you so convinced that things in Naples can change just like that? I agree with Bassolino when he says that in order to change this city, not even one hundred years are enough. It's not easy to eradicate a whole mentality," observed Mariano Coppola, taking down his Malvasia in one gulp.

"That's just a way of safeguarding himself from blame. This way, he has a nice excuse ready and waiting to cover his own failings," De Nittis told him.

Augusto Argentieri was taking all of this in as angelically as a papal emissary, with a smug smile for the skirmish that he had incited. With his hands interlocked under his chin and his elbows resting on the table, he kept nodding from time to time. Then, as though he had pinpointed the crux of the matter, he waded in.

"You see, that young Alleanza Nazionale politician with the expression of someone who met defeat head-on with a smile on his face really caught my attention. This wasn't his election to win, and I think he knew that. Let's suppose that he wasn't even looking to win, but in reality, well aware of his inevitable defeat, he was biding his time, stockpiling arms for a future run. So . . . Bassolino is in his final term and his mistake is that he didn't prepare a generation to replace him; he didn't leave an heir to his legacy. And so, while Italo Bocchino is getting in shape for a new battle, he has a reserve of good contacts and support for the next election."

"Well, if we follow your theory, we need to take into account that after all is said and done, this young man knows more than he's letting on," said Eugenio Castelli on his soapbox, before disappearing beyond the balcony curtains to have a cigarette.

"Yeah, and let's hope that he holds out and doesn't get discouraged by the opposition in these shark-infested waters," the host concluded.

From across the room the duo of Di Francia and Belladonna belted out their rendition of Ray Charles. As they modulated their voices like Brother Ray, the notes of "Georgia" permeated the air, while the litany of Shostakovich became more and more distant. In the meantime, the lawyer, Marruocco, who had boxed me into a corner, carried on undaunted in affirming that the times were just right to lay the foundations for an outpatient clinic that included physical therapy and speech pathology units. The work permits wouldn't be a problem: he bragged about having pull with some managers of a public health administration to whom he had granted many favors, as well as with some heavy hitters from the region of Campania whose wheels had already been well greased.

Through the glass that divided the sitting room from Augusto Argentieri's study, I caught sight of Costanza and her mother confabulating in private. They were holding each other's hands, laughing, and seemed rather moved.

Contrary to my innate ability to fall asleep on command, I was in for a sleepless night. From the moment I had put my head on the pillow, one thought led to another, and yet another would quickly take their place to the point where these thoughts were bouncing around my head, nonstop, like pool balls on a billiard table. Unable to extricate myself from the quiet hornet's nest during those hours, the only thing I was able to discern, though not without some dread, was that those thoughts, fleeing the evanescence of conjecture, had been transformed into reality—a reality that was about to be the next chapter of my existence. Yet the awareness of it didn't take hold until the break of the following day, when my eyes lingered to examine Costanza's finally relaxed face. It was as though the night had erased her features and with them her latest anxieties and fears; she was sleeping next to me and breathing normally. Her anxieties, which normally would push her to relegate me to the edge of the bed, were placated and now she was lying still next to me, curled up on her side. She had her back to me with her arms across her waist and her knees pointing out, almost as though carving out an inviolable, protective space for her womb. One minute, her breathing would be heavy and long; the next, it would be light and short. But after a while it would stop short in her throat and become a tenebrous grumbling, as though, summoned by a distant voice, she had sunken into a remote part of herself in order to happily merge with someone. A half-smile hinted to the fact that she must have been enthralled in the amorous web of a conversation that was fluttering through a delicate yet everlasting dream.

Taking care not to wake her, I slipped out of bed and quietly tiptoed over to the bathroom. Based on her somnolent burbling, she seemed to be in the middle of an oneiric amorous tryst.

The boiling-hot water from the showerhead put my thoughts from the previous night in order. In the steam, an image of Costanza and her mother appeared. I could see them hugging behind the glass—a loving look, followed by a tender caress on the doorstep during the previous evening. And I can't say how it occurred to me to do what I had been intending to do for quite some time, nor what drove me to do it. I only know that I suddenly felt it like a vital necessity, as though the entire meaning of my existence depended on that action. As though only by defining that moment could I take control of my past. I don't mean all of it but at least a part so that I could fill that void that always followed me around. It was an idea that I had always relegated to my list of resolutions. There was something epic about it; I could just taste how damned significant it was, even though it was alive for just a moment. Now and then it would emerge within me and carry me away from the drab grayness of a path that is always the same, and provide me with the illusion of being able to, against all odds, give my life the colors of a dream.

That morning, though, it appeared to me in the guise of a legacy, reminding me of who I was and where I came from but, most of all, who I was born from. So I decided that the time had come to ask my mother to finish something she had put on hold for some time, to pass the baton of an art that had its roots in her childhood.

With matted hair, Costanza joined me in the kitchen where I was staring into the black swirls of my espresso, like a fortune teller trying to shed light on his own future.

"Why didn't you wake me?" she asked, yawning.

"I don't know," I replied. "You were sleeping so soundly. . . ."

Essentially, she had a new air about her. Her face was more relaxed, with no traces of swelling under her eyes that she would have upon waking. And she even moved with a lackadaisical sluggishness. Wherever it was she had just come from, it was a place that had changed her for the better.

Seated before me, she started to fiddle with toast and marmalade, taking a healthy amount of the latter. She asked me to fill her espresso cup to the brim. Then she finally focused on me.

"Already dressed? Where're you going?"

"To see my folks."

"At this hour? But aren't we going to their place for lunch?"

"But first I wanted to talk a bit with my mother."

"Sorry but . . . let's tell her together."

"Of course . . . I have something else to do."

"Ah . . ." Costanza added, her mind drifting elsewhere.

Then, after telling her how she had done nothing but talk through the night, I asked her whether she recalled what she had been dreaming.

"I don't remember what I dreamed," she replied. "Why? What did I say?" she added.

"Nothing!"

I got up, kissed her on the forehead, and started to walk out when she called me back.

"Michele . . ."

"What is it?"

"I haven't heard you even say two words about what I told you yesterday evening."

And how could I have? The previous night, just back from that intolerable dinner at her parents' place, seated on the bed, she had slathered on her face cream, staring into space the whole time, as though I didn't exist next to her. Just after shutting off the light on the night table and slipping under the covers, I had heard her utter some words that sounded like a threat: "I'm pregnant. This time we are going to have that child." And her tone was the sort that wasn't asking for feedback. Then, wishing me a good night, she had turned so quickly to the other side as though she had hoped to run into her child in who knows what remote place deep inside of her.

~ 12 ~

I knew that one day, all that I would have left of my father and my mother would be a faint memory at the bottom of my heart, or at best some worthless object that might quickly stop speaking of them. And I was certain that for me and my siblings there would be no legacy, no house, no stash of money to divvy up, aside from a couple thousand euros of liquid assets put aside for their final expenses—all the works: hearse, flowers, wreaths, funerary lamps, and some offerings to the church.

I had my eye on something else, something that wouldn't appeal to anyone else. It was something that my mother possessed and that I wanted to make mine. I wouldn't have let the others get their hands on it since only I would make use of it, and for that reason I considered it priceless: the art of sewing.

My mother's talent was already obvious in the way in which she handled the materials right from the start. She would bend the fabric to her will to create new shapes.

She wielded rulers, chalk, scissors, and cotton with utter focus and confidence; with the stubborn patience of an artist who visualizes the image to be realized in his head and sees it slowly take form just as he had conceived it. As a child, fascinated by the creative acts of that genius, I would nestle myself among the folds of material and go off into daydreams of faraway places. As time passed, living and breathing those fabrics, I grew fond of the elegant Prince of Wales check, the bizarre houndstooth, the rustic herringbone of tweeds; at the same time, the flannel and the shaved carded vicuña were pleasant to the touch, and I liked to run my hand over the bulkiness of Tasmanian wool. Then I learned to distinguish spring materials from summer ones, like plain weave gabardine and the sturdier English drill. The refinement of poplin and the fresh suppleness of Irish linen would even send me into raptures.

Once upon a time, almost everyone granted themselves, if only once, the pleasure of a nice pair of tailor-made trousers, and despite the poverty of the small town where I lived, my mother could even get by on those earnings. But when my father decided to leap into the unknown of the big city, he couldn't even imagine subsisting on that work.

Once in a while I let my imagination get the better of me: if she had thought about the big picture, I would have become a tailor; she would have taught me and together we would have expanded. In time, I would have opened a shop of my own, which would have gradually grown, along with the clientele throughout the neighborhood. Rich and famous, I would have joined the ranks of the greatest, most famous tailors in the city. I would have competed with Isaia. I would have been more important than Attolini and the one and only Kiton, who stitches suits for Clinton and Prince Charles. I owe it all to her if, to this very day, I still take great joy in wearing, whenever possible, hand-made trousers that rest just so on the hips and fall flush on the legs. Ones with lined pockets cut into the sides and, if necessary, with a little coin pocket just below the belt; with or without a cuff, depending on the style; with or without pleats, as the fashion of the day requires. In my wardrobe there are at least two pairs of them: one for summer, the other for winter. They help me remember who I could have been.

When I get to my folks' house that Sunday morning, despite the hum of activity in the kitchen, my father is still shuffling around the house in his slippers, with his thinning white hair falling uncombed over his face, which is more sulky than usual.

The room is flooded with light and the sun filters through the windows, warming my back. As though under a spell, my mother has laid out over the table right before my eyes a double-wide bolt of tobacco-colored linen. Upon my request, she pulled it out of a closet as though that piece of fabric had always been there waiting for me. I straighten it out and repeatedly run the back of my hand over it. Under my fingers I feel the rough yet delicate weave. And I seem to notice the scent of wood and leather coming from afar. I am ready. Under my mother's watchful eye, my steady hand starts to work the chalk, marking the centimeters for the waist, the crotch, the legs. After that, a mark for the creases, a line for the pockets, and one for the little watch pockets, and voilà! There it is: the outline of what will be the first pair of trousers ever made with my own hands. Then, inviting me to move to the cutting stage, it is actually she who gets things underway with a swift snip. My hand trembles, but the constant swooshing of the linen beneath the blade instills confidence in each cut. After just a half hour I'm there, thimble on finger, going over the pattern with needle and thread. But she's the one who uses the machine. Working the Singer's pedal furiously, she begins to give life to the waistline with the belt loops. And I follow every move of her hands.

I've always seen her like that: my mother sitting at the sewing machine, in her little corner near the window, caressed by the cold light of a fluorescent bulb, surrounded by odds and ends, and by garment bags and dresses; at her feet, fabric remnants and spools of white, black, and gray cotton thread within arm's reach. I've always seen her like that: her head nestled between her shoulders; her eyes focused on the hem of cloth to skillfully hold and turn under the shiny metal presser foot while the Singer's piston, with its gentle rhythmic rattle, sends the needle up and down.

And I can still see her like that, while she winds the thread around to knot it at the ends, moistens it with her mouth, to pass it through the eye of the needle on her first attempt with a precise flick of her wrist. And then she maneuvers the fabric, joins it, connects it in a masterful thrust of her fingers by suddenly raising her forearm.

I have seen my mother resurrect all sorts of garments. A truly extraordinary ability: she would unstitch them piece after piece, reshape and modify them, changing the characteristics of them according to the needs and desires of their owners. And when the endeavor presented difficulties, she would always find a solution all her own. Judging from a protrusion that appeared below the nape of her neck, I could quantify every hour, day, month, and year spent sewing— one adjustment after another, one leg crease after another; a zipper, the shortening of a shirt sleeve, a finishing touch on the side seams of a jacket, turning a collar, taking in a skirt by an inch or two across the hips. At all hours of the day until late in the evening, a procession of people came and went in my house. And it was always the same rigmarole: "A little longer here, a bit tighter there, a half inch shorter and a half inch wider, there, yes, pull it a little more this way and move the buttons there." In front of a mirror her clients would try on garments over and over, visually satisfied by the accuracy and precision of her work, and yet they would still haggle over the price, which was already low. However, she would always give in. And there was no way of convincing her that the compensation for her work, unlike in the various tailor shops in my neighborhood that charged handsomely, was not commensurate in terms of labor, nor in terms of her inordinate quality. Especially considering her clientele consisted of engineers, architects, and doctors who, when the time came to settle the bill, hemmed and hawed as though they were penniless. My mother's reaction was always the same: "It would seem like stealing. . . . I don't put much into it, and I don't want to lose customers." I was always defenseless to that innate graciousness of hers, and more often than not, I would swallow my anger and quietly walk away.

One time, though, I wasn't able to stifle my indignation. It was one of those rash youthful acts that you feel rise up from your bowels, when you're overwhelmed by a sense of justice that hasn't been corrupted by the prudence and cowardice that come with the age of reason. It remains one of the few impulsive actions—not that there have been many—that I do not regret, and without hesitation, I would do it again once, a hundred times, even a thousand times.

I was more or less twenty years old. It was a typical Neapolitan day: the sky was clear, the sun was shining, the sea looked like a postcard, and I was just about to sit down to eat. My mother, who had worked until late at night, had gotten up early to finish the pile of alterations for the lady who lived upstairs—the wife of the lawyer, Mr. Rinaldi. (Because shortly afterward, before setting off for Capri where she would spend the Easter holidays with her family, she would be stopping by in a frightful hurry to pick up what had become a practically brand-new wardrobe of clothes.) Right away she had begun slaving over meat ragout, eggplant parmesan, and homemade gnocchi. My father, tired from ranting about how late my mother had started cooking, had taken his place at the head of the table. The television, meanwhile, was broadcasting Nanny Loy's good old friendly face; he was wishing Italy a happy Sunday with a segment that took its name, *Il rododendro*, from the name of a plant (rhododendron) and would promise to be the format for a whole new program where people would air their grievances, or what's eating at them (a play on rhododendron and "rodo dentro"): *What's Eating You?* As usual, egged on by the director through the airwaves, my father never failed to rattle off a laundry list of things sticking in his craw, starting with how my mother was overworked, sitting in her corner sewing all day long; then on to the lies that, according to him, she would continuously try to sell him; and finally how late we all sat down to eat on Sundays. In truth, he didn't need an excuse to kick up a fuss like that, and even when things were going well we would hardly get through lunch without dodging the occasional profanity. And, at times, the plates—and anything else within his reach—would fly.

But my father saved his best for the religious holidays. For a long period of my life, Christmas was an honest-to-goodness torment. I've never been able to understand why he would get so ornery during those particular days. Maybe it was the frenzy of the celebrations, the crowds in the local markets when he went out to grocery shop, the traffic that would run amok in the streets. Who knows. Even today, when that time of year gets closer, such sadness comes over me that I would just as soon skip it all to reawaken when it's all over.

That day, though, lunch was proceeding calmly. Nevertheless, when the doorbell rang insistently, my mother stared at us, white as a sheet, got up, and disappeared, closing the dining room door behind her without my father even batting an eyelid. Several minutes passed, during which both he and my siblings showed no signs of impatience. However, anticipating an angry outburst, I got up to hurry my mother along. I found her in the *stanza dei miracoli*, the room where all the miracles happen: she was stuttering in an attempt to fend off the attacks of *la signora*, who was negotiating the price of three trousers, two jackets, some shirts, and a pair of curtains adjusted to fit the new house in Capri, with the ferociousness of a vendor in an Arab bazaar. Seeing my mother overcome by humiliation broke my heart. It was a blow to her dignity and to mine. Thought and action became one: I grabbed the bags with the garments, came right up to the wife of Mr. Rinaldi, Esquire, and placed them in her arms.

"Here, consider this an Easter present from my mother," I said, leading her all the way out to the elevator. "Now, go away and never set foot in this house again."

My heart beating through my chest, still upset by what I had just done, I shut the door and stared at my mother. She didn't even show a hint of disappointment at my impulsiveness. I caressed her and accompanied her back to the table where my father—I have no idea why—welcomed her with an affectionate demeanor. "Eat before it all gets cold."

My mother seemed so beautiful on that April afternoon. A ray of sunshine lightened her hair and lit up her blue eyes. I saw a face from her younger days and the sweet features that I can still see in an old photo: in a nice gray tailleur, smiling and leaning against a rosebush in the courtyard of our house.

It was then that I swore that in the future I would never end up in a position to argue about a subordinate's work. My mother never said a word about what happened that Sunday many years ago; nor did I ever know what was going through her head at the time. Yet, later on, during frequent family squabbles, whenever the topic turned to me and my supposed qualities, she never failed to mention humility. And then I would know that she was reliving that moment.

My father starts to fiddle about around the table, paying attention to the smallest details, though not complaining, contrary to his usual habits, when he sees me spending too much time shadowing my mother. He just tries to make his presence known, now and then, bustling about in the kitchen: a clinking of plates, a knocked-over glass, a carelessly slammed cabinet. The trousers are nice and basted in a tack stitch. All that's left is the fine-tuning: the buttonholes and choosing the buttons; finishing the fly flap and the back pockets; adding the grosgrain ribbon inside the waistline; reinforcing the cuffs and giving it a first fitting. Small details that my mother, with a certain apprehension, prefers to put off until the next day. Behind on the finishing touches for lunch, she's afraid that she'll put my father in a bad mood. But her face suddenly darkens when she plunges into a well of memories into which I had pushed her by merely alluding to Geppina. All it took was that name, which I mentioned, not even giving it much thought, out of the blue, to set off something inside of her. Something that was pressing to be brought out into the light. Something that was connected to her younger years, during the first months of her marriage when she had decided to do what she believed necessary and no longer postponable.

She can recall that day, she says, as though it were yesterday because she had found herself experiencing a vivid premonition of misfortune that would stay with her and me for the rest of our days. She was about twenty and that morning, upon waking, my mother had felt the ground slipping out from under her feet. She didn't feel well at all and she would like to have stayed in bed, but she told herself that she had to put an end to the matter. So, lugging her swollen belly, she had gone out bright and early with her husband. My father had accompanied her to the cross street at the Church of the Assumption, bombarding her with advice. In her current state, she needed to be prudent. She had passed her due date by a few days, and with a paunch like that, at the very least she risked giving birth to me right in the street. Her mother's house on Via Sant'Anna, where she had lived until just a few months earlier, was not far and she proceeded at a brisk pace. But at the intersection of the side street, her sister Francesca came racing toward her in a panic. She was mumbling something about the car having arrived from Pescara but that Geppina, having barricaded herself in the attic, wouldn't listen to reason. My sisters' and my mother's pleas had gone unanswered. Not even two nuns had been able to coax her out; not even Don Attilio, the parish priest from the Assumption, who had been chased away by spitting and cursing. From the window, Geppina broke up the calm of the side street, launching whatever she could get her hands on at anyone who came near her. Below at the front door a mob of neighbors and the usual busybodies had gathered: some ran over, still in their pajamas, some half-dressed or without shoes. Only when she caught sight of her sister's silhouette appearing at the end of the street did Geppina suddenly fall silent, restoring peace to the neighborhood. Then my mother entered the house and, making her way through the crowd of relatives, friends and neighbors, climbed up the ladder to the attic. In the half light, she glimpsed her standing on a wicker chair, one leg resting on the window sill, staring at her, her eyes full of hate. For a moment they just stood there, one in front of the other, without saying a word. Meanwhile, down below, their sisters' prayers, mumbled under their breath as though at a funeral, rose up to them. Staring her straight in the eyes, my mother came closer with an outstretched hand. Geppina seemed frozen in place. One step away from her, my mother grabbed her and pulled her in. Holding her tightly against her chest, where a sobbing Geppina found her refuge, she just stroked her disheveled hair and her tear-streaked face.

Then they started to descend the ladder, one after the other. My mother came down first, clutching her belly, her heart beating a thousand miles an hour. Suddenly, she felt a light tap on her shoulder and the rungs buckling under her feet. Accompanied by her sisters' frightened screams, she found herself in a heap at the bottom of the ladder, flat on her back and the whole world spinning around her. Between her legs she could feel the flush of viscous liquid. She was about to pass out when she heard Geppina's voice whispering in her ear.

"*'A fine che fai fa' a me, l'addà fa 'sta creatura che puorte dinto 'a panza.* The way I'm ending up because of you is the same way that child in your belly is going to end up."

In that same instant in which Geppina was forced into the car and carried off to the convent in Pescara where my mother had taken great lengths to keep her cloistered forever, I was coming into the world.

Listening to my mother's words as she spoke about Geppina, I think how she has consumed her days, her months, her years running the rosary through her hands, each bead representing a wound that life had inflicted on her. One after the other, each bead became more bitter than the last. The morning on which I ask my mother to bestow her art of sewing upon me, I'm not sure why, but I can see my own reflection in one of those beads. It doesn't take much thought for a doubt to creep into our minds: maybe some devious destiny pulls the strings of our lives at will, manipulating us like marionettes.

"Michè, you've gotten all caught up in this issue on my account. I know it," my mother says. "But I'm really worried about you. . . ."

Perhaps she's considering that invisible thread of hatred, which she fears connects each of us to the other. And her sister, through her, to me.

Seeing her like that, I can't find the words to tell her the news that she, just like my father, has been waiting to hear for a lifetime: that her firstborn son, himself getting old right before her eyes, is about to become a father.

I don't know why, but when Costanza joined us for lunch, I told her to not say anything—not yet, at least.

~ 13 ~

I have to call Michele, Geppina had probably told herself, not expecting to find the tone of my voice so eager and obliging. The phone call—a collect one, as always—caught me in the middle of a therapy session with a spry little old lady, fresh after a stroke. The woman stared insistently at me with the smile of someone who, having come to terms with being at the end of the line, didn't want to waste any of the time she had left by modulating her breathing, or focusing on the positioning of her lower jaw, or with vocalization exercises that demeaned her memory of her youthful beauty from long ago. But I was in such a good mood that not even Geppina's disjointed stammering, with that coarse, thick dialect of hers, could get to me.

The connection was bad and it was difficult to understand much, except that she was in the hospital in the company of a crew of police officers, and the matter concerned her daughter Maddalena. However, I clearly grasped that she was so scared she couldn't even speak. And I knew quite well that being in the presence of a policeman, forced to offer explanations and justifications for the umpteenth time, she was coming dangerously close to losing control and maybe even committing some hotheaded act. And she could not afford to do so. Moreover, since the "long arm of the law" was involved, she would end up convinced that the whole world took pleasure in stirring the pot. And in her case, it wouldn't take much for something nefarious to come to light. I assured her that I would be there right away, reminding her not to do anything until I got there.

When I crossed the courtyard of Cardinal Ascalesi Hospital, the sun was almost at high noon and I couldn't even make out her shadow. I was riding so blissfully high on the peacefulness of that day that my thoughts fluttered in a listless array all about my head.

Beautiful. What a beautiful morning it was. From on high, a beam of light descended and set the palm tree in the middle of the courtyard on fire. From which direction, I can't recall, but a spring breeze blew softly, gently, giving the heart some false promise. From the PA system under the vaulted ceiling of the porticoed walkway, I could hear the notes of an "Ave Maria" infusing the chatter of people crowding the café in one corner of the cloister. All around me there were the usual comings and goings of patients with their visiting relatives, and clusters of doctors and nurses in their windswept white scrubs. All of a sudden, disrupting the serenity in the courtyard, an ambulance pulled through with sirens blaring and slammed on its brakes right in front of the emergency room. And then I finally saw Geppina, who was sitting motionless on a bench, hands on her lap and vacant eyes staring into nowhere. The inconsolable motionlessness of that woman with her straw-yellow hair, a tight flowered dress, and cork-soled wedge sandals that were way too high all provided a complete picture of just how alien she was in a place where all the others were doing all they could to cheat death. Deep down she must have wanted to cheat life *with* death.

Getting through the police detail at the hospital was easier than I had feared. A uniformed officer with a five-o'clock shadow and the benevolent nature of someone who has seen it all just asked for some personal information. First my information, then Geppina's, which he didn't pry into. Right after, digging through a pile of documents held together with string in front of him, he opened a folder and put on his glasses:

> May 17, 2005, at 17:00 hours, after being transferred from the City Hospital in Rieti, Maddalena Piccolo—born in Naples, September 14, 1985 to Giuseppe Piccolo and Giuseppina De Nicola, resident of Volla (in the province of Naples), at 37 Via De Gasperi (formerly Parco degli Oleandri)—was admitted to the neurology unit of Ascalesi Hospital in Naples.

At that point the man took off his glasses and stared at Geppina for a moment. "Can you verify that you are the mother of this patient?"

Without waiting for an answer, he looked down, moistened his fingers with his tongue, and went back to flipping through the paperwork.

Geppina, worrying that at any moment he might look into her priors, said nothing. Afraid that something about her past involving contraband cigarettes might come to light, not to mention her son Lello's long rap sheet, she just turned to me with her eyes wide open. Most likely she was afraid, or she was intent on holding back her anger, because a vein in her neck started to bulge.

"Ah, yes. Here's the fax from Rieti," the officer said with the relieved expression of someone who just found a needle in a haystack. "Ma'am? So can you verify the information? Is this your daughter?" he added, adjusting his cap.

"Yeah, yeah. It's her daughter. Sorry. You know how it is: all the anxiety," I intervened.

"How is she?" asked Geppina, her tense lips rolled inward and almost invisible.

"Ma'am, how do you think she is? The report is quite clear," he observed, removing his cap as though it were burning his forehead.

February 12, 2005, at approximately six in the morning, at the Cavalotti overpass, in the proximity of the Rieti-Roma highway bypass, a young female who appeared to be twenty years of age was found on the shoulder of the road. According to investigators at the scene, she was found without any identification, nor with any unique identifying features—only a photograph of a young girl, presumably of five or six years of age, dressed in Spanish costume attire. Upon admittance to the trauma unit of the City Hospital in Rieti, she presented multiple fractures and a cranial concussion with resultant comatose state. The cause of the accident remains undetermined. However, given the injuries suffered, signs point to a violent impact with the ground attributable to a fall from a significant height, presumably from the aforementioned Cavalotti overpass. Currently the inquiry to establish the facts has been suspended owing to the impossibility of interrogating the abovementioned subject, given her comatose condition.

"We are circulating this report to the appropriate authorities, et cetera, et cetera," he concluded, looking at us with his eyeglasses resting on his forehead. "They were only able to determine her identity a few days ago, when she came out of the coma. And then we tracked you down," he added.

"But how is she now, Officer?"

"Uh, how is she? . . . What can I say? . . . Alive, but she must have suffered quite a bit. I saw her two days ago to confirm her personal information."

"Were you able to ascertain what happened?" I asked.

"Look, the situation is a bit complicated. At first she claimed she couldn't recall anything, neither what she was doing on the overpass nor whether she was with someone else. At least that's what our colleagues in Rieti gathered from the interview," he answered, as his eyes refocused on some piece of paper within his arm's reach. "Yup, that's exactly what's written here," he continued, but then he raised his finger. "But she told me she was in a car with some guy who was drunk at the wheel. No, they were both drunk, and the car drove off the overpass. . . ."

Geppina looked at him impassively, showing no emotion on her face.

"And now we get to the strange part. When I called the police headquarters in Rieti for clarification, they confirmed that at the time your daughter was found, there was no sign of a car or anything to corroborate her version. The doctors feel that this business about the car could be something she made up. The fact that she dropped from the overpass is certain, but I think the how will remain a mystery . . . I mean, whether she threw herself off or whether someone else was involved."

After telling us in which ward we could find Maddalena, the police officer took us down a long, dilapidated hallway. There were some construction materials piled on the floor, probably for restorations that would never be carried to completion. In the meantime, the Ave Maria prayer, now set to celestial music, was playing again on the PA system. In the doorway that led to the covered portico, the man said good-bye to us with a cordial tone, but not before he described the way to the ward. We hadn't even taken one step when his voice stopped us in our tracks.

"Oh, I almost forgot. . . . Who's Martina?"

Geppina wasn't discouraged. She just glared at him angrily, turned her back, and went on her way among the others in the hallway, shuffling her loathsome wedge-heel cork-soled sandals. For a moment I just stood there, shocked, staring at him, afraid that he might have changed his mind and wanted to grill us for more information.

Instead, he said, "Poor kid . . . probably something she concocted in her head."

"Yeah, just another one of her concoctions," I confirmed with downcast eyes.

There are certain words that give you chills and that take your breath away.

"Spinal cord injury, brachiocrural hemiparesis on the left side, moderate cognitive impairment with grand mal epilepsy."

That is what the doctor had said about Ironhead's condition, accommodating us in a narrow little room full of boxes in the neurology ward on the third floor. It's astonishing how certain words lose their meaning immediately, allowing us to erase them from our heads without even giving them a second thought. Maddalena had tons of such words to toss into the wind.

A deafening buzz stayed with us as we walked down the hallway, peeping into the rooms here and there. Lying in rows of four beds apiece, one positioned to face the other, were the neglected bodies of women, young and old, who no longer served any purpose to anyone. Just piles of meat to throw away. And if they were still there, it's because no one had enough time to get around to it.

We found Maddalena's room right at the end of the ward. At first glance all the beds seemed occupied, except the last one next to the window. But there was no sign of her. An imposing platinum-blond woman, compassionately intent on spoon-feeding an emaciated old woman, welcomed us like a lady of the manor and led us right to Maddalena's bed, tottering on extremely high heels, which seemed on the verge of snapping under her bulky mass. After offering us two chairs, she told us that she never failed to check in on Maddalena when the nurses made themselves scarce, which was almost all the time. She would feed her, help her out of the bed, and settle her into the wheelchair. When necessary, she would even change her diapers. Although Geppina had shown no emotion on her face up until then, her heart almost skipped a beat when she recognized the creased photo of Martina in her Spanish dress on the bedside table.

"Where has she gone now?" I asked in an attempt to stem the woman's rambling enthusiasm.

We would be able to find her at the end of the hall, near the big window.

"She's always there, looking out the window," the imposing woman added, adjusting her leopard-patterned blouse, which was so tight it could burst open over her chest, along with the sequined tiger.

That's where we found Maddalena, abandoned in her wheelchair, below the open window. She was slumped over with her head on her chest, her arms resting in her lap, lost in who knows what kind of escape fantasy. Of all the afflicted bodies I had the opportunity to see that morning at Ascalesi Hospital, hers seemed the most useless in the world.

"*Matalè? Song'io, so' mammina.* . . . Maddalena? It's me, your mama. . . ."

When her mother appeared before her and knelt down to whisper her name, she just barely lifted her head and looked at her with a distant stare, as though floundering in the middle of a sea of nothingness. Who knows, perhaps she was focused on concocting another one of her stories, one of those really powerful ones that can block out the tough times, the missteps, the desperation, and the solitude, along with the longing to throw herself into the void and die. Or maybe she was dreaming about walking hand in hand with her little girl on a beautiful sunny day on the desolate streets of Volla.

Geppina's legs buckled and she slid down the wall. Then she went and sat on the balcony with the photo of Martina clutched in her hands. She realized that tears were suddenly welling up in her eyes. The surge of emotion was different from how it would grip her when Maddalena would return home after being gone for days. I wasn't in the mood to talk. As sadness corrugated her entire face, I could feel the senseless bliss with which my day had begun suddenly melt away, and I sank into the shame of who knows which burdensome privilege.

Maddalena unexpectedly stretched out her arm toward her mother.

"Maa-mm-màà," she said in a cavernous voice, while two large tears began to roll down her face.

"Is-isn't M-Maa-ar-tina p-pre-tty?"

That was the last time I ever heard her say her daughter's name.

~ 14 ~

Gian Maria Villari from the Operational Unit of clinical psychiatry was the doctor who handled Martina's complete psychological workup. With his indisputable expertise he evaluated both her personality structure and her cognitive development, without omitting any mention of any potential scarring attributable to her post-traumatic condition. His clinical assessment was naturally forwarded to Judge Giuliana Conti.

Martina is a roughly five-year-old girl with a frail appearance. She demonstrates no apprehensions about following me into the consultation room. This denotes that she is comfortable being separated from her role models and that she easily trusts unfamiliar people. Martina utilized the toys at her disposal without, however, being able to employ them in any organized structure of play. She never asked for my help, even when she faced difficulty with the toys, which leads me to conclude she is a child accustomed to spending long periods of time alone. All of this indicates her familiarity with conditions in which she is unable to rely on the help of authority figures. Martina is a child who presents a hyperkinetic disorder, a common coping reaction in the face of a baseline of extreme duress. Evident signs of a marked emotional and sociocultural deprivation are present in the subject. Her language skills are poor; she utilizes a limited, basic vocabulary. Her lack of familiarity with colors and crayons is notable. She is unable to express organized thoughts, but she responds in brief utterances to specific questions.

Doctor Villari had the opportunity to talk with Martina about herself and about her family affairs; yet, as can be expected from reading her report, she avoided dwelling on the composition of her nuclear family and on family relationships, let alone shedding light on names, even of strangers, that the girl attributed to her various authority figures.

I don't live with my parents because Maria made me go to foster's home. Maria is my mother's cousin. I'm in foster's home because my mommy is sick and she goes to the hospital. Grandma Claudia hurt her head. Grandpa gave her some slaps. Before I lived at Anna's house, the blond one. I slept at her house. Sometimes I go sleep at Emanuele's house. He brought me here. He has a daughter. Her name is Rosa. Mommy goes to the hospital because Grandpa yells at her. Concetta is my mommy. Grandma Claudia always goes to the hospital. Maddalena is my Grandma Claudia's cousin. Papa's name is Grandpa Lino and he's Grandma Claudia's husband. Giuseppina is Grandma Claudia's cousin. Grandma Claudia always gives

me shots with a needle. Now I live in foster's home with
Aunt Clara. I like foster's home.

Therefore, Martina confuses roles and people, places and situations. Some characters that she evoked seem to be the
fruit of her imagination. Is her apparent escape from reality
caused by traumatic events, or is it simply attributable to her
exuberant infantile imagination?

During my professional studies I was taught that among
the various methods of personality assessment for children,
the most effective projective test is analyzing their drawings,
just like observing them at play. A drawing, just like a game, is
a privileged channel of communication between young
peers and adults. Drawings and games are an external stage
on which children project their modes of existence and their
problems. They are also a means by which they can drama-
tize, represent, and communicate their own anxieties, a way
of giving voice to their traumatic experiences.

The doctor stressed that Martina's artistic display was
characterized by a very uneven line, almost primitive, with
no inclination toward highlighting details. And when she
had been asked to draw a human figure, Martina drew what
resembled a head to which she attached two very long legs.
The figure had no torso or any arms. It is common knowl-
edge that this manner of attaching limbs directly to the head
is typical of much younger children. The doctor maintained
that Martina had not been able to demonstrate the rudimen-
tary emotions that he proposed, such as joy, pain, and fear.
She said that she did not know how.

Martina's answers to the projective tests are extremely
spare and pithy. Martina appears to be an insecure child
who hardly speaks. She is incapable of expanding on and

developing her brief and laconic observations. In fact, when I showed her some images of animals, Martina revealed a complete ignorance of familial associations, confirming the fact that she felt like an abandoned child, in constant danger.

In one image there are three bears pulling a rope: an adult and a cub on one end and another adult on the other end. Martina says, "They are getting the cord to attack; they have to attack the little one. They want to kill it."

Then, an image of a lion seated on an armchair: "A wolf is eating his hand because he wanted to bite a mouse."

At the sight of a bear cub in the foreground with the silhouette of two adults in the background of a cave, Martina seems to get restless and confused; she stammers, tries to speak, and shuts down. She is experiencing an obvious moment of anxiety. Then she says, "It's a war. Him, the little one, he want to kill this one. He wants to take this thing where spiders go."

Before an image of a bunny in its little bed in a second-floor room with its door open, levels of anxiety linked to episodes of violence and abuse resurface. In fact, Martina tells of someone who knocks on the door while "he was in the bed. He wanted to kill him. He said that he couldn't come in because he was getting undressed."

As one can deduce from all of the picture images, the main theme here is violence, both suffered and acted out. When, instead, I showed Martina a series of images depicting people, her answers made two themes quite clear: the perception of a man touching a little girl and the perception of war. As a matter of fact, Martina has often repeated, "Then there's a war" as an expression indicating moments of confusion and violence.

And, once again, when confronted with a drawing of a woman seen from behind in the vicinity of a crib, Martina says, "A man was touching a little girl because she has to get undr . . ." She stops and then reiterates, "She has to get dressed. There's a war, there's everything on the ground. The man was waking her up, that thing is happening down there."

I believe that numerous post-traumatic indicators are evident and ascribable to child abuse and mistreatment. This persuaded me to introduce, in a successive session, that specific topic. However, her stories are confused and nonspecific, notwithstanding the clear evidence of her past involvement in many promiscuous and dysfunctional family contexts. She tells me about Grandpa Enrico whom she defines as "Grandma Claudia's husband" and adds, "Grandpa Enrico used to wash my tushy and my little coochie. Grandma Claudia gave me little kisses on my cheek. You don't give kisses on the mouth. Grandpa Enrico gave me some on my cheek," pointing to her mouth.

In the account he sent to the juvenile court, Doctor Gian Maria Villari reached the conclusion that Martina presented poorly integrated personality traits, with obvious and marked signs of emotional and sociocultural deprivations, which contributed to a general retardation in her psycho-emotional development. Her cumulative past was tied to events that were frustrating, related to abandonment, and often violent, all the while in the complete absence of a two-parent home and a nuclear family.

Nonetheless, he claimed that Martina did not demonstrate any signs of psychopathology worth noting. In the end, however, in two lines—which, when read carefully, would seem to challenge the previous judgment, if not contradict it altogether—Doctor Villari wrote, "Numerous post-traumatic indicators ascribable to situations of sexual abuse have surfaced in the subject."

In short, he believed that Martina, though not exhibiting significant scarring, could have, at any rate, endured sexual violence. And that's where the plot thickens. Who could have abused her? When? And most of all, where? Yet another veil of mystery obfuscating her story. Is it possible that such abuse can be left in a cloud of doubt? That no investigation was opened? And that no criminal proceedings have been launched by anybody?

Anyway, a doctor speculates about a trauma of such severity, and no one bothers to dig into it? The indifference was unexpected because I'd be inclined to believe that the majority of those called in to weigh on this case would have bet their life on the guilt of Geppina's husband. For various reasons it probably occurred to the social worker. Or maybe in her heart Judge Giuliana Conti knew. Surely the people from the foster home let their minds run wild with that one. I suppose that deep down—figuring it was one of the many incidents that unfortunately slip through the cracks of the legal system—even Counselor Serra deemed him responsible for that abomination. I have no qualms about admitting that even I had a nagging suspicion that was chipping away at those fleeting certainties that were struggling more and more to hold water.

Martina is lying in the bathtub. She looks at the window. One of those long bathroom windows that only allow you to see the sky. The water is barely warm. Her eyes are fixed on the clear glass—no shower curtain—while Geppina keeps repeating the same abrupt, matter-of-fact motions. Lather up, massage, rinse it away with your hand, rinse again, more carefully, all the hard-to-reach spots. Scrub in your creases, your elbows and knees, where dirt and grime always build up. All the while she just looked outside: a vast expanse of blue, a cloud, two clouds, three clouds, and whatever chance had in store for them; one bird, two birds, three birds, and a blinding light—the same as always. The house is quite noisy. The buzzing of the television mixes with Geppina singing without the words—she simply lets the modulated, relaxed sound resonate from her throat. In her head there's the rush of the faucet. She feels Geppina's lather-covered hands slide over her body. Over her arms and legs and through her hair. Grandpa Lino is in the doorway watching her and smiling at her. The soap gets in her eyes. It burns. She closes them. The phone rings. Geppina's voice says, "Who could it be at this hour?" She steps out. Now there are other hands touching her. On her chest, her stomach, her legs. They are rough. It's a pleasant sensation. She opens her eyes. Grandpa's face is right there in front of hers. Behind his lenses, his eyes seem enormous and they watch her. The water gets colder . . . and colder. . . .

I've never succeeded in moving beyond my imagination about what might have happened to Martina, if it had even happened. One day, having stopped by Geppina's place to review some documents, for no apparent reason I thought of Miss Clara, the director of the foster home; she had told me how Doctor Villari's recommendations really worried Geppina. Looking right into their eyes, I asked her and her husband how much of this story was true. Was Martina really in the bathtub? Had Lino effectively taken Geppina's place? Is that all that had happened, or did he do more?

They didn't answer me. They lowered their heads and seemed to be in pain—the sort of pain of someone who cannot fathom how his life, leading up to that very moment, might fit into destiny's arcane plan. But in that glimmer of pain that flushed over their eyes a moment earlier, I felt I had witnessed all of their time come to an end. And I thought they knew it, too, because I saw them resigned like moribund dogs on the side of a road just waiting to die.

At this point, perhaps I'm exaggerating, and it wouldn't be difficult to do so, all things considered. Perhaps out of concern for being overcome by all of this horror, perhaps out of fear of seeing myself transformed into a pillar of salt once some unknown inner part of me revealed itself—that unknown part that hides in all of us. And how could you blame me?

~ 15 ~

The decision to introduce Costanza to Giuliana Conti, by now, like all the decisions I would happen to make—including the one to learn how to sew a pair of trousers—was exclusively based on my reaction to the new set of circumstances. Circumstances in which a man suddenly sees his life turned completely upside down.

For example, Costanza's firmly established behavioral patterns seemed to have completely changed over the previous month. She had forgone any activities that were not directly related to her prime objective. In other words, she carried on with a pregnancy that had sprouted among the ruins of her, and my, hostile nature. And I don't think it was merely ascribable to her tenacious personality. Like many women expecting a child, in order to dedicate herself to maternal nesting instincts and to establish the new mother-child bond, Costanza was responding to a primordial urge that can lead to relegating the husband to the background. However, since she had waited so long for this child, her instincts were exaggerated to the point in which the husband was almost entirely erased from the picture.

So she had arranged for those upcoming months—and it was only natural for her to do so—down to the smallest detail. They were changes that surely involved me, too. Her plan would begin with restructuring her duties at the office so that she could get home earlier in the evening. This would entail new rules at home, including the schedule and makeup of meals. This meant a new inclination toward household chores. She was like a cleaning lady each day. This meant a complete reshuffling of our private life, which implied seeing friends and relatives according to a strict timetable that also necessitated reminders for our romantic interludes, which were to be held strictly once a week, sheltered from the excesses and madness of the outside world. And don't get me started on rearranging the apartment in order to free up an extra room, complete with a crib and bassinet, a playpen, glow-in-the-dark star decals on the ceiling, and all the accoutrements that would brighten up the future child's life until its twelfth birthday. Among other things, her intention was to acquire a new stereo with an advanced sound system, and corresponding headphones with extendable *bellybuds*, or padded earphones, to apply to her tummy. New studies were revealing that exposure to music in the womb, even in the first weeks of gestation, was an ideal way to influence the fetus's emotional and psychological development. In short, according to her, listening to Mozart and Beethoven would give our child all the tools he would need to become a more balanced man with superior logic; and so, the music would help him forge a personality that was both mild-mannered and determined, in keeping with her expectations.

And that's how I was able to appreciate who Costanza had become in that period, while she would walk alongside me, completely clueless about the ideas percolating inside of me.

As for me, it would have been rather complicated to explain what I had brewing in my head. Later, I would repeat it all to myself, on the way up the stairs that would lead us, floor after floor, to my objective. Later, when she would hear Giuliana Conti explain the best option for Martina. Later, when I would be able to offer her better justifications and beg her to listen to reason. In other words, just because we were expecting one child didn't mean we had to rule out adopting another. That's what was bouncing around my head. An idea that fully matured a number of weeks earlier, while sitting right in front of the judge. And she was calm enough to hear me out to the end that I was certain that I could make her see why I had decided to take responsibility for Martina's future, instead of letting her fate be decided by laws that would have little or no regard for the pain they might cause. I would make her see that there was nothing wrong with my decision to celebrate a new life by saving another. And for someone who had accepted living between two worlds, it seemed like the most natural thing to do. I wanted her to know that Martina represented a chance for me to reconcile who I was today with who I should have been. In the end, I would assure her that in this way I would avoid having to navigate, at who knows what cost, the convoluted bureaucratic complexities of adoption and that I would immediately back off if any of it became a major sacrifice for her.

That's what I would like to have told her. But I was concerned that if I had done so earlier, she would have thought it was all nonsense—a lie that was providing cover for some unspeakable fear about our new reality, or at best a feeling of inadequacy that was masked behind a foolish decision. Since Giuliana Conti knew Martina's situation quite intimately, as soon as Costanza was sitting with me across from her and hearing what she had to say about this being the best course of action for Martina, Costanza would agree on her own terms. But just short of that, anything I might have confided to her earlier would have seemed like the rantings of a troubled mind. Nonetheless, I was even more convinced that if I cared about her and about the child we were expecting, I would need to do something brave. Besides, I had been preparing for that moment for a week, with the same single-mindedness that years ago I would use to prepare for the 400-meter hurdles final.

The juvenile court is located in a hilly area of the city, in Via Colli Aminei. It can be accessed by passing through a gate, which is constantly guarded by the municipal police, after providing identification and verifying a valid appointment with the property authority. An alley snaking uphill through some greenery leads to the top of a hillock where a low, two-story, red-brick building sits. From the large windows overlooking the grounds, you could almost touch the foliage of the fir trees planted behind it. In the lobby, you could already feel the heavy air of mournful silence just by looking at the gloominess on the faces of the people occupying it.

On the second floor the chatter was deafening. The waiting area was packed. From behind a desk, the bailiff barely lifted his head.

"Do you have an appointment?"

"Yes!" I replied. "Judge Conti is expecting us at ten."

"One moment," he said, rising from his chair. "In the meantime, take a seat, if you can find any room," he added before slipping into the throng.

Through an open window, a sweet spring breeze wafted in, while a ray of sunlight seemed to hover in mid-air. On a row of chairs, beneath the watchful eye of two nuns intent on saying the rosary for who knows what sins, some kids hung their heads like men on death row.

"You could have told me that you had an appointment," said the man, who returned out of breath after a few minutes.

"Well, that's what I did," I replied nonplussed.

"No, that you have a real appointment. I mean, that she was expecting you and that you know the judge, that is," he retorted, directing us to a hallway off to the side.

Before knocking on the judge's door, as I stared into Costanza's eyes, I found myself saying, "It's easier than it might seem." Judge Conti opened the door with a smile and the tone of someone who had read my thoughts the whole way over. Even though she was driven by a sincere interest in Martina's case, Giuliana Conti—known for her rigid adherence to procedure and a strict sense of fair play—was not able to completely hide her astonishment at my determination in getting custody. Not that she didn't recognize my moral character, but what truly surprised her was discovering the bonds of kinship that the girl and I shared. Actually, I understood quite well how the Michele Campo she was seeing before her after so much time might be difficult to take in.

I knew it didn't take much for prejudices, including the most secret kind that we don't even reveal to ourselves, to flame up from under the ashes of class discrimination. In that sense, I feared Giuliana Conti's prejudice, even though part of me after so many years was still ready to trust in her open-mindedness and in her clarity of vision.

On the other hand, if I had shared with Costanza my reluctance regarding my old friend, she would have attributed my lack of lucidity to my new torment about my roots.

Her being there at my side, at any rate, beyond triggering Giuliana Conti's feminine curiosity, helped to corroborate the expectations I was secretly harboring. She would witness the care Judge Conti was taking to express herself for the entire meeting. Beyond their common expertise, they seemed to speak the same language and to get along swimmingly. It was obvious that they liked each other, and for a moment I saw them as animals who belonged to the same species.

And the fact that Costanza was a practicing child neuropsychiatric was no minor factor in paving the way for the plan I had in mind.

"My aunt's lawyers are still hoping that the court might reconsider. They believe that if they could just speak with you, you know . . . to reexamine the state of her home life, they might be able to convince you that . . ."

"Look, Michele, as I already told you the last time, I'm not sure there are any grounds for allowing Martina to return to her home environment. On the contrary . . . I'm sorry to say it, most of all in light of the fact that you're a relative. . . . But I believe that the best course is finding her another family unit. Trustworthy and stable. You see, despite the documentation that Ms. De Nicola's lawyers keep sending me, the action that began with the order of removal is considered an irreversible process that leads to adoption. The foster home is just a transitional step."

"At this point I need to ask you something," I told her, looking her in the eyes. "Are you sure that removing Martina from her family was the best choice?"

She didn't skip a beat. She closed her eyes for a second and then cracked a half-smile.

"Just for the record, I am legally obligated to do this. And I think that for Martina, as painful as it might be, it's the best thing," she replied. "How 'bout you? Be honest, what do you think?"

She caught me off guard. "I don't know!" I said, lowering my head in a vain attempt to hide the embarrassment that I knew would appear when faced with such a question. "According to her grandparents, Martina was better off with them."

"From where I stand, things are quite different. . . . There are specialists who described a truly dramatic situation in their reports: an untenable, unlawful situation that had already gone on for too long. . . ."

"Maybe so, but I know for sure that they have good intentions."

"You know what they say? The road to hell . . ."

I was about to tell her it was probably no different for people like them, who struggle to make things better for themselves. But I didn't.

"Michele, let's analyze the situation," Giuliana Conti continued. "At first, Martina had been entrusted to her aunt, but she was living with the grandmother along with the mother from the time she was about a year old. And this was in contempt of strict instructions of both the juvenile court and the presiding judge, who had given custody precisely to the aunt . . . Concetta Piccolo, right? . . . Who, among other things, is separated from her husband. . . . Not exactly in the best shape to take care of Martina. Actually, she has never been in that kind of shape . . . along with two small children, to boot. Ultimately, Michele . . . the indigent conditions in which they live are disastrous, and that's not to speak of the violent arguments between the mother and her daughters . . . apparently over Maddalena's pension money. . . . I heard that her siblings forced her to withdraw all her unused funds from her bank account . . . and maybe with their mother's complicity. Michele, we all know quite well how economic hardships can influence behavior, but . . . can you imagine the effect this has all had on little Martina?"

At this point Costanza came to my rescue.

"A delay in psychophysical development, signs of deprivation, fear of abandonment . . ."

"Exactly, and I need to fix all that."

"I agree. But if you give me a chance. . . . In reference to the likely sexual abuse involved, I must tell you that I don't completely agree with Dr. Villari's observations. I could cite many cases in which . . ."

"But even so, that's not the point," Giuliana Conti observed.

"Her grandparents seemed rather doting and protective when it came to Martina," I said, touching on the family issue. "Plus, the fact that she attended a private school seems rather significant to me in this regard."

Giuliana Conti listened quietly, not even blinking an eye, even though her expression betrayed a certain impatience for inopportune meddling in the juvenile court's deliberations.

"As I was just saying, that's not the point. . . . We're not talking about the appropriateness of what has been done—which is out of the question—but about what might be the best option for Martina, going forward," she hastened to add. Then, turning to me, she continued, "Martina will be placed with a new family. My task is to find a suitable one."

I was about to apologize, telling her that my intention was not to doubt her judicial authority or her professional authority or what have you. Yet another of Costanza's interruptions proved providential: once again, she was able to change the tenor of the conservation.

"We are here precisely to understand . . . to identify the most helpful trajectory for Martina," Costanza observed. "I am quite familiar with the dysfunctionality of this family," she added, turning to look at me. "The two of us have spoken at length about them, even if I don't personally know any of them."

I'm not sure why she said she didn't know any of them. She had met Geppina a few months earlier, right at our house, when I decided that the moment had come to introduce her to my mother. I thought she had some hidden motives that were beyond my grasp at the time, but they must have been part of some meticulous strategy of hers.

"If you want to help Martina, put her with another family. And though the adoption process is slow and weighed down by lots of bureaucracy, I will try to locate a suitable family as soon as possible," the judge iterated. "Of course if you two, for example, were interested in taking care of her, and I'm speaking hypothetically, the matter would be rather straightforward, given the biological relationship between Michele and the girl . . . not to mention by doing it that way she wouldn't suffer the traumatic separation from those who have been her parental figures up until now. And it could bridge the gaps in her life that she's had to contend with."

Costanza caressed me with her eyes and then flew into an impassioned debate with Giuliana Conti.

"Judge, I'll say it again: if we are here with you, it's because we have talked about it," she added, turning toward me with a look of complicity. "Of course it's a matter of thinking this through carefully, especially in light of our own situation—as a couple, I mean—and there's a new development: we're having a baby."

"Ah, I didn't know that," Giuliana replied. "Congratulations! At any rate, though, that doesn't affect your situation. On the contrary . . . Every single event that occurs within a family contributes to the educational growth of a child, even the birth of a younger sibling."

"I am ready to do my part," I added, glad that Costanza and Giuliana were doing their best to find common ground.

"So what do you suggest?" asked Costanza.

"I don't think you should go with adoption straight away. At first, you could try custody. Then, once you've gotten over the legal hurdles, which are unfortunately an unavoidable reality, I will be at your complete disposal for a definitive adoption."

"Which hurdles?"

"Well, marriage, for example. The law does not permit adoptions by unmarried couples."

Costanza looked at me. Then, turning to Giuliana Conti, she said, "No impediments whatsoever here. At any rate, I think it's essential to meet with the child first, so she can get to know us better and so we can get a sense of her personality. What do you say?"

"That's not a problem. Michele already has the opportunity to see Martina at the foster home, but I can arrange some authorized visits for both of you, especially if they are leading to custody. You just need to let me know. . . ."

A phone call interrupted her. Before answering, she gestured with her finger, asking us to excuse her, and picked up the receiver.

Costanza turned and smiled at me. Her glowing face indicated she had some ideas of her own. Watching her, I thought back to that morning in the kitchen, when she had joined me with a relaxed expression and her head peering down at a child whom she'd met the previous night in some dream. Now she had the same dreamy demeanor from then, with none of the sullenness that usually overtook her. Oddly complacent, I wondered what she was thinking about. That was the question: about what?

"Excuse me," said Giuliana Conti, hindering my thoughts, after hanging up. "But there's so much work to do that—"

"I'm sorry," I said, interrupting her. "We are taking too much of your time."

"No, no, not at all. This is part of my work. In fact, I am reassured to know that Martina might come into an ideal situation. Anyway, as I said before, think about it and let me know. Keep in mind, however, that we don't have much time. The less Martina stays in the foster home, the better. I must also tell you, just to be clear, that you are not the only ones on the list. But don't worry about that. You have all the right credentials, and if all goes as expected, I think we'll be able to ensure a good future for Martina."

"Judge, give us just a little time and you will hear from us," said Costanza, rising from her chair.

At the door, before saying our good-byes, I asked Giuliana about her parents and her sister, Marina.

"They're fine. They age well. Marina is always traveling for work. In fact, she needs to come to Naples for some performances next month."

"Give her my regards, will ya?"

"I told her you had come by to see me last month. Call her. She'll be happy to hear from you. She'll be at my folks' house for the entire run of the show."

Then she cordially sent us off. She kissed me on the cheek and was affable to Costanza, who reciprocated with a bright smile, which she drew from a repertoire of pleasantries that would have been unthinkable up until very recently.

All around us the mood seemed to suddenly change, from the waiting room to the hallways and the stairwells. There was no sign of the noise from earlier. Now, only silence hung in the air. Everyone seemed to be walking on tiptoes. The children with downcast eyes whom I had noticed a bit earlier were still there next to the nuns who were also still sitting with their hands interlocked over their laps. And it was almost as though in that wait that separated them from the gallows, the whole world were taking part in their suffering—everyone, including the bailiff behind the desk, the law clerks who came and went, and the policemen keeping watch over the offices.

"You know what I was thinking about?" Costanza asked, going down the stairs. "About how destiny takes pleasure in toying with my life," she said, staring at me without waiting for me to answer. "Before, fate didn't want to give me any kids, but now, it's got two in store for me," she added with an overjoyed expression.

So that was the reason for her dreamy disposition when she was beaming at me in front of the judge moments earlier. So that's what she was thinking about, I thought. In saying what she said, she had taken me back in time to the free-thinking nonconformist whom I had first met. What had become of that decisiveness, which was a reflection of her razor-sharp thoughts? Where, I wondered, had that Amazon firebrand of the family line gone?

"Your friend was very kind. It's obvious that she cares about you," she said, tripping on the last flight of stairs. "Has it been long since you've seen her sister?"

"It's been so many years by now," I replied. "Jealous?"

She laughed and looked up to the heavens.

While walking back down to the gate, with her by my side, along the shady lane that was besieged by the echo of footsteps and the sound of traffic in the distance, I finally understood how easily one's life can turn in one direction rather than in another; I finally understood destiny's tyrannical randomness. Costanza's was inexorably tied to mine.

And beyond giving her a child, destiny was chaining her to the life of Martina, a living testament of what I could have been but had never become. Conversely, at that point, it wasn't a stretch to think that if, on the one hand, I was about to prevail over a shit life that I was born into by chance, on the other hand, I had done all I could do to pollute her life. If she had only pondered the issue, even for a moment, I'm sure she would have completely disagreed with my hypothesis.

~ 16 ~

Thinking about Judge Conti without also imagining her sister, Marina, before my eyes is impossible. Meeting that fatally beautiful girl—tall, thin, green eyes, a Neapolitan Brigitte Bardot, a goddess—dragged me out of the world of shadows that I came from and to which, at that time, I still belonged. It was she who sanctioned my entry into the circle of young scions from the well-to-do of Naples. And she was also the one who, inexplicably in love with me, sparked my ambitions at twenty years of age by drowning me in the incandescent magma of youthful, and therefore unmitigated, passion.

Back then, around the middle of the 1970s, where I'm from, guys like me came a dime a dozen, but few were well versed in the art of survival and determined enough to undertake the risk of social climbing. It wasn't a matter of a playboy looking for a good catch but a wager on a young man who was stubborn, tenacious, and capable of making sacrifices and blending in; a young man who would quickly learn how to imitate those around him and to win over, through sweat and hard work, the world he wanted so very much to be a part of.

Marina Conti, daughter of a lawyer and a schoolteacher from the middle-class Vomero—the neighborhood in which I also used to live as the son of a doorman—was one of the most sought-after girls in the city. She was perennially surrounded by indefatigable admirers, and I had to keep looking over my shoulder for them. They were guys with whom I had to often engage in battles of the sort where my rhetorical weapons would have been superfluous. When I met her, Marina, barely sixteen, was in her third year of her *magistrale*, or education training, in a high school run by the nuns of Saint Maria Ausiliatrice, an almost mandatory choice in those days for anyone who showed even a slight propensity toward learning. But if, on the one hand, her education progressed unspectacularly and without controversy, on the other hand, the myth of her beauty grew to the point of commanding a following. Not just from the boys. At school, her female classmates imitated her behavior, her movements, her style of dress, and even her hairstyle, all as a way of vying to get into her good graces. Inevitably she ended up becoming *the* model in all the fashion houses in the city, and in no time at all she was drumming up very lucrative engagement fees to walk the runways for the big designers.

I was always by her side, playing the part of the unbridled playboy, on the altars of an ephemeral, albeit highly coveted, notoriety that summoned the casual attention and frivolous flattery of women who were enticed more by their desire to compete against Marina than by my putative charms and suntanned face.

As for me, well, I felt totally out of place, like a trespasser in their world who stunk of poverty. Yet, I think the others saw in me a handsome guy who toiled to prove himself always affable and seductive, even elegant to the point of obsession. I was her mysterious little curly-haired *Saraceno*, an exotic Neapolitan cross between Don Juan and a bronze-skinned Arab who had learned to sway his hips to the rhythm of the timeless Bee Gees, to the "father of Italian disco," Giorgio Moroder, and to Donna Summer's rapturous "Love to Love You Baby." An enterprising type who exuded worldly self-confidence when in reality he lived with the fear that if they had figured out where he was from, he would have been immediately sent packing and into the arms of a father who kowtowed to the upper class as a doorman and of a mother who slaved over a sewing machine day after day.

I was able to keep up the charade with everyone but not with Marina. Naive and skittish as I was, I revealed my secret to her. I took her to my house and introduced her to my father who fell in love with her right away, my brother who couldn't take his wide eyes off her, and my awkward and reverential sisters. But the real fireworks happened with my mother. It was not just a matter of an affinity between two women with a capacity for great emotion but a fatal attraction between a seamstress and a perfect model. No sooner would Marina flip through an edition of *Vogue* or sketch a dress that she had seen in a shop than my mother had already started stitching it. And she came into my world—that world I had always experienced as a threat, a form of original sin—with such a genuine delight that the clouds of my insecurities finally dissipated, and my yearning to fly the coop and my vindictiveness began to transform into more pragmatic approaches to life. I was learning to be appreciated for my personal qualities, my pleasant demeanor, and of course, my kindness, but most of all for how determined I was to improve, to grow, to build a future for myself. To the point that once in a while

Marina's father, a truly unyielding man, granted me an indulgent look.

Despite my tenacity, my vocational certification had proved useless, and that's to say nothing of my career as a 400-meter runner being nipped in the bud. But all those years on the track helped me gain admittance to the College for Physical Education with hopes of landing a job teaching in a public school.

It was a long, happy period of my life—a period so close to perfect that it was naturally destined to end. With the passing of time, though, Marina continued to gratify me with her unlikely choice to stay with me, even showing me great affection—which meant preferring me each day to a multitude of guys who were infinitely more handsome, richer, and more interesting than me. I began to have an ominous feeling that she would drift far away from me and rise way higher. A premonition that turned into a reality because in the span of a few months, Marina spread her wings. Off she went to Milan for fashion week, to Florence for Pitti Donna, and to Rome to get her feet wet with television commercials and maybe even in the movies. Now and then I would receive a phone call from her in the evening, then nothing but silence for days. But most of all there were the sleepless nights spent thinking about her in someone else's arms. And seeing her on the streets, laid out in actual size on a billboard advertising some lingerie or perfume, all while smiling flirtatiously with people rushing past. These thoughts had transformed me into a jealous, petulant, insecure, and aggressive man, to the point that my suspicions and recriminations were spoiling even the scant moments we spent together during her fleeting visits home. The more I grilled her with questions and underhanded insinuations, the more antagonistic and secretive she became. The more reason cautioned me to back off, the more that nagging doubt took hold of me. Until one evening when I slapped her, thus putting an end to our relationship.

She left, leaving no trace behind. Nothing. And I plummeted into the clichéd gloomy desperation of a rejected lover; I would whine, looking for sympathy from friends and relatives, scrounging up information about Marina and getting in return, as though they had been scripted, sermons about how I should consider the end of one relationship the beginning of a new one, that I should get on with life even though I just wanted to die.

What saved me from sinking into the abyss was the unexpected intervention of Giuliana, her nerdy older sister, who was constantly immersed in her law school books, always so standoffish that she seemed invisible. It was she—one evening when I had met her for yet another session of venting about my broken heart—who had the bright idea of greeting me at the door wrapped in a white towel that left almost nothing to the imagination. And before letting it drop to the floor, with a gentle twist of her hips, she summoned up the courage to admit that at night, when I used to bring her sister home, she would stay up so she could spy on my every movement, shuddering at each step I took through the quiet house.

But as erotically passionate as it was, our liaison was short lived. Giuliana always initiated things: more than just knowing how to use my body, she showed me that she could read my thoughts. She sensed how doggedly determined I was to stay connected to her sister, and so, with majestic altruism, she vanished from the scene.

In the years following our breakup, Marina became a rather successful actress. She would work in the movies and on television, but most people thought she gave her best performances on the stage. I even ran into her for fleeting moments during which each of us would remark how all that time away from each other had turned us into perfect strangers. I never saw her again. As for Giuliana, there's not much to say. That was the last I heard of her, except that she had married, that she had had a child, and that she was headed toward a brilliant career as a minister of justice.

~ 17 ~

Going to Geppina's place had never been easy for me. As soon as I made my way through the tangle of elevated highways that plunged into the bleak landscape, I would become sad. Not to mention the surrounding countryside, crisscrossed by unevenly paved roads and the continuous rumbling of trucks. A landscape that was made all the more hostile by transient trailer parks and makeshift shanties slapped between the cement pylons, by the heaps of garbage at cross streets, and by the abandoned buildings that served as refuge for scores of emaciated dogs, homeless people, and prostitutes warming themselves by bonfires in the light of day.

That morning was no different. Except for the fact that I was headed over there with a car full of cans of peeled tomatoes and tuna, pasta, meat, fruit, vegetables, and bags full of secondhand clothes for the kids and grandkids. And my mother was with me. She considered this cornucopia of goods to be more an offering to placate the wrath of a vindictive deity than to help out a sister suffering economic hardship. For a good portion of the trip over, she did nothing but rattle off all her anxieties about how in Geppina's heart the embers of hate might still be glowing under the ashes of time. She continued to believe that Geppina had never forgiven her for having locked her away in that convent forty years earlier. By contrast I felt that she was more or less the same as she would have been if my mother hadn't separated her from the family. But the way my mother saw it, once you get a taste of hatred, you can't do without it. The problem was that my mother was the one who had introduced her to that hate. And she was convinced that it was still there in her eyes when they met at my house, one month earlier right in front of Costanza.

After the initial awkwardness came the impenetrable wall of mistrust. As much as Costanza and I had tried to put them at ease by making small talk, they wouldn't even give each other the time of day. So we decided to leave them alone in the living room, where they sat at the mercy of some feeling of edginess that caused them to cast their eyes downward, avoiding each other. It was my mother, though, who caught Geppina by surprise, breaking the ice by asking her, not without getting all choked up, what she had been doing that whole time. At first skirting all the details, Geppina stuck to talking about her husband, the one and only Pino Piccolo, a lowlife known to everyone in a street market in Caserta who, for years, had put her and her four kids through hell. However, when he had started to go in and out of jail, regularly tormenting her with requests for money for lawyers, she had gotten as far away from him as possible. She told my mother that to put bread on the table for her kids, she had wandered around from town to town getting by any way she could. And that one fine day, Lino appeared on her horizon, and she was still grateful to him for his saving her from that life of hardship.

They had met on the docks at the port in Naples where he would make ends meet as a street vendor. Without the courage necessary to approach her, he had followed her around for weeks while she wandered through the offices at the ferry terminal; he would spy on her as she yapped with this or that sailor; he would sneak into the cargo holds of ships docked at the piers, or else he would duck out of sight in the storage depots with one of his buddies. But when he finally decided to come out of the shadows, calling her "ma'am," the only thing that came out of his mouth was a lunch invitation at a local watering hole near Piazza Mercato. And he always treated her with kindness, as no one had ever done before. He didn't ask her where she was from or what brought her to those parts, and he never even asked her to join him in the old silo of the dilapidated cotton mill on Pier 14. In the early days of their relationship, Lino would just wait hours on end for Geppina to come back from her usual rounds, just for the pleasure of taking her for a bite and sit with her and watch the forest of cargo cranes that reached to the sky on the eastern edge of the port. Later he even gave her a chance to make some extra money with the black-market cigarettes that she would resell by trolling through the offices and shops on Via Marina and on Corso Umberto, aka the "Rettifilo." Then one beautiful spring morning while sitting on the pier, their eyes following the purple silhouette of the *Caribbean Queen*, which was leaving the Bay of Naples, he told her that he would be happy to take care of her and her children. He was offering her a roof over her head and a bit of affection. It was all he had, but it was hers if she wanted it. That man, Geppina confessed to my mother, was like manna from heaven, and even though she wasn't attracted to him one bit, in time she grew fond of him and she was glad to have given him four children.

When I pulled the car up to the Parco degli Oleandri in Volla, we were met by a flutter of flags that the wind had buffeted against the balcony railings. Hanging from them were sheets and remnants of banners exalting the soccer glory of old: even an old effigy of Maradona wearing a crown graced the building's facade. On the asphalt some little kid had painted the whole starting lineup for Naples, which just one month earlier, following the fratricidal defeat in the playoffs with Avellino, had miserably missed their bid for promotion into Serie B. And on a wall of that nautical-looking church someone had written in block letters, "Capparella, your face alone will forever haunt us in our worst nightmares." The unknown graffiti artist was upset with the attacking midfielder who, during the away leg of that home-and-away set of playoff games, after a mesmerizing run down the right flank in which he'd left some Avellino players in the dust, ended up one-on-one with the goalkeeper and the best he could do was send the ball high and wide. The whole stadium was speechless.

Suddenly, just as we were arriving at Geppina's building, a voice on the radio broke a news story about a series of suicide attacks in the London Underground. Estimates were already numbering the dead in the scores and the injured in the hundreds. The likely suspects included Al Qaeda, Bosnian mercenaries on the payroll of some homegrown British Muslims, and even Al-Zarqawi, who very likely could have provided the explosive materials. The journalist did not fail to remind listeners that in Italy the threat of attack remained very high and that the interior minister had proclaimed a red alert.

A few people appeared on the sunlit second-floor balconies, while others kept watch on us from the windows on the upper floors. Still others did the same right in front of us from the splotchy neglected lawn. Each time I had gone to Geppina's house, I had intercepted some curious looks, but on that day they all seemed to be waiting to witness who knows what event.

Just as I was trying to unload the boxes, bags, and the sundry supplies that wouldn't fit in the brimming trunk, I was surrounded by three women followed by a brood of children. The first to come forward was Concetta.

"*Buongiorno a zí, io so' Cuncetta*. Hello, Auntie. I'm Concetta," she said, hugging my mother. "*E chisti ccà so e figli miei*. . . . And these here are my kids," she added, pointing to a little girl with braids and a little boy with a weaselly look.

Then came Monica's turn. "The Redhead," as she's known, threw her arms around my mother's neck, waving her tousled amber hair. The third sister, children glomming onto her legs, waited timidly in the wings before finally heading toward the building's shadowy lobby. I had never seen her, but I recognized her from the black hijab on her head that only revealed her pale, oval face. It was Susetta, one of Geppina and Lino's daughters who was married to a Tunisian immigrant named Mahmud. He had done time with her stepbrother Lello. As soon as he was out of prison, he had asked her if she wanted to date him. In his mind, Susetta had defied all sorts of prejudices: her father's, her mother's, those of the neighborhood, and even of the entire town. According to those who had described her to me, she had to be the most introverted and level-headed of the siblings but also the most stubborn. Not giving in to pressures from the others, she had even converted to Mahmud's religion and, in turn, he had gone on the straight and narrow and had resumed the trade passed down to him by his father on the Kerkennah Islands: furniture restoration.

Beneath my mother's startled eyes, the children began to swarm the merchandise, grabbing whatever they could. In no time at all, they swept up the fruit, vegetables, and meat, the clothes and toys, going up and down the stairs like a colony of industrious ants. A sign written by a shaky hand and hung on the door of the elevator gave notice that it was out of order. A kitchen smell permeated the stairwells, and on each floor I had the distinct feeling that all the tenants were eavesdropping on us from behind closed doors or spying at us moving past their peepholes. When we got to the fourth floor, we found Geppina waiting for us in the doorway. She was wearing a tight-fitting orange blouse with white slacks, and her straw-yellow hair was gathered at the nape of her neck. Behind her, Lino's yelling ordered children and grandchildren alike not to touch any of the God-sent bounty that they had just unloaded in the kitchen.

"*Buongiorno!*"

"*Buongiorno!* The elevator's always busted," said Geppina, looking right past me toward my mother. "Come in. Take a seat."

My mother smiled at her and followed her into the apartment.

Despite the blinding sun of July, their hallway was awash in cool shade; the wall on the left was plastered with photos. Walking one step ahead of us, Geppina brought her fingers to her mouth and then extended a kiss to Salvatore, who was smiling behind the glass in the splendor of his eternal youth. She did the same with the photo of a little girl dressed in a Spanish costume, wearing a ton of lipstick and blue eyeshadow. I recalled having seen that photo of Martina; it was on the night table next to Maddalena's bed at the hospital. But there, framed on the wall, it gave the impression of her being a departed soul. At least that's how it must have seemed to my mother because she lingered to look at it with devotion and curiosity, as one does with the dead.

In the kitchen, Concetta had already put the coffeepot on the stove, while Monica and Susetta just sat there at the table, doing nothing, staring wide-eyed at the mountain of groceries scattered on the floor.

"*Uèhhh, e basta cu st'ammuina* . . . Heyyyy, enough with all that racket," Geppina yelled at the children coming and going from the balcony. "You'll wake Uncle Lello."

"Yeah, right, *his lordship* had a late night," Monica commented with a hint of sarcasm.

"Miss Anna, make yourself comfortable," said Lino, turning to my mother while sliding a chair toward her. "You shouldn't have gone to all that trouble," he added with the tone of someone who always feels out of place. "Doc, by now you're one of the family," he tacked on, looking at me with a dazed expression from behind his thick lenses.

"*Mammìì, ma che te ne fai 'e tutta 'sta roba?* Ma-maaaa, what are you gonna do with all this stuff?" asked Monica while she pushed the bags aside and assessed the value of their contents.

"*E poi tutta 'sta frutta, cu 'stu caldo va a male* . . . And all this fruit will spoil in this heat," Susetta added, arranging the veil on her head.

"We'll give it to the gypsies who live under the bridge. *Accusí non va a male, ma statte nu poco zitta.* That way, it won't go bad, but why don't you pipe down a bit," said Concetta, while shushing her and contending with a tray and espresso cups.

Geppina was seated right across from my mother, looking at her askance as though trying to suss out some hidden thought. For just a moment, they started to size each other up as they had done the first time at my house, but it was just a brief moment since Concetta showed up and interrupted their stare-down challenge.

"*A zí, pigliatevi 'o cafè*. Hey, Auntie, take some coffee," said Concetta, placing the tray on the table. Then, extending a cup to that weaselly eyed son of hers, she added, "*Tiè, porta chesta a zí Lello*. Here you go. Take this to Uncle Lello."

"This is his second cup," said Geppina, looking up at her daughter. "*Tiene tanta cazzimma pe' quanto è secca*. For someone so skinny, she's got a lot of chutzpah," she added, turning to my mother.

"I've got chutzpah? *Si teneva a cazzimma chill'omme 'e merda nun me lassava*. If I had that much chutzpah, that piece of shit would never have left me," Concetta ranted, getting her hackles up.

"You're better off without that one, believe me," Monica said. "And if you really wanna know, it's all your fault. You called it bad luck. . . . Always saying, *If he goes back inside, how will I get by?* And *if he goes and leaves me for someone else, what will I do?* You never did anything. Not a thing. And in the meantime, he just did what he wanted," she added, using her hands to preen her reddish mane.

In fact, Concetta feared the worst from her husband, and she had gotten the worst. Tonino had gotten some really young girl pregnant, and he had taken off with her six months ago. She would never say a thing, nor complain, hoping that sooner or later he might change his mind and come back. And who knows, maybe she would take him back.

"You need to take your mind off him. You've got kids to raise," added Susetta, who was there with her back against the wall and her hands folded on her lap like a saint.

"*Ma chi 'o penza a chill'omme 'e merda*. Who cares about that piece of shit."

"You've God to thank since you even found work," Monica chimed in.

"*E già, parla buono tu? Volesse vedè a te a pulizzà a merda da gente per quattro sorde . . . hai mai lavato 'o culo e nu viecchio? No, eh? A vuò sapè a verità? Fa schifo. T'avota 'o stomaco.* Oh, yeah? Look at you talking all nice. I'd like to see you cleaning the shit off people's asses for a few bucks. . . . Have you ever wiped an old man's ass? Oh, no?! You wanna know the truth? It's awful. It turns your stomach."

"*Ma che vuò? È 'na fatica.* What do you care? A job is a job."

"*Ma va fa 'e bucchine . . . ma chiamme fatica chella che faccio io? Pulizzà 'a merda da gente ma chiamme fatica?* Why don't you suck it. . . . You wanna call what I do a job? You call cleaning people's asses a job?" Concetta retorted, all in a lather.

"What is all this?" my upset mother butted in. "*Ma che sono 'sti parole, ci stanne 'e creature . . . e po' 'na femmina non parla così.* What kind of language is that with the children here? And a woman shouldn't talk that way."

Having already had opportunities to witness their arguments in the past, that morning's profanity had certainly not shocked me. However, my mother, afraid they might tear each other apart, was white as a sheet. And she maintained that same funereal paleness the whole ride home. The whole time she sat next to me not saying a word, hoping Martina never returned to that house.

"*A zí, nun ce facite caso . . . stanno già 'mbriache.* Auntie, don't pay them any mind. . . . They're already drunk," said Lello, appearing in the doorway, still in his pajamas. "Hey, what's all this stuff? Did Santa Claus come early this year?"

"*'O principino s'è scetato . . .* His highness is awake," was his father's greeting. "*Vatte a vestì, che è mala educazione!* Look at your manners! Go throw on some clothes!" he added, lowering his head.

"*Eh, guarda ccà, ce sta pure 'o vino* . . . Oh, look what we have here. There's even wine," the boy muttered, peeking into the bags that had been laid on the floor. "*E qua non dura manco nu jorne, ccà so tutti 'mbriacone* . . . None of this stuff will last a day with all these drunks. . . ."

The shrill voice of one of the little girls looking out on the balcony cut him off. "*Stanno arrivando 'e 'nfame . . . o zí, stanno arrivando 'e 'nfame.* The rats are here. . . . Hey, Uncle, the low-life rats are here."

In fact, leaning out, I saw *rats*, or police in their slang, park a squad car in the clearing. I saw two officers enter the building, while a third, who had stayed behind in the car, looked up and made eye contact with me.

"They've come for me!" commented Lelluccio, little Lello, curtly before disappearing into the shadowy hallway, followed by his father.

Monica and Susetta, nearly losing control, clung to their children, visibly shaken, while Concetta, fearing for her own kids, threatened to throw herself off the balcony if they took them away from her. With one loud yell, Geppina silenced her daughters. Then she looked at my mother with steely, piercing eyes and walked off closing the kitchen door behind her. We heard the doorbell ring and, immediately after that, some agitated exchanges. Then voices were raised, and raised voices turned into yelling. You could make out Geppina's insults and Lino's anemic pleas for her to stay calm. Someone slammed a door violently. When silence was restored to the house, Geppina and her husband found my mother motionless in the chair, their daughters speechless, and the children crying. From who knows where, the theme music of a television news broadcast reached our ears, and an anchorman's voice read off the latest death tally in the London Underground.

"They took him again," said Geppina, collapsing in a chair.

Lelluccio was under house arrest and he was serving the last three months of a two-year sentence for having taken part in an armed robbery. But they had just taken him away because of an accusation of attempted murder and all they were waiting for was the nature of the sentence since he had copped to the crime. Since he was a boy, Lello had learned that life was a game to play according to strict rules and that if he didn't want to get played, he needed to be on the right side of the table, to side with the right people, for better or for worse. Because of this code, he was on his way to serve fifteen years in jail: he was covering for the real culprit, a local crime boss who, in addition to guaranteeing him an instant career in his clan, had promised to take care of his family with a monthly check.

From the little balcony where Geppina had taken cover, the row of tenements slowly faded into a geometry of gray concrete. Clinging to the railing, her eyes were lost on the horizon, perhaps looking for a hiding place off in the distance. Before she left the kitchen to join her with a glass of water in her hands, my mother's eyes had told me she wanted to get out of that house as soon as possible. With just one look and a gentle caress of the skin, they picked up the pieces of a conversation that had been interrupted so long ago. They went on and on, whispering things that we could not hear. They were two sisters who had drifted apart and were reunited again.

There was something decisive about that moment: they needed space and silence. Even Geppina's daughters were quiet. Susetta took care of the children, taking them to play in another room, Concetta started to arrange the groceries that we had brought, and Monica had busied herself at the stove. I stood there for a bit, watching my mother and Geppina, who were, by then, completely engrossed in an infinite stream of unspoken words. While the same television from before broadcast the gravelly, choked-up voices of the survivors from the London Underground bombing.

~ 18 ~

Two, maybe three, months had passed since I had gone to the foster home the first time. That morning I parked my car just beyond the gate, next to the large palm tree in the middle of the flower bed, telling my mother I would be right back. I needed to take her to see her sisters and that stop was on the way. Either way, I was in a hurry. While walking at a good clip, I saw Martina with a woman dressed in black with blond hair and hands on her hips; she seemed quite sad, as though she were carrying the weight of the world. They were walking side by side through the orange trees on the side alley, heads down, without talking. It was the first time I saw that woman and when I ran into Miss Clara, I asked her who she was.

"That's Martina's grandmother. I told you about her. Remember? As usual, she showed up without warning and started yelling that she wanted to see Martina. . . . To avoid any problems, we let her in, but we warned her that the next time we will call the police."

I asked whether she had been forbidden from spending time with the child.

"Of course not, but we need to stick to the monthly appointments so as not to upset Martina," she replied bluntly.

"Well, but if it's her grandmother . . ." I objected.

"Doctor, if Martina is here, it's for a reason . . . don't you think?" she explained with a peeved tone.

On more than one occasion, remaining rather vague with the details, she had made it clear to me that she did not appreciate intrusions in matters regarding the children, much less in how the foster home was run. The bitterness with which she spoke about Geppina proved it. But when it came to my and Martina's relationship, for some odd reason, she had decided to bend the rules a little. She would always let me spend some time with her before swooping in to reestablish her authority. At any rate, the thought of my mother waiting for me in the car led me to cut to the chase: I handed her Enzino's evaluation to be sent to the juvenile court and quickly said good-bye to her. When I reached the first flight of stairs, she stopped me to tell me that there were some developments about the young boy but that she would tell me the next time.

I headed to the gate, taking the long way around the flower garden, just to get another look at Martina who was on a park bench with her grandmother. She seemed at peace, as though everything happening around her had nothing whatsoever to do with her. I smiled; so did she. But the woman dressed in black turned to show me the steeliness of her blue eyes. I nodded my head almost imperceptibly at her.

When I got back to the car and found my mother pale as a sheet, I thought she had suddenly fallen ill—one of her usual spells of low blood pressure. "*Mamma?* Is everything okay?"

No reply. She turned and looked at me with a vacant stare. Then, looking out of the car window, she said,

"Shall we go?"

At the end of the ring road, in a glare of sunset that seemed destined to engulf everything in flames, I slipped onto the first stretch of highway that ran toward Rome, keeping an eye on the road signs. After a couple of exits, I ventured into the vast outlying plains overlooked on one side by the bluish silhouette of Vesuvius and on the other by the hills in Cancello; the towns rolled by one after the other like flowing lava.

Contrary to habit, my mother had withdrawn into an incomprehensible silence. Her eyes followed the narrow patches of countryside, the rows of vines that snaked through plots of haphazardly cultivated land, the crumbling farm houses, and junk heaps frying under the sun in auto graveyards. And all the while a nauseating stench of carrion assaulted our nostrils.

"Mamma, what is it?"

Silence.

"Mamma?"

"Her name is Geppina," she mumbled, her voice cracking.

"Who?"

"That woman . . . the one who was with the little girl," she replied, without taking her eyes off the road.

"What, do you know her?"

She turned and looked at me with frightened eyes, as though she had just witnessed the apparition of a ghost who'd come back from the afterlife to demand justice.

"She's my sister!" she said. "I hadn't seen her in a very long time," she added, averting her gaze and her heart from me.

Even though I force myself to believe that life is just the result of a series of fortuitous, chaotic, and random events, how could I attribute Geppina's sudden appearance before my mother as anything but the work of fate? In some elaborate plan, had destiny appeared out of nowhere to collect on a debt too steep to repay? One little thing could have changed everything. What if that day, for example, I had not agreed to take my mother to see her sisters? Or, if Miss Clara hadn't insisted so urgently that I bring her Enzino's monthly progress report? Some insignificant mishap, like a flat tire on the highway, and all those voices that had subsequently begun to hound me simply wouldn't have ever existed. The world would have gone on transmitting echoes of some far-off music, instead of collapsing right on top of me. I would have continued plotting my existence on a straight course, and consequently, there would have been no Geppina, no "Ironhead," no Concetta. No juvenile court, not to mention no Giuliana Conti or a lawyer, with that office of his in the Centro Direzionale. Instead, right or wrong, I find myself struggling with my regret for having been, at least in part, responsible for the abrupt detour in my mother's life, for having burdened everyone else's. And what about Martina? I know that our two paths would still have crossed. But without being caught in that intricate tangle of kinship, at best I would have spared a sad thought for her. I would have filed her story in the category of the many things that just happen.

Hands on the steering wheel, I stared at the road with a befuddled expression. I got scared for a moment. They say that we fear that which we do not understand. I rather believe that fear comes from finding out something that you didn't even know about the day before. And I didn't have the fortitude to save my mother from the abyss into which I suspected she was plummeting.

Her sister? What in the heck was she talking about? No way that could be. And if it was really true, that meant just one thing: the blood in that woman's veins was the same as mine, the same as Martina's.

"Your sister? What do you mean?" I asked her, and I'm pretty sure I was yelling.

It was right then, on that sunny June morning, along that desolate stretch of land, that I heard about Geppina for the first time and about that huge boulder that was weighing down my mother's heart. She started to slowly rehash everything, as though she were struggling to find the words hidden in some remote place inside of her. Now and then she would interrupt herself and look into the distance, then she would resume, even more tired, as though she were walking uphill, and her voice would grow fainter. For her entire life she had guarded the secret existence of that woman by keeping her treasure chest of memories under double lock and key.

The youngest of five children, Geppina had demonstrated a rebellious streak right from the beginning. She was a problem child in a family that was not doing well at all. My grandfather, Angelo De Nicola, known as *Michele 'o picciotto*, or Michael the Kid, his nickname reflecting his Sicilian origin, was a drunk and a whoremonger. He would leave the house first thing in the morning and come back in the middle of the night—at times with a chicken he'd pinched from a country farmhouse, at other times with a bag of fruit and vegetables scrounged up in some farmer's fields while dodging the latter's buckshot. However, just before he hit fifty, an unexpected heart attack ended his life, casting the whole family into misery. Not so much because of his passing as much for the depression that overtook his wife—that is, my grandmother. The daughters found themselves forced to take care of her like a lifeless doll. They washed her, dressed her, groomed her hair with almond oil and bone combs; at noon they would feed her what little they had and leave her by the window to stare out into space, and there she would stay until nightfall when they would undress her and put her into bed.

The young daughters made some provisions to survive this poverty. My mother convinced the owner of a tailor shop, where she had worked since she was ten years old, to give her a few hours of overtime each evening. Meanwhile, when necessary, Rosa and Francesca would earn a few *lire* by helping out old lady Maria, the town's mattress maker. And, finally, it was up to Filomena to keep an eye on their mother while the others were out. I imagine that each one of them cultivated her own dream—the only one available to a young girl at that time—that sooner or later some guy would show up and rescue her from that squalid life.

"Do you know how many times we would go to bed hungry? But nobody knew our family business. In the morning, when we would leave the house, I would scrub my sisters' faces with a cloth to give them healthy rosy cheeks. . . . But Geppina . . . you want to know what she would do? She would go out into the street and scream that she was hungry and that her mother and sisters didn't give her a thing to eat."

Her prime concern, my mother went on, was for her sisters to be able to maintain just enough dignity to stifle any gossipmongers. This earned her the only dowry possible in a chest full of nothing: the aura of respectability needed to find a husband.

However, out of the blue, the household was thrown into disarray. Geppina was barely a teenager when people in town started spreading strange rumors about her.

"*Alla guagliona ci piacciono gli uomini.* That girl really likes her men."

"What do you expect? No father and with a mother like that."

"Why don't her sisters keep an eye on her? That guy's even married. . . ."

"Now who's going to want her. . . ."

Word had it that she'd been seen hanging around the shadowy underbrush at the castle. In another version someone in a car claimed to have seen her on some deserted side roads in the countryside. Yet another person swore to have run into her as she was going into an old electrical power station with some slobbering geezer behind her, humming and happy as a clam.

"*Nanní, ma perché non ti stai nu poco piú accorte a chella guagliona?* Annie, why don't you look after that girl a little more?" people would always ask my mother.

In those days, idle talk like that translated to dishonor and shame. And my mother was desperate: she was already engaged to my father, who was little more than a boy then; but she worried about her younger sisters, all marrying age— as they used to say—who were facing a future as outcasts.

Geppina was like a rotten tooth that risked infecting all the others. According to what my mother told me that morning, she had tried everything to keep her out of trouble: she had hidden her clothes and tied her to the bed. She'd even beaten her with a cane, almost breaking her back. But Geppina started running away from home. One time she disappeared for a few days, frightening my mother and her sisters almost to death, not to mention giving the gossips something to talk about for weeks. Until one day, when she got the idea of extracting that decayed tooth, before it was too late—before everything went to rack and ruin. It was my grandmother who took care of it, one morning when she suddenly came out of her catatonic state. "You need to lock her up," she said. "It's the only way," she added, her head drifting back into the clouds.

And the responsibility fell on my mother. Even though she wanted nothing to do with that solution, she convinced herself that the family would have been better off, and that far away from that house, more than just coming back to her senses, Geppina would have the chance to study and, after a couple of years, return home lucid and even grateful. They thought about it over and over and ended up seeking advice from Don Attilio, the priest at the Church of the Assumption, who found Geppina a convent in Nola, with the sisters of the Redeemer. During the first year, she ran away three times, and all three times my mother sent her back, engaging in a personal battle with her sister. One time, after she had already gone to the other convent in Pescara, the nuns there found her bed empty one morning and no sign of Geppina. Geppina's sisters and her mother never mentioned her name again. They simply put her out of their minds. My mother was the only one who would see her again. My mother had always kept her close to her heart and Geppina would forever remain there, but mother never spoke about it with her family.

It happened one sun-drenched August morning. It was at the beginning of the 1970s. By then, we were living in Naples and my father had decided to bring the family to the sea to celebrate his first new car—a metallic-blue Opel Kadett 1000. He was driving up the coastal road to Domizia, around Varcaturo. He was driving through the rows of pine trees that separated the road from the reed beds when a blowout forced him to pull over. It was there that my mother saw Geppina. Twenty years had passed. She was on the shoulder on the other side of the road, sitting on an overturned garbage can, with the indifferent expression of someone hoping time goes gentle as it runs roughshod over her. My mother couldn't believe her eyes. She simply couldn't fathom that the woman with a cigarette in her hand, sitting so vulgarly with her legs apart, could really be her sister. She told herself she was wrong—that it was just someone who resembled her. Meanwhile, the whole world was turning around her: the trees, the reed beds, the Opel Kadett, my father, and us kids gallivanting through the courtyard of the roadside restaurant. She had tried to get those thoughts out of her head all day and even all night, but the ghosts of her past wouldn't let up, and so she had made up her mind. My father had never seen her like that; she almost scared him. He offered to take her back there, agreeing to be nice and stay in the car without intervening.

That morning on the state highway in Varcaturo there was no trace of wind. The tree branches didn't move an inch and the heat was awful. My mother remembers cold sweat on her back and a terrible sewer smell emanating from the road that mixed with the salty sea air. For the whole ride they hadn't seen a single soul, almost as though the entire world had decided to keep out of their business. A few yards away from the clearing where they'd seen her the day before, she ordered my father to stop. She was afraid of startling her, so she had gotten out and walked along the scorching hot shoulder. They had instantly recognized each other. Neither of the two dared to take a step. Then Geppina had run off into the reed bed. My mother had followed her to an abandoned little farmhouse, where three children—whom my mother inferred to be Geppina's children—were playing on the bank of a malodorous swamp.

My mother refused to tell me what they said to each other once they were face-to-face. Except that my mother had been angry with God, with a rage she'd never expressed before, for not having watched over her sister.

The following day she had shown up at the same spot along the road but no sign of Geppina. Having overcome her modesty and embarrassment, she had even asked for information from a woman squatted down close by in the same clearing. But seeing the woman's terrible smile, like a festering wound on her face, my mother had just kept going.

She had returned to the abandoned farmhouse. Slipping through the thick bullrushes, she had scrambled up to the barrier of dunes that looked out to the sea. No sign of Geppina or her children. On the grassy space in front of the restaurant, under a blazing hot expanse of sky, she had waited hours with my father, startling with each passing car. She had returned the following day and the one after that but nothing. Geppina had disappeared once more, never to be found again.

~ 19 ~

The morning when they took Enzino away, Miss Clara reached me on my cell phone while I was still daydreaming about the whitish blotch that I had just seen twitching on the snowy screen of the sonogram. It was not much more than a shadow for the moment, but in a few more months, it would transform into a child. My child. We had just returned home and Costanza had lain down next to me on the bed in a state of bliss. My first thoughts turned to Martina, and it took me a while to understand that Clara was talking about little Enzino, my patient. They had found him sitting on the edge of his bed with what little he had packed into shopping bags. He was refusing to go home with his new parents. Clara was decidedly shaken and her agitated tone made it difficult for me to follow her; she was mumbling something about a train that brought children somewhere or other, she was accusing me of having filled the boy's head with absurd stories, and in the meantime she was asking me to run over there to remedy the situation. I tried to convince her that I had to stay put—that is, until Costanza, who had been listening in to our conversation, encouraged me to tell her "yes" with a subtle nod. Then I promised that I would be there in less than a half hour if she would just hang up the phone. So, leaning over Costanza's belly, I whispered to my child that when I got back I would tell him the story of Enzino and the choo-choo trains. In the courtyard of the foster home, a police car was idling behind the palm tree, while Miss Clara, who must have seen me from the balcony, was right there in the doorway with a rather unfriendly expression on her face. She led me to the kitchen; a man and a woman were seated there with the doleful look of someone who, after repeatedly dodging bullets coming from the left, realizes that there are more coming from the right.

"Doc, come with me. Now!" Miss Clara urged me on, as her voice echoed through the entryway of the building. "Now, let's see how we can resolve this situation. . . . This morning we were supposed to hand him over," she added, showing almost no tact. "Here, these are Mr. and Mrs. Izzo, Enzino's new parents."

The man got up and extended his hand. But the woman didn't budge. She just stared at me with eyes that appeared to be floating on a sea of fear.

"*Buongiorno*. . . . I didn't know the date was set for today," I said, apologizing, though for what I didn't know.

"But I had told you about it," an irritated Miss Clara shot back.

"Well, you had told me there were some developments, not that this morning Enzino would be leaving. And we still have to complete his therapy. . . . The boy has made much progress, but he still has work to do."

"Of course, I realize that," the man interrupted. "But you see, we have worked out a treatment plan with some doctors. A phoniatric specialist, a neuropsychiatrist . . ."

"May I ask you whether you've met the child, you know, whether you've had a chance to establish contact?"

"Yes, yes! Last month we met with him four times and he seemed, despite some initial difficulties, rather . . . how shall I say?"

I shot a hateful look at Miss Clara since, by now, I was really pissed off at her for having kept me in the dark about these meetings.

"We just want to make sure that this transition is not traumatic for him, if possible," the man added.

"Exactly. That's why I called you here," Miss Clara jumped in, turning toward me. "The fact is that Enzino won't budge. . . . He insists on taking a train. . . . Can you tell us what that's about? He says that you told him about it. And then there's Martina who won't leave his side. She's also going on with this nonsense about a train. They're holding hands and won't budge."

"Oh, the train . . ." I said, cracking a smile. "If this is his big day, he needs to take the train."

"Listen, Doctor, this is no time for games," Miss Clara intervened angrily.

"On the contrary, this is precisely the time for games. And if you'll allow me, among your many tasks, this one involving Enzino is the most important today."

"I think the doctor's right," Mrs. Izzo said, seeming to have recovered. "So what shall we do?"

In that moment, with perfect timing, we could hear the sound of a train rattling down the track in the distance.

"Come," I said, moving toward the balcony.

In the meantime, the train cars of the Metro Flegrea line, heading from Pozzuoli to Naples, were whizzing by, their outline standing out distinctly against the blue sea.

"You see, trains hold an irresistible charm over the children here. They aren't just background noise for them. The kids watch them pass by for hours on end and day-dream about what awaits them on the outside. Maybe they think about how one day a train will take them far away, perhaps to some unknown location or even to a new house, to a mother. At any rate, to some happy place. I just told them that the day when they would go to their new homes, to their new families, to their new mothers and fathers, a train would bring them there. And for Enzino, just as for Martina, trains represent their last hope. What can I say? I invented a little fairy tale to make their departure more encouraging."

Miss Clara stood up straight and abruptly twisted her body to look at the man and the woman with incredulous eyes. And, not having perceived my hostility, hastily asked me, "Okay, then. Now what?"

"We take the train!" the woman replied with a glowing smile. "Doctor, I just have one favor to ask: I want you to tell Enzino, to calm him down," she added amicably, taking my hands in hers.

I found him motionless, sitting on the bed, his slender little legs hanging down and the plastic shopping bag at his feet. Next to him, Martina was squeezing his hand, and they both looked at us anxiously but with a touch of defiance in their eyes that made them irresistible. Two little scared war-riors awaiting their sentence. I squatted down next to them and explained to Enzino that his train had arrived that morn-ing. And it was the right train. I can't say that he was happy.

No, not happy, but I believe he felt relieved by the fact that I hadn't lied to him.

From the balcony, Martina and I watched him go across the courtyard, hand in hand with the Izzos, dragging his feet on the gravel and looking at the ground. Before getting into the car, however, he looked up, and holding the hand of his still unfamiliar mother, he waved good-bye for the last time. Tears rolled down his face.

"What about me?" Martina asked, seeing the car vanish beyond the courtyard.

"Soon," I replied. "Hopefully soon."

It was quite some time since Judge Conti had authorized my visits with her every fifteen days, and the visible, positive changes in Martina were taking place on a daily basis right in front of me. Now she would willingly go to kindergarten. She had learned to spell out simple words with the magnetic letters on the board, and she seemed almost cheerful, even if she was still suspicious around adults whom she didn't know. All in all, the recalcitrant little wild animal she was when I had first met her was transforming into a malleable being, eager for attention and affection, and was thus capable of being agreeable and charming to get them. She had stopped asking about Geppina and about her mother. Perhaps she had given up. But I like to think that she had hidden them away like a secret; in order to survive, she had decided to fool us all.

There we were, side by side, sending off her little friend who was leaving us. And perhaps for the first time, right there, behind the curtain that would shelter us from that intense, late-August heat, we were sharing the same sad thoughts, feeling equally lost. The sun was shining, but it was oppressive. It didn't enlighten anything or bring any cheerfulness with it. We stood there waiting for the train to pass. When we glimpsed it cutting a swath through that stretch of coast, distinct against the backdrop of blue sea in the distance, it was as though Martina could see Enzino waving to her from the window. In a reflection on the glass, who knows why, I thought I saw him, too.

～ 20 ～

Only a month had passed since I had told her, "Soon. Hopefully soon," referring to a train that would carry us away from there together.

"But where's Costanza?" Martina asked, without taking her eyes from the glassy sea, which that September evening was melting into an incredibly clear sky.

"She's sick. She has a fever . . . but she's coming next week," I replied, walking her inside. Miss Clara was busy with a half-dozen unchained furies, who wanted no part in sitting down for dinner.

"Michele, they always put up a fight," Martina observed maturely. Perhaps she already felt distanced from the other children. "I don't. I've learned to be a good girl," she added, running toward the dinner table.

She was wearing a pair of jeans and miniature tennis shoes, with colored socks and a blue-and-white T-shirt on which the blue was just a shade lighter than her eyes. I had told her that they were a gift from Costanza. That wasn't true. She had wanted to put them on right away, even though bedtime wasn't far off.

"Martina, go take off these clothes or you'll get them dirty," said Miss Clara, fussing over the stove.

"But I've learned how to eat good. I won't get dirty," Martina replied, looking for a sign of confirmation in my eyes.

"If you get something on you, I won't let you wear them again, okay?" Clara retorted in a strict voice.

The look that I shot her ended that discussion before it could begin. Considering the fact that in the not-too-distant future we would be bringing Martina to live with us, Miss Clara often gave in to the temptation to indulge her, at least in front of me. However, these concessions didn't automatically make her into the expert pedagogue she thought she was, nor the curmudgeonly sheepdog with a heart of gold looking after an unruly herd. To put it simply, she was just going with the flow. Yet for just one moment I glimpsed a flash of satisfaction in her eyes when, at the end of dinner, she realized Martina hadn't dropped one crumb.

At nine o'clock an unusual silence engulfed the house: the children had hit the sack, including Martina who before going to sleep, however, had dug in her heels about wearing her new little outfit to bed. In the calm of the dining room, I stayed behind to speak with Miss Clara, whose legs, by now at the end of her day, were beginning to wobble. She flopped down on the armchair, asking me for news about Giuliana Conti.

"I spoke to her last week. . . . Nothing's changed. She's waiting for our marriage license so she can begin the process."

"And when will that be?"

"Next month, at the town hall."

"Don't forget: we wanna hear those wedding bells."

"Yeah," I replied without much enthusiasm, while my stomach churned into a triple knot of anxiety that made me gag.

With a sigh Miss Clara observed that despite her predicament, Martina should consider herself a lucky little girl.

"You see, Doctor, it almost never goes like this," she added. "Not all of these children meet someone like you on their journey. And she's absolutely smitten with Doctor Costanza. All Martina does is talk about her. She says how beautiful she is, that she smells nice. Yeah, that's what she says. . . . That's a sign from God, believe me. . . . You know what happens when adopted children grow up? In most cases they want to know who their parents are," Miss Clara continued. "And how can you blame them? They might even run away from the home where they grew up to look for their mother or father. Blood is a powerful thing. Never forget that. This is a sign from God!"

Of course, a sign from God. Now, what should I have said to her? That Martina, contrary to what she believed, was one of the most unfortunate human beings to have ever crossed my path? That Costanza would never see her again? Was I to let on that the real reason for which she hadn't come there that afternoon had nothing to do with a fever? Of course, since Costanza's fever wasn't the sort that constrains you to bed, the kind that you cure with lots of rest, hot broth, someone doting on you a bit, and a good dose of subtle sarcasm. So what should I have told her? The truth? Yeah, right, the truth. Sure, that her kind of fever was more insidious and dangerous, that it starts in the pit of your stomach, works its way through your sides, and creeps into your heart and your mind, hour after hour, day after day. I should have told her that her fever was called fear—fear of not having what it takes to endure Martina's eyes, her smile, her fragility, her being a little girl with a whole host of catastrophes in her past. I should have told her about a usually strong, generous woman who had surrendered to the pain of losing that whitish shadow on the sonogram, that losing the baby had crumpled her soul and embittered her thoughts.

How could I have told her that in losing that baby Costanza no longer wanted to be the mother of a daughter that wasn't her own? Would she have understood? And if I had revealed all of this to her, would she have continued blathering about how lucky Martina was?

As though restored after a long rest, Miss Clara bolted up from the armchair: "You know, Doctor, this morning, Professor Izzo called me. You remember him, right? Enzino's new father. He says that the boy seems at peace, that he's starting to smile. . . . Enzino smiling . . . Can you even imagine that? I've never seen a single smile on that child's face."

"Well, that's good, right?" I responded listlessly, standing up. "It's late. I'll see you in fifteen days." And I started to leave, after gathering my bag. Exhibiting an unusual vigor for that late in the day, she accompanied me to the door and saw me off with a probing look.

"Say hello to Ms. Argentieri for me."

～ 21 ～

When I came to the Vomero hill, I was seven years old and enthusiastically occupied the lowest rung on the social ladder. I attended school and spent my free time with children of greengrocers, laborers, delicatessen workers, and butchers who lived around Piazza degli Artisti and the public market in Antignano. They put us all together in one class, united by our common social background, under the careful supervision of a teacher who was quick to administer corporal discipline. Since I came from the countryside, they must have thought that was the best place for me.

All I have left from that first year on the Vomero is a cold, dark memory, the memory of an incredibly unforgiving winter spent in a dank basement apartment on Via Luca Giordano. Two bedrooms, a bathroom, and a kitchen that would flood every time it rained because of the terraced landscape next door that would gather the rainwater. A number of memories have stuck with me besides loneliness, like my enchantment before the baroque spectacle of candies in the window display of Bellavia and the dismay I felt in the toy department of Standa where those delinquent classmates of mine would force me to shoplift. Other things resurface, too, like my mother quietly sneaking into the house, her long silences, her unhappiness, the brassy taste of fear whenever I happened to find blood-soaked towels left in the bathtub.

One day, Pagnozzi, a nutty classmate of mine, explained that "women are all sick. My mother does nothing but bleed."

"Really?"

"Yeah, sometimes I go in the bathroom and the toilet water is all red. It's natural. It's their curse. Relax! They're not going to die from it."

Then a ray of sunshine broke through that blanket of darkness. We moved nearby, to another area of the Vomero hill, where my father had been hired as the doorman in a high-class building. Coming in contact with those people, I learned that in order to survive in the hustle and bustle of that world, it would take convincing as many people as possible to indulge my fantasies. That was the secret of combating prejudices. I became so good at it that I was like an acrobat leaping through rings of fire. I made it seem so easy I could do it with my eyes closed since that fire won't burn you. That fire doesn't hurt.

I began to train as a tightrope walker when I was roughly ten years old, right on Via Kagoshima, which I learned to pronounce like everyone else—with the accent on the *i*, even though the *o* was supposed to get the stress. It was named after the Japanese city nestled in Kinko Bay, which sits below an active volcano, Mount Sakurajima. According to some people, the city resembled Naples in its climate and in the character of its people—though that seemed fairly implausible. But either way, toward the middle of the 1960s the leaders of both places decided to form an alliance as sister cities. Now, somewhere over there in Kagoshima there's got to be a Naples Street, overlooking the bay and the volcano. There has to be because Via Kagoshima is a street no longer than a few hundred yards, perched among twelve-story high-rises, which snakes all the way down to Via Aniello Falcone, a street on the hill with a panoramic view of the Gulf of Naples.

The day that the Japanese delegation arrived for the plaque-hanging ceremony was a sunshiny May morning. In the bay were an aircraft carrier and a frigate from the American navy. The entire street was draped with the Italian tricolor and white banners with red suns in the middle. On the sidewalks and looking over balconies, a crowd of curious people followed the procession of foreigners, fascinated by the women wrapped in flamboyant kimonos who teetered on their wooden sandals and by the servicemen from the NATO base—tall and blond, standing starched in their blue uniforms with dozens of medals on their chests. For a little kid like me, who came from a small inland town and had lived through a cold winter in a moldy basement apartment, that was a confirmation: I had landed right in the middle of a party that promised to never end.

Halfway down the street was number 72, where I used to live with my family in an apartment with four bedrooms, which was well lit, even though it was on the ground floor. From the sparkling main lobby, you could access my father's doorman station. There, my father, who was a big supporter of class differences, trained me to keep my head down and to deferentially greet the doctor on the fifth floor and the engineer on the sixth, and the professor, the architect, and the accountant. They were the ones who inspired me to take my first leaps through the fiery rings of prejudice. Behind the gentle aloofness of some, the haughtiness of others, the ostentatious generosity of this person and the open-mindedness of that person festered their common will to keep the impenetrable borders of a caste in place.

I recall a certain Mr. Parini, a fabric merchant in Piazza Mercato who lived on the fourth floor. One day, after seeing me running out in the front courtyard of the condominium, he gave my father a brand-new pair of Superga sneakers, urging him to cultivate what he considered an inexplicable talent for a boy as scrawny as me. On the other hand, Ms. Del Buono, the school principal, lived on the seventh floor. Faced with my mother's complaints about my poor academic standing, arguing that there are no dimwitted students, only incompetent teachers, Ms. Del Buono offered to tutor me in Italian and French, though she gave up after only a month, advising my parents to get me into a trade as soon as possible.

On the second floor lived a lawyer named Taglialatela. He had a son about my age who wore enormous eyeglasses. Even though he was extremely intelligent, the lenses made him look like an ignoramus. His name was Antonio. He was a really big kid for just ten years old. Forced to wear his British-style short pants, awkward and shy as he was, he made an easy target for bullying by our peers. Since I was just as inept and stood out, too, I liked Antonio. And we began to play together more and more often: table soccer, toy trains, or with what he called "board games," which I had never seen before in my life. But our partnership did not last long. It ended one afternoon when I overheard his mother scolding him: "Antonio, I don't understand you. With all the other children in the building, you have to play with the doorman's son?!"

Finally, on the top floor, there was a certain Lorevain, nicknamed Crackpot by the whole condominium because of his decidedly extravagant ways and because of his irritable temper, which, all too often he unleashed on my father. He was Mrs. Altieri's lover, and she was a rich widow who was a decade his senior. She was the talk of the building for how nonchalantly she wore bizarre pastel-colored little outfits, but since she was lonely she tolerated him and welcomed him into her home. However, the epithet Crackpot became synonymous with consternation throughout the building when he started to launch plastic bags full of water from the seventh floor with the intention of protecting his afternoon nap from the racket that we boys would make as we ran around boisterously in the courtyard below. The final straw came one day when one of his aerial strikes grazed a little boy who, upon hearing the explosion of the "water bomb" at his feet, almost died from fright. But when his father, a journalist who lived in the next building, rushed to the man's apartment to give him what for, the solitary avenger apologized, saying that his intended target was not that gentleman's boy but the doorman's—that is, yours truly.

The matter did not end there. Through word of mouth, Lorevain's intentions reached my father's ears. My father was determined to confront such hostility his own way, once and for all. Not so much to take back the dignity that he had forsworn for some time by then but because the thought of seeing his son humiliated like that was unbearable. But how could he get even without losing his job? He lost sleep over it. With a rap sheet like his, full of pending charges and a rigorous repeat-offender rehabilitation plan in progress, he risked undoing years of sacrifice, throwing away all hopes for a better future for himself and his children.

At that point, my mother intervened: deeming unacceptable both her husband's involvement and the injustice suffered by her son, she had devised a plan that was certainly way more refined than anything my father could have scripted. In fact, she decided to send my father away from the house; she figured that by sending him to visit his mother in the country, he wouldn't be back before evening. She phoned my grandmother, asking her to play along with the excuse that she had suddenly taken ill. She convinced her husband she could look after the building and sent him on his way. Then she prepared her children for school and took a seat at the doorman's desk, wearing one of her flowered dresses as though it were Sunday. She took care of the mail, answered the intercom multiple times, greeted the doctor from the fifth floor and the engineer from the sixth, said good morning to Professor Russo, who was going out for his morning walk, and stopped to chat for over an hour with Mrs. Gandolfi—the one from the ground floor—who could not help noticing how kind the doorman's wife was.

It was about one o'clock when she spotted Lorevain coming through the main door on his way home for lunch. So she shot up on her feet, crossed the lobby with a wide smile on her face, and greeted him affably; she took the shopping bags from his hands and accompanied him to the elevator. Once the man was inside, without any time for him to react, my mother was at his throat, digging her fingernails into his skin. With a ferocious look, she told him that if he ever hurt her son in any way, she would not hesitate to take out his eyes. Lorevain tried to push her way, but in an attempt to slip from my mother's clutches, her nails ended up gouging his face. A terrible scream echoed through the stairwell.

A few hours later, as expected, two officers showed up. They took her to the nearby police station to respond to a complaint of assault and injuries. The sergeant who interrogated her dredged up her husband's turbulent past, reminding her that they were no longer in the land of criminals where they came from; now they lived among respectable people and esteemed professionals, so they had to behave. My mother didn't give much weight to how she was treated— she was used to it. But as soon as the sergeant asked her for her version of the facts, with disarming candor she claimed to have behaved with kindness and respect—exactly how the administrator of the condominium had told my father to behave the day he was hired. She said that seeing Mr. Lorevain returning with some shopping bags, she had rushed over to help him but that once they were in the elevator, he had put his hands all over her breasts. Then, looking him straight in the eyes, she told him that no doubt, his wife would have defended herself that way, if she had been in the same situation.

As far as Lorevain's inconsiderate behavior, the officer had a desk full of complaints, but he found the story about her molestation hard to believe. It was the woman's word against the word of a respectable, albeit eccentric, person. And only one or two witnesses would have lent any credibility to what she was saying.

Within two days, my mother delivered to the precinct a statement attesting to the reliability of her version. It had been signed by all the residents of the condominium.

I've always wondered about what motivated their goodwill, and although I have never been able to verify it with certainty, I am inclined to believe that those respectable professionals had preferred to sacrifice a deranged man kept by a rich widow than lose the service of their loyal subjects.

However, after the Crackpot incident my mother seemed different. She stopped getting lost in the labyrinth of her thoughts and she suddenly lost all of her sadness, as though the disease that was holding her prisoner had liberated the spirit of a changed woman. It was at that time she decided to learn how to write. I taught her how to flourish her *A* when she signed something. She also stopped bleeding (or perhaps I didn't notice it anymore), and although Pagnozzi had educated me about how women were cursed, I stopped feeling that sense of panic, imagining what it would be like living without her.

~ 22 ~

The temperature was really hot. Oppressively hot.

The rage that had taken hold of me after that whole afternoon spent with Martina kept me awake for most of the night. I was hypnotized by lights flashing onto my bedroom walls from outside. I would give in to sleep for a bit, but after a few minutes I would reawaken, dripping with sweat, while Costanza never stopped tossing and turning next to me. She must have been having a terrible nightmare because she was muttering incoherent phrases, moaning, and choking up with tears. I was even tempted to wake her, but I preferred to get out of bed, savoring that bit of refreshing coolness from the floor tiles. Barefoot and in the dark, I started wandering about the house. Everywhere I turned it was as though invisible barbed wire were barring my path, just like that lump of future that had already died before even getting a chance to be born.

Wherever I sought refuge, I was tormented by the flickering image of my child on the ultrasound or by the image of Martina, who bore the expression of a little girl who confidently placed her life in someone else's hands.

Costanza's note was still on the kitchen table: "The chicken breast is in the oven. Sorry for not waiting for you, but I'm very tired. I'm going to bed." I read it and reread it, as though I might find a secret message in those insignificant words. A message that might help me understand the reasons why everything I thought destiny had always kept in store for me had suddenly been whisked away. But what had destiny kept in store for me? At that point, I no longer had a clue. Maybe nothing. Or whatever was left of nothing. I felt profound pity for myself. For what I had become, as well as for the man that I had never become. I wondered whether Costanza had ever loved me and if I had truly loved her. I felt overcome by a flash of heat. I thought how neither of us, in all that time spent together, had ever uttered the word *love*. If she had ever truly loved me, I am certain that she never would have turned her back on Martina so cruelly. On the other hand, if I had seriously loved her, I would have been consumed with plans for our own child, and maybe I wouldn't have had any time to entertain any dreams of adoption. Incontrovertible truths. Nothing would come of either one. If at times I had ever despised her, now I was feeling something very close to hatred for her. I'm sure that she also felt something similar for me.

A light, shuffling sound behind me told me she was there. For an instant I was tempted to cast out all doubts by asking her directly, point blank, 'Costanza, did you ever love me? Did we ever love each other?'

"I had some strange dreams. I can't really remember, but I know that I was crying nonstop, and you were there, too."

"Yes, I noticed you were agitated. You were tossing all night long."

"Was I keeping you awake?"

"No, that's not why."

"What, then?"

"The heat . . . and a really difficult day . . ."

"What time are we leaving tomorrow?" she asked while yawning.

"I'm not leaving. Today, before going to see Martina, I went to visit Maddalena at the center in Arpaia. . . . They asked me if I could take care of getting her to some medical appointments. There's no one else who can bring her."

Costanza didn't say a word. She moved out of the dark and toward the sink. She drank from the faucet, holding her hair behind her head. She splashed water on her neck and forehead, then she sat down on the sill of an open window, staring into the blanket of darkness in the garden. Her detachment made me regret mentioning Maddalena. Only then was I seeing clearly that she wanted to reestablish, quickly and permanently, distance from that world that didn't pertain to her and in which she had to play her part, perhaps for my sake, not all that convincingly. On the one hand, how could I blame her? But seeing her so brazenly indifferent rekindled that flame of hate in me, which I could barely keep at bay. And the more she flaunted her detachment, the more I longed to plunge her into the vortex of her suffering.

"And how is she?"

"Who?"

"Maddalena"

"In a wheelchair. The workers at the center say that she just sits motionless, with her head slumped over her chest. If they didn't pull her out of that torpor, she would stay like that all day long. They told me that at times, when they try to stimulate her with memories, the only person who surfaces in her mind is Geppina. Yesterday I sat with her for a half hour, and I started to describe the landscape visible from the patio. I told her that the sky was clear, that all around us there were hills covered with trees, and that in the countryside there were fruit trees: pears and peaches. And then I described the color of the calendula flowers visible on the untilled fields. But it was as though she didn't even hear my voice. Then I plucked a flower from the plant in front of me and laid it on her lap. And you know what she did? First she sniffed it, then she lifted her head a bit, and looked at me out of the corner of her eye and told me in a cavernous voice, 'Gr-ra-z-zie.' A trickle of saliva was dripping from her mouth. So I took a tissue and dried it, reflecting on her voice. . . . Yes, a voice, anyone's voice . . . It's sort of like feelings. We don't have them because they exist on their own, end of story. No, we create them, with devotion and care."

"I'm suffocating from this heat," Costanza interrupted me. She put her feet back on the floor and went back to tiredly sticking her head in the sink. As she turned back to me, a flash of light crossed her wet face, and she added, "You know, it's not good for you to be so close to all that suffering. Pain loves emptiness; it feeds on the sound of itself. Be careful."

"That's just what I did for too long. Now I don't want to be careful; I can't . . ."

"If you let yourself get too involved, you'll only get hurt. After all, that world isn't yours anymore. And you're not used to suffering."

"Why, can someone get used to pain?"

"Yes, when you're born into it. Or when you live with it for a long time . . . you stop feeling it at a certain point. You become part of it. And you're too close to see how dreadful it is."

"Exactly why I wanted to adopt Martina, but you refused to. I suppose there was too much pain in her, and you didn't feel like getting caught up in it. . . ."

"That was a low blow. I get it. Maybe you're right. But I couldn't have done it. Martina would have always been a constant reminder of failure, not related to her but to someone else. It hurts to have to say it, but as they say, sometimes it's better to be hurt by the truth than consoled by a lie."

"Listen, I've thought a lot about this. I think we should annul our marriage. I mean . . . yeah, that it's not too late. . . . Well, being that it's not urgent . . ."

For a moment Costanza seemed to be swaying.

"Yes, I think so, too," she said disappearing into the darkness of our home. First, though, as she passed behind me, I got the impression that she had lightly caressed my head.

That night I couldn't fall asleep. Feeling fear, guilt, and rage at all my doubts, I kept wondering whether I had to do something to put an end to our relationship; I wondered whether for some reason unknown to me, Costanza had delegated me as the one to turn his back and leave. A dark shadow had surrounded us. It was separating us and making us each sail alone through a long night, and the morning was so far away that it didn't seem real.

～ 23 ～

The simple fact that "Ironhead" Maddalena was in a wheel-chair had led the staff at the center in Arpaia to believe that taking care of her was no more or less difficult than taking care of the other patients there. Already after a few weeks, though, Maddalena had been transforming herself into a despotic invalid, drooling from her mouth and always with a lit cigarette between her trembling yellowed fingers. Taking advantage of her condition, she had learned to dominate anyone in order to get the only things that were of interest to her: coffee, cigarettes, and Neapolitan songs. For her, nothing else mattered.

During those first months of her stay in Arpaia, then, the staff at the center did not log too many noteworthy incidents. There were a couple of burned sheets from her having fallen asleep with a cigarette in her hand, some dishes thrown on the ground when she was denied telephone privileges, and there was the time she purposefully ran over some eye-glasses in her wheelchair. The glasses belonged to Emilia, a forty-year-old mental patient who looked sixty and who subsequently went berserk. Last, there was the time she launched the television remote against a living room window just because Maria, Emilia's equally crazy twin, insisted on passing hour after hour staring at the blank TV screen, thus keeping Maddalena from watching her beloved soap operas. In short, nothing irreparable, nothing that could not be remedied. They were almost routine occurrences for a place like that frequented by life's rejects. But what really stirred up the hornet's nest of discontent and what threw the workers and the managers of Il Boschetto (as the center was called) into a panic, was Maddalena's revelation about the alleged filthy behavior of an attendant who, in the middle of the night, had undressed himself to show her the fervor hiding inside his breeches. As Maddalena's guardian, I too was informed. In concert with the directors of the center, however, we agreed to keep what happened just between us, forgoing any investigation for two reasons: "Ironhead's" congenital habit of lying and to not ruin the life of a family man, even if he was a degenerate. Given all the uncertainty, we decided that if I didn't utter of word of this to the probate judge, they would have pushed to have the filthy sleazeball transferred to a different facility.

Yes, I had been Maddalena's legal guardian for a number of months. After finding her at Ascalesi General Hospital right after Costanza discovered she was pregnant and after Giuliana Conti would inoculate in me the desire to adopt Martina. About the time when the flame of hope, flaring up, had set fire to my life, as well as Costanza's. It just happened, out of the blue, without time to reflect. One day a certain Adriana Tamburi from Nola, the probate judge who was in charge of Maddalena's case, for who knows what mysterious design by fate, was talking about Maddalena and her unbelievable recovery with none other than her colleague, Giuliana Conti. It wasn't difficult for Giuliana to piece together my connection with Martina and, therefore, with her mother. And so, the long-awaited search for what she called a "reliable" person had finally come to an end. But I accepted the role of guardian with the stipulation that the plan would include a provision for reuniting Maddalena with her family.

Now, with a clear head, it seems extraordinarily clear how that decision fit perfectly into the big picture for me. It would be easy for me to claim that I had not planned it that way, that I hadn't even given it any thought. But the indisputable truth is that by getting everyone on the same page, that decision would have coincided with everyone's needs—closed the circle, so to speak. Maddalena would have someone to take care of her, the court would have a trusted representative in the day-to-day management, the social worker would no longer have to carry the unbearable weight of dealing with her family, and likewise, the family itself would be glad that, along with Maddalena, they would have an unexpected cash flow. (In effect, by suggesting that Geppina take her daughter in periodically for a few days, I had dangled out there the possibility of lavishing a few hundred extra euros on her, given that my role was to administer Maddalena's meager pension.) In addition, in my mother's eyes, that decision would help to placate her sister's hatred, the same hatred that my mother feared would be heaped on me. As far as I was concerned, with Martina's approaching adoption, it would have been natural for me to also deal with her mother. I imagined that in this way, though they were sailing on a course to different shores, they would never lose contact with each other. A painless mother-daughter separation would have allowed the uncanny thread of consanguinity to keep them bound together in some way. I imagined it all . . . over and over and over.

Even today the overpasses that cross Via Argine form a sort of lid, against which the roar of car engines and the frenzy of the car horns ricochet back to the ground in a deafening echo.

As oppressive as the early-morning heat was and as much as the automobile exhaust fumes wreaked havoc on the lungs, that morning Maddalena seemed to be at peace. Seated by my side in the car, her head slumped over her chest, she had her eyes shut as though veiled by a swirl of bliss while, in that network of roads surrounding us, all hell was breaking loose. The mountains of garbage gathered like hedgerows along the sidewalks and sloped right into the middle of the street, releasing a pestilent stench that reached our noses, despite the windows being shut tight.

Now and then, Geppina would reach forward from the back seat to shake Maddalena by the shoulders. "*Matalè, stai durmenno? Madonna mia, ma 'sta figlia mia dorme sempe. Matalè, scetate a mammina.* Maddalena, are you sleeping? Oh, good Lord, my daughter's always sleeping. Maddalena, wake up for mommy."

After many years, all the medications had produced devastating effects on Maddalena. The most harmless of these, for example, was an antiepileptic drug, which had the capacity to make her sleep continuously. Not that it was a deep sleep—definitely not; rather, it was a sweet drowsiness, like an irresistible call to abandonment, a sort of vacation from reality that Maddalena was powerless to resist. Seeing her like that, I figured that such mental numbness was the least a person could wish on someone in her state. At least she wasn't forced to torment her soul with memories.

"'O cca-a-fè . . . S-some c-c-cof-fee," she said with a hiss, while the usual rivulet of saliva dripped from her mouth.

With one eye on the highway, I grabbed a tissue from the glove compartment and put it to her lips. With a slow movement, she lifted her right hand and started to dab herself, while Geppina held her head from the back seat.

"*Matalè, aiza 'a capa, a mammina.* Maddalena, lift up your head for mommy."

A ray of sunlight lit up her entire face. Furrowing her eyebrows, she revealed a large forehead, a cranial depression below her thinning hair, eye sockets that were way too big for her incredibly small eyes, a snub nose, and a fleshy, curled mouth forming a grimace. Then, suddenly, her head slouched back over her chest.

"Some espresso," she repeated with a hoarse tone.

"Mommy's got no espresso for you. You drink way too much."

We had just moved past a bottleneck when Geppina pointed out a secondary road, just beyond the intersection, which cut toward the hospital. The signs prohibited access, but given the absence of cops and the bustle of cars, she claimed it was the only way out of that inferno. Dodging the cars on the wrong side of the road, I took off at high speed for a few hundred yards. Then the road widened as we skirted some fallow parcels of land, some apartment houses, and aluminum warehouses. We drove alongside a cemetery with a low, crumbling retaining wall, beyond which two rows of poplars stood out. On the other side, heaps of garbage followed the curves and plastic bags covered almost the whole lane so that cars would run over them. From that point on, the trip became easier. On the state highway, the roadway turned into two lanes in each direction, and after a number of curves we caught sight of the Sacred Heart of Jesus Hospital, clearly visible on the summit of a verdant promontory over which Mount Vesuvius cast its shadow. Had Geppina not been there to guide me through the maze of small little towns, it would have been difficult to find, just as it would have been impossible to reach the center for mental health, where we had gone a few hours earlier for a neurological exam.

When I introduced myself at the reception desk, pushing Maddalena through a crowd of elderly people exhausted from the heat, the young employee was engaged in a friendly conversation with a nurse. Based on how she played with the pen in her hair bun, she gave off the vibe of someone with her mind in a different place. Their dry, relaxed faces made me think that beyond the counter window there had to be cool conditioned air. Only after the woman had rearranged her rebellious coppery hair, the staff member explained that we had to wait our turn. But when, after much insistence on my part, he was able to ascertain Maddalena's condition, he assured me that the urologist would let us go through before the others. We just needed to wait for him to get there.

Meanwhile, it was almost noon, and because of the excessive heat, Maddalena had fallen asleep in her wheelchair. I, on the other hand, kept pacing back and forth in the waiting room, pondering what sorts of thoughts were hidden behind the old, wizened faces of the people around me. Such tired, contracted faces. As their glazed-over eyes suddenly met mine, they made me think of what Costanza had told me the night before—about the suffering of the world and the fact that my being so close to it was not healthy for me at all. I thought she was right because there I was, cowardly wishing to be in Capri with her, in the town square drinking an aperitif, perhaps along with her father and mother, or having dinner at Achille's, savoring those famous agnolotti and then in the hanging garden at the Siniscalchis' house, "where the nights on Capri are magical," talking about this or that artist on the island for culture week, or on the terrace of Villa Paradiso for one of those concertos for piano and strings under the moonlight.

I was pondering all this while Geppina sat outside on a bench in the flower beds next to the parking lot where she had sought refuge, she claimed, to get a breath of fresh air. To see her that way, staring off into the distance, a cigarette between her lips, I wondered, on the contrary, what she was thinking at that moment. Who knows? Maybe one of her thoughts had to do with what I had just revealed to her about Martina's future and about the fact that she would never get her back.

Without warning, an August morning from many years ago resurfaced in my mind. I could see the metallic-blue Kadett 1000. I could hear how quiet my father was as he drove. I could sense my mother's impatience with us kids sitting in the back carrying on with lively chatter and exuberant laughter. I could see a long road that ran along the sea, the thick reed beds, and Geppina sitting on an overturned barrel waiting for time to pass over her. That image was a by-product of my mother's evocative storytelling, and now it ended up taking on the vivid features of one of my own recollections that had resurfaced all of a sudden from who knows which tunnel of memory.

From the look he gave to Maddalena, the doctor did not seem too happy with her general condition that morning. On such a hot day as that one, it was best to move as little as possible, and so dealing with someone like Maddalena would have been a less-than-ideal situation. That is why, as he greeted us with a half-peeved, half-polite tone, he immediately picked up the phone and begged a nurse to join him.

The space in the emergency ward was rather cramped. With the desk and the cot on the other side of the partition, there was little space to move in. The wheelchair could barely pass through, and the only place for Geppina and me was next to the open window, one of us on top of the other. Somehow I extended my arm to hand over Maddalena's medical records, trying to explain why we were there.

"How long has it been since the girl's been seen by a doctor?" the urologist asked, flipping quickly through her file.

"About seven, eight months, Doc. Since when she got out of the hospital," Geppina replied.

"Hmm. Have you noticed anything out of the ordinary? Do you know whether she has any leaks? Whether she's incontinent?"

"She wears a big diaper, and when she pees, there is an awful smell."

"Hmm . . . Maddalena, can you hear me? Do you understand me?" the doctor asked, doubting her cognitive abilities. Then, when Maddalena answered him by grumbling and faintly nodding her head, he added, "Hmm . . . let's have her lie down."

The nurse, already drenched in sweat in his white scrubs, arrived just in time. He lifted her up and laid her on the bed like the hind quarter of an ox that he was going to butcher. Although he seemed rather sturdy on his legs, by the way he panted and turned red, he was clearly struggling more than he had expected. Then, after slipping off her sweatsuit, her underwear, and her diaper with some help from Geppina, he made room for the doctor and joined me on the other side of the partition and stood at attention in front of the door. In a few moments, a nauseating smell of pus invaded our nostrils, and each time the doctor probed and asked whether she felt any pain, Maddalena groaned. After a few interminable minutes, while asking the nurse to help Geppina redress her, the urologist peeked out from behind the partition. Removing his latex gloves, he approached a tiny sink mounted on the wall and soaped up his hands while shaking his head, dejected as though he were suddenly realizing the pointlessness of his own actions. Then, losing his detached demeanor from a moment earlier, in a subdued voice he said that Maddalena was really in rough shape. The infection had affected her entire vaginal apparatus, but with a good regimen of antibiotics and some very careful hygiene, he would be able to get her right as rain.

"The bigger problem lies ahead. She needs more attention, someone who can take better care of her daily needs, to wash her regularly, to make sure that she drinks a lot of water. Moreover, her kidneys are functioning poorly. That's why she continues to have stones," he added, by now back at his desk.

"Doc, when she stays with me, I keep her squeaky clean," Geppina said. *"Nun è accussì, Matalè, nun è 'a verità? Diccello tu 'o duttore, diccello quante volte ti lavo.* That's the truth. Right, Maddalena? Tell him. Tell the doctor. Tell him how much I wash you," she continued, shaking her daughter, whom the nurse had, meanwhile, gotten back into the wheelchair.

Maddalena just replied by mumbling that she didn't like water. "I l-like c-c-cof-fee!"

On the road back, safely belted into her seat, Maddalena started shaking her head and becoming rather difficult while I reiterated the doctor's orders. Water, a lot of water. Large quantities of fruits and vegetables. Very little coffee. She emitted an even more cavernous grumbling, knowing that I give in easily. Then, with a loud sniffle, she mumbled something like, "M-mind y-your ffuck-king bus'ness."

"*L'acqua ... sí, a voglio propio vedé, chesta pure 'e pillole se le piglia senza acqua.* Water ... yeah, that's a good one! She even takes her pills without water," said Geppina, who by then was rather quiet in the back seat, exhausted from a long, hard morning. "*Chesta è 'na prepotente, vo' vincere sempe essa!* She's a real bully. She always has to get her way!"

The day's exhaustion had a different effect on me, though.

"Oh, yeah. She wants to be a bully, huh? Okay, if she doesn't do what the doctor says, I'll tell the staff at the center to take away her cigarettes, her coffee, and her headphones. . . . And good-bye to her Gigi D'Alessio songs."

Giving her a sidelong look, I told her that I also had some legal obligations in her regard, and to ratchet things up a notch, I threatened to not let her go home again. Maddalena seemed to ignore all the warnings. In fact, with her one good hand, she fumbled in the fanny pack she had clipped tightly around her waist, pulled out a cigarette and lit it. Unperturbed, I pulled it from her mouth and tossed it out the car window. With a stern voice, I reminded her that I did not like the smell of smoke in my car.

Then, lifting her head just a bit, she looked at me askance. "*Ja, pe' piaceeere ... fam-me fu-fu-mà. . . .* Come on, p-pleeease ... l-l-let m-me sm-smoke," she said, drying her spittle with the back of her hand. "*Te faaacce 'n bu-u-cchin'.* I'll suck you off."

A sword seemed to go right through my chest and pin me to the seat. However, what really hurt wasn't so much her words as the awareness that they were just the tip of the iceberg of all the horror that resided within "Ironhead." A few weeks earlier, reacting to my questions about how she was able to feed herself when she wandered around the train station, she had used the same words: "I s-suck-sucked p-p-people off."

Since a car's horn fortuitously blared and drowned out Maddalena's words, I hoped that Geppina hadn't heard them. But when our eyes met in the rearview mirror, I glimpsed the shame of the whole world in the back of her sky-blue eyes. It was a shame that I suspected she might want to transfer to me for who knows what mysterious reason. Meanwhile, the traffic in the town center had diminished. It was two o'clock and the shops were closing. There was just one truck in front of us, moving at a snail's pace and making a clanging noise, while waves of a heat mirage were rippling the asphalt.

After the latest of Maddalena's never-ending requests for an espresso, I didn't put up a fight. Near a café, I pulled over and got out, only to return in no time with a to-go cup. Meanwhile, Geppina was outside the car, leaning on the door as she smoked and stared off into the distance. She had the most pained expression I had ever seen on a human being's face. And something was telling me that her shame, which was still flickering in her eyes, had nothing to do with Maddalena. Pretending not to notice that she was crying her eyes out, I found something to distract me in the glove compartment. She got back into the car after Maddalena took her last sip of espresso and lit yet another cigarette.

Once we were back at the Parco degli Oleandri, the desolate streets were sizzling beneath a blanket of suffocating heat. I parked right near the main door, while from the usual open window, Gigi D'Alessio's voice lingered in the air: "quando calienta el sol mon amour, mon amour. . . ." Before getting out of the car, I stuck my hand into the glove compartment, took out a package wrapped in brown paper, and passed it to Geppina. It was the gold that I had bought back from the pawn shop—her gold, which she had sacrificed to pay the lawyers, Castaldi and Serra, for handling Martina's case. The receipt I gave her listed a gold chain and crucifix, a bracelet with charms and alternating little medallions, and two white gold wedding bands, for a total of 580 euros.

"I bought them back from the pawn shop with some of the money from Maddalena's account. But now I have to find a way to finagle some receipts for medical payments to show this as a legitimate expense . . . but this is the last time. Last month I even paid your water bills so they didn't shut it off. . . . How can I justify all these expenses? Maddalena receives seven hundred euros of welfare pension per month, and when she comes home every fifteen days, I leave her an allowance of two hundred. Beyond cigarettes and medication, Maddalena doesn't spend much on anything else."

Suddenly, Geppina's eyes filled with a flash of rage. Her face turned red and her forehead was beading with sweat.

"What do you even know about Maddalena's expenses?"

"I know that two hundred euros are not much, but you need to make do with them because I don't want any trouble with the probate judge."

"Problems? And what do you know about problems? You can't even imagine what real problems are!"

Without saying a word, I opened the car door and got out. I took the wheelchair from the trunk, lifted Maddalena by her waist, and set her down, while Geppina was on the apartment intercom asking for help. The fast shuffling of feet echoing through the stairwell anticipated the arrival of her son Lello, who showed up all out of breath.

"Mamma, we have to be quick about it. With my house arrest, I can't even leave the front door. *Se passa 'a polizia so' cazz' amari.* . . . If the police drop by, I'm in deep shit. . . ."

With him on one side and me on the other, we lifted up Maddalena, wheelchair and all, and after making it past two flights of stairs, we loaded her into the elevator. Before the elevator doors closed, I reminded Geppina that the arrangement with the staff at the center in Arpaia was that they would pick her up on the following Monday.

"We will see each other in fifteen days, though, when I bring her back."

As I was leaving, I felt a vague contempt for those two lives. They were part of me, and I was bound to them without even asking to be.

~ 24 ~

When the phone rang, it was almost eight o'clock. Costanza had already gotten out of bed—for weeks she had been looking for a way to avoid me and my dark mood—and she was in the shower. At least that's what I thought from the sound of rushing water. I, on the other hand, had gotten back under the covers and was sipping my usual espresso, reflecting on the days that went by relentlessly, one after the other. By now they were all the same. They were days during which everything seemed pointless and empty. Days when I could feel quiet rage welling up inside of me; days when, instead of simply shutting a door, I would slam it; or when I wouldn't even notice I had raised my voice, when all I wanted to do was talk normally. Maybe that was just my way of filling the void that was threatening to swallow me up, like a child who stamps his feet when he's afraid of the dark.

Coffee cup in one hand, I raised the receiver with the other.

"Hello?"

"Michele? Good morning. It's Giuliana Conti."

"Ciao. How's it going?"

"Sorry for calling you at this hour. It's just that . . ."

"Any news?"

"Yes, I wanted to tell you . . . Well, I wanted to notify you that we found an adoptive family for Martina."

Silence. I placed the coffee cup on the bedside table . . . with too much force. It broke.

"Hello, Michele . . ."

"Yes, yes! I'm right here," I said, lying.

"I know how painful it must be, but . . ."

"For when?"

"Tomorrow . . ."

Silence.

"Tomorrow?"

"Yes, that's why I called you at this hour. I thought that maybe you'd like to say good-bye to her, see her one last time."

"One last time?"

"Yes . . ."

"Who are they?"

"Michele . . ."

"Are they from Naples?"

"Michele . . ."

"What do they do for a living? Do they have other kids already?"

"Michele. Michele, enough! You know that I can't tell you that. She will be fine. Don't worry. I chose them very carefully. I am sure that she will fit in well. Now, however, I have to go. I have a hectic schedule today. Don't forget to go see her. . . ."

"Okay."

"Ciao. See you soon."

When I hung up, I heard the bathroom door open and footsteps echoing through the apartment. Costanza. From a distance she asked who was on the phone. I didn't answer. I jumped out of bed and went to the window. Sky, clouds, sea. I meditated on a distant point, in my own world. I'm not sure how long I stayed still like that. I felt alone. By myself. By myself. I felt like crying. I needed attention. Warm, constant, loving attention. Probably what Martina felt she needed, I thought. No matter how hard I tried, self-pity inevitably turned into self-loathing.

And Costanza tried to mitigate my bad mood by reading off the list of contemporary English artists being exhibited at the Palazzo delle Arti Napoli, written on the invitation I'd received the day before. Then I turned around and yelled at her to quit it with her usual cultural socialite frivolities. I didn't give a shit. On the contrary, I had never given a shit. I was fed up with always having something to prove. Keeping up with the others. Toiling. Pretending. Convincing myself that being close to pain wasn't bad for me. That pain loved emptiness and fed on the sound of it. Costanza had never wanted Martina and now I hated her for it. I hated that she considered my suffering to be inconsequential. Or did she believe that by virtue of having placed all her hopes of being a mother in that stain of blood nothing else mattered? My mistake was in still staying with her. Yup, that was my mistake.

Costanza looked at me without saying a word. She just stared. Disoriented and afraid, like old Coleman Silk staring at Faunia Farley when, during one of her rash outbursts, she threatened that she never wanted to see him again.

Then, moving her espresso cup away from her, she got up from her chair and said, "I'm going. I'm late."

~ 25 ~

After a stretch on the bypass, the state highway that leads to
Licola seemed like molten lead poured over asphalt. A truck
had dumped a whole load of gravel on the roadway, creating
an endless line of traffic. The foster care facility was not far
as the crow flies, but to get there you had to drive quite a bit
on the backed-up section of the state highway. From where
I was, looking far across the expanse of countryside, I could
make out a row of apartment houses along the coast and the
palm tree in the center of the courtyard that provided shade
for the building where Martina would live for only a few
more hours. It was just a few more miles, but judging by the
comings and goings of police cars, the wait promised to be a
long one. So, after a hundred yards, I veered toward some
unknown dirt road. To the east, the direction visible from
my window, it was getting darker. To the west were thin rib-
bons of wandering clouds tinged with orange and crimson.
Just beyond some dense reddish brush, there was a column
of smoke rising from a two-story house. A sign nailed to a

tree trunk read, "Building Material for Sale," "Greenhouse Plants," "Fruit for Sale." I passed by it, bouncing over the rough road surface. I skirted a pond that was walled in by tall reeds, but as the lane was ending, some downed trees forced me to detour through some dense brush. My wheels sank into the muddy ground. Game over. I tried to pull the car out by accelerating, but it was useless. Darkness was beginning to fall, and I wanted to get to Martina at any cost before she went to bed.

So, having abandoned my car, I decided to take the path that bordered the pond, making my way through the tall grass and being careful where I stepped. A little farther ahead, hanging between two trunks in a ring of trees, were large fishing nets. All around there was an intense odor of burning brushwood, and the closer I got to the farmhouse, the more deafening a chirping sound got, as though an invisible flock of happy birds were hovering in the sky. The courtyard of the house was horseshoe shaped. In a tin-roofed shack, a group of people, covered in swarms of gnats, was busy turning a crank over some wine-making barrels. A stream of wine issued from the press, cut across the ground, and ran into a sewer grate. The odor of wine must mixed with the burning smell saturated the air while the birds' chirping had become unbearable. Under the covered porch the wall was jam-packed with tons of little cages—in each one a little goldfinch flitted around frenetically. At the end, an enormous aviary was covered by a dark drape, and based on the frightful flapping of wings, it was easy to imagine hundreds of birds fluttering inside of it. As I approached, I made out two men next to the aviary; the first poked his arm through a narrow slit, quickly grabbed a bird, and passed it to the other, who sat on a stool with his eyeglasses perched low on his nose. In the dim light of a lamp, the man kept turning and turning the bird in his clenched hand, examining it with the expertise of an ornithologist. Then, lightly tapping the goldfinch on the head, as though blessing him, he placed it in the cage by his feet. But when I arrived a few steps away from him, my blood froze in my veins: the man who appeared to be blessing the birds was actually blinding them with a red-hot needle. And what had appeared to be happy warbling was a horrible cry of pain.

Seeing me retreat, terrorized, into the courtyard, one of the farmers got right in my face with a menacing air. He had brown, sunken eyes that were a bit too small for his head, and when he fixed them on me, I got scared.

"What do you want? Who're you looking for? This is private property!"

I told him about the accident on the state highway, about my bogged-down car, and about my intention to get on the road for Licola.

In an unceremonious deadpan, he indicated the way out of the farmstead.

"A hundred yards and you'll run right into it."

"Do you know whether my car—" I asked, before he cut me off.

"You'll have to call a tow truck, and take the same road you just took. You can't go through here."

On the horizon, the sun had set the whole sky on fire, and in the distance the dark sea was furious with whitecaps. Darkness was falling, but the last glow of light gave everything a permanence: the nearby residential area, the gloomy green countryside, the lit streetlamps on the side of the road, and the asphalt that was robbing some blue from the sky.

I walked at a steady pace on the side of the road. I was thinking of Martina, and I hoped that the memory of everything she'd experienced up until that moment would quickly vanish from her mind, like a bad dream. That evening, I would see her for the last time, and I wondered whether she was thinking about me, too . . . whether, not seeing me show up, she was about to completely forget about me, like a bad memory. And I started to run. It had been years since I ran. All the noises around me went silent, my breath was rhythmic, my heartbeat started throbbing in my head, and my blood pumped through my veins. A voice in my head told my body to keep going, told my legs to keep a constant rhythm, to not let up, to keep going without stopping. Faster and faster. Finally the world disappeared, along with the heartbreaking song of the birds, along with the steel serpent winding in agony on the state highway, along with the heaving sea in the distance, and along with the multitude of lights starting to stipple the countryside.

Miss Clara proved to be very understanding. Despite her brusque mother superior act and her usual litany of admonitions, she let me bring Martina out with me. Since she found out about my failed attempt at becoming a foster father, she had begun to treat me with a tone somewhere between contempt and pity. And of course she loved to repeat that violating the "strict house rules," when necessary, was not a sign of weakness but proof that a true act of justice often consisted in not doing the right thing.

As I crossed the courtyard at the foster home while clutching Martina's hand, a procession of clouds passed in front of a magenta moon, and the cool evening air gave off a violent scent of roses and jasmine flowers. I was almost positive that Miss Clara was spying on us from the balcony, but Martina removed all doubt when she turned around and shook her hand to wave at her. And until we left the property, when the woman disappeared from sight, she continued to wave at her, skipping on the gravel, with the pride of a dog that had finally found its master after wandering a great distance. Yet all I did was repeat to myself, like a mantra, what Miss Clara had told me in the doorway: Martina didn't wait so enthusiastically for anyone else, just for me. She waited. Just for me. Enthusiastically. Just for me. She waited . . . What would I tell her? How would I tell her? Are there even words to tell a child who believes you to be her father that it was all a joke? That not only would she not come to live with you but that she would never see you again?

That you will part ways from each other?

In the crowded piazza, I felt surrounded by an obscenely happy display of humanity, which was absurdly unaware of our pain. A stream of people was coming out of the subway station, and children were chasing each other around in the park, while a shining merry-go-round and a multicolored little train captured the attention of scores of children.

We ate a pizza. Then an ice cream. And aside from a few words, we didn't talk much. Afterward we went on the merry-go-round. Once, twice, three times, while the sky was lit up with phantasmagoric fireworks: red, white, green, and silver crowns and cascades streamed downward as rockets shot into the sky with deafening whistles that would burst into thousands of sparks only to burn out in the night. When we got off, Martina stood there in front of me and stared at me, probably no longer than an instant, but I think it will forever be one of the longest moments of my life.

We sat for quite some time on a bollard, looking up without saying a word. "When I get big, will you come see me?"

She sat poised at my side, and her little face, lit up red, white, and green, showed no sign of emotion. I got a lump in my throat and sank into a pit of shame. The same shame I had seen in Geppina's eyes. If she had only understood, I could have asked her for forgiveness. For having deceived her.

For having disappointed her. For having failed to keep her with me. But she was just five years old. Five years and with an odd smile on her lips.

"Yes, of course I'll come see you."

"Are we going back now? Miss Clara said that tomorrow I have to get up early. My new parents are coming."

On the drive back, when the shadows of the night surrounded us and the ruckus of the merrymakers became a more distant buzzing, Martina began humming the nursery rhyme about the train. The one I had taught her. She seemed happy. But even the warbling of the goldfinches a few hours earlier had seemed happy at first. I thought back to the furious look she had shot me in the reflection of that mirror the first time I had met her. I struggled to comprehend why now she was so overtaken by a wave of joy that was like a gust of wind throwing open a thousand doors. I had tears in my eyes.

I stayed with her until late in the evening. In her bedroom, the other children were already asleep. I folded down her covers and kissed her forehead. Before I turned out the light on the night table, Martina grabbed me by the hand and said, "I love you." As I closed the door to her room, I wondered whether that was how forgiveness blossomed: with pain packing up its things and moving out unannounced in the middle of the night.

Before I left the foster home forever, Miss Clara, in wishing me good luck, had whispered that I shouldn't worry about it. The next day Martina would take her train.

~ 26 ~

Christmas season was unavoidably upon us, and with that realization, once again, came my mother's need to buy off her sense of guilt with an offering to her sister. But no matter how hard I tried to fill the void, I was still suffering from an absence that refused to become mourning. Martina had disappeared from my horizon. So had Costanza, even though I felt her close to me. This forced me to rethink things, to get everything in order, to bring clarity to my life. I tried to rationalize, to get enough objective distance to make reasonable choices. In light of all that had happened and, more painfully, what was going to happen, what would be my role?

It was two days since I had picked up Maddalena from the center in Arpaia to have her spend the holidays at home. And, as usual, I had made sure that she had everything she needed, like diapers, medicine, and gifts for various family members, which she had insisted on buying from IKEA. While we were getting on the highway interchange, by pure coincidence, her attention had been drawn to a tower lit up with Christmas lights that rose high into the sky. She was so happy, so unusually in good sorts that when she gave me a lighter—though it made no sense for me as a nonsmoker—I was obliged to accept it. When activated, it produced a flame along with a wave of multicolored lights and an interminable hip-hop melody.

With all the frenzy of Christmas shopping drawing people out of their houses in droves, going to Geppina's meant taking the usual state highway, clogged with cars, being stuck in traffic for who knows how long, and having time to dwell on the crumbling tenements, the elevated roadways that went off into nowhere, the desolation of the landscape with the same streets forever crisscrossed by the rumbling of truck engines. Most of all, it meant having plenty of time to think about Costanza, about the irreconcilable rift that had come between us, about how little we had talked, about all the sleepless nights we shared. Which is what I did up until the entrance of the Parco degli Oleandri, interrupted only by the din of all the ambulance sirens and by the comings and goings of police cars. Not that such confusion could alarm me; by now shootings were a common occurrence in the outskirts of the city. But the closer I got to Geppina's building—thinking about how many trips the kids would need to take to carry the supplies up the stairs— the more unruly the throngs became. I struggled to make it past people who were running to join a gathering crowd, crossing without first looking for cars. Proceeding at a crawl, I thought I recognized two women who were my aunt's neighbors; outside a small grocery store decorated with pyramidal displays of panettones and multicolored holiday lights, they were crying and holding each other.

A few feet from Geppina's building, a car from the fire department barred access, forcing me to drive past. I parked near the supermarket a bit farther up and I headed through the waves of people, but in the droning all around me, I perceived the sound of genuine pain. Real trepidation and not the vacuous nattering of simple, and in the end morbid, curiosity. Elbowing my way through, I made it past the police cordon: from the windows and balconies in Geppina's building, in a collective silence, people stared down at the gurneys that exited the lobby one by one to be loaded onto the ambulances. Four gurneys. Four bodies. All wrapped in white plastic sheets. On Geppina's balcony, where I had often pondered how dreary that place was, Concetta, Susetta, and Monica were petrified, with the look of horror still in their eyes.

Based on the reconstruction of the incident, the forensics team had concluded that a carbon monoxide leak had taken all four in their sleep: Geppina, her husband, Lino, Maddalena, who was home for the holidays, and Lelluccio, who was under house arrest awaiting trial. However, as further information came to light from witness testimonies, the office of the prosecutor didn't take long to conclude that this was not a tragic accident.

The knobs on the kitchen stove had been left on, just like the ones on the gas heaters in each room, while the windows and balconies had been closed tightly. Another clue that confirmed the theory was that the main electrical panel had been shut off, evidently for the purpose of avoiding a larger tragedy—namely, the whole building going up in smoke. So whoever had designed the plan, even while committing a deranged act, had taken care not to cause harm to others. But who among the victims could it have been? The investigators were not able to determine the identity of the perpetrator with any certainty, even if the biggest clues pointed to Geppina.

According to Concetta, who had gone to her mother's early that morning, the strong smell of gas was already detectable in the stairwell, and once she had gotten to the third-floor landing she had almost fainted. But by no means did she have any premonition of tragedy. What alarmed her, though, was the apartment door locked from the inside—something that her mother never did—and the fact that the doorbell was not working. Only then, fear began to take hold, and she started banging on the door and yelling. Not receiving an answer, she started to rummage desperately through her bag, hoping to find the extra set of keys that Geppina advised her to keep on her at all times. Her screams, echoing through the stairwell, had made the neighbors come running just at the moment in which she opened the door and a billow of gas was overtaking her, forcing her to back away. Her mind was cloudy and she was struck deaf as though trapped in a bad dream because people around her were moving their mouths, but she couldn't make out what they were saying. Suddenly, a rush of rain and a gust of cold wind coming from the windows that someone had opened on the stairway struck her in the face, bringing her back to reality. Then she dashed into the house.

Concetta testified that once inside, she stood petrified at the sight of those bodies curled up in bed with contracted faces. And she swore she could not remember anything except the inexplicably serene expression on Geppina's face and her floral dress, perfectly ironed, as though she had worn it for a party. A few months earlier, under the same gray sky, Geppina and Lino had walked off into the shadows of the Centro Direzionale, with a part of me by their side. Now they had taken that same part of me with them forever, leaving me with the torment of not having understood, not having foreseen, not having done anything to avoid what was perhaps inevitable.

I am well aware that according to the laws of men as well as divine laws, Geppina is to be considered guilty, but I don't have it in me to condemn her for this act, just as it would be useless to inveigh against a merciless wind for having uprooted an old, hollow, worm-eaten tree.

I think that some people remember while others dream. For me, Martina, Geppina, Maddalena, and all the other ghosts of that world have an almost dreamlike quality; I have no doubt that they existed, but I live with the constant fear that they might vanish from my mind at any time. With the same evanescence of dreams. Forever.

This is what really happened around Christmas 2005. At least it's what I remember most clearly. However, I recall a distant echo of yet another investigation into Berlusconi, suspected of bribing an English lawyer so that the latter might lie on his behalf in some deal or another. And I have a vague inkling that in the midst of all the general chaos, there was some tragic news about the artistic separation of Massimo Boldi and Christian De Sica, the comic duo of Italian cinema. Rivers of ink had been spent writing about them in articles by intellectuals and cinephiles who were as divided as the Montagues and the Capulets. But what I do definitively remember, thanks to Costanza's pressing lectures, was the opening of an installation in Piazza del Plebiscito by Sol LeWitt, a world-renowned artist who with his *Walls* "was rebuilding a visual itinerary by deconstructing urban space in which the spectator was absorbed by the idea of movement." That's all. Everything else is still wrapped in the dense blanket of an indissoluble fog.

In the ensuing months, the shroud of affliction that had enveloped me to the point of near asphyxia had slowly given way to a sense of inescapable loss. And that was already an improvement. I had stopped flagellating myself, and I had begun licking my wounds, begging for some certainty in every direction, begging for an ounce of inclusion in a world in which I had sought acceptance for so long. At times I was even content; at others, though, I was like one of those dogs that wag their tails from one master to another, happy just to be stroked. I would distance myself from mere acquaintances, making promises—more to me than to them—about some unlikely get-together further down the line. Or I would comply enthusiastically with any piece of advice, suggestion, or point of view; or, better yet, with a giggle of flattery I would comment on every little stupid conversation, which meant that I was "never better." But then I would throw aside my surprise and my repulsion and I would move on, thinking that there was nothing left to do but thank God for what little He'd left me and beg Him to keep it that way for all eternity.

During that period, Costanza and I even seemed to recover a climate of mutual understanding, which transformed our shared silence into peaceful tolerance, which then turned into a sort of solidarity as a way of protecting the desire for belonging to which we had both succumbed.

I have to give her credit for having done so much to pick me up after the deaths of Geppina, Maddalena, Lino, and Lelluccio, all of whom she never mentioned again. And for having stopped hiding behind her moralizing about pain that feeds on emptiness. As for me, I did my best to resign myself to a rich and full existence, without yielding to solitude and, above all, without getting too caught up in life. What was in the past was in the past. Impossible to erase, impossible to carry around. We never even spoke again about Martina—except one time. I was the one who began; Costanza indulged me. We could picture her sitting properly at her new parents' dinner table or doing her homework in her little bedroom full of stuffed animals, while humming the theme song to some cartoon. Then we imagined her growing up and becoming a girl dealing with her first acts of transgression and her first loves; then turning into a woman who demands a lot out of life, who never shows signs of past suffering, nor ever reveals the disappointments and broken dreams of an abandoned child. We visualized her living her life. Then we never spoke of her again.

~ 27 ~

Moored in the sea just beyond the Faraglioni, those ancient vertical rock formations that breach through the surface like little lighthouses, the boat was pitching sleepily. Gusts of wind rippled the surface of the water and ruffled Costanza's hair as she lay sunbathing on the bow. Next to her, Linda and her friend Mimí, who had flown in from Milan that morning, were dozing. Or maybe they were just pretending to sleep, aware that at any moment something might happen to "upset the family harmony," since Costanza's sister had expressed her concern about it earlier.

Under the canopy, Augusto Argentieri sipped a glass of wine; looking around him with a disgusted air, he was complaining how by now too many of the nouveaux riches were visiting the island and they whizzed by too closely in their extremely gaudy speedboats.

"And the islanders don't mind. They only think about money, and the more these people visit, the more money they make," Marisa commented, careful to not let the wind ruffle her bun freshly done up with hairspray. "Once upon a time, as soon as we set foot on Capri, they would come running to collect our suitcases. . . . Augusto, do you remember how helpful Gigino was? He would come to the pier with his little three-wheeled Piaggio Ape and unload everything at the house. And all day long he would come and go to see whether we needed anything. Now you have to beg him to find the time. . . . He could not care less about us."

"Of course! There are those who will pay him three times what you give him." Donato De Nittis's comments never failed to include a hint of embittered irony.

"What's money got to do with it? It's a matter of respect. . . . They've known us for thirty years. But they know whom to call when they need a doctor's appointment or a hospital room. . . . 'Professor' this, 'Professor' that . . . And Augusto is always available."

"Ah, well, what's that got to do with it? . . . That's something entirely different," her conciliatory husband replied.

"Something entirely different if they at least paid. Instead, they come bearing a goat or a fish. . . ."

"Marisa, don't you know your husband really believes that being a doctor is a mission, a special calling? Money is not important to him," De Nittis had chimed in with a teasing tone. "Augusto is too good."

"What do you mean 'good'? . . . He's foolish!"

"At any rate, those people never call me," said De Nittis.

"Because you're loathsome," Marisa had told him. "He's foolish. You're loathsome. . . . What a nice pair of friends you make."

"All right, enough of this nonsense!" Augusto Argentieri cut them short. "The more important question is, do you know what Mimí does for a living?" he added, glancing over at his daughter's friend.

"She's an art conservationist. You happy? Now, quit it. . . . Please, let's not ruin our weekend."

"Mind you, I'm happy to see my daughter, but the rare time she deigns to visit us, she could at least come alone," Argentieri blurted out. "Not that there's anything wrong with the young lady whom she brings along. . . ."

"Augusto . . . Are you serious?" Marisa had intervened again.

"What? Did I say something wrong? . . . I'm just pointing out that she's always the same: for example, because of her, this morning we came out to the boat at noon."

"Actually, it's not her fault," I intruded cautiously. "This morning the flight was late. Costanza and I had to wait more than forty-five minutes at the airport. We had to run to the ferry. . . ."

With a grimace of disappointment, Augusto Argentieri was in the middle of getting up to adjust his white linen jacket. Then, after a long sigh, he turned back to his wife.

"Did you tell Consuelo that we're having dinner early this evening? Remember that I want to follow the early election returns on TV."

"The results are no big deal," Donato De Nittis added with a yawn. "The latest polls show them outdoing . . ."

"If I were you, I wouldn't be so sure."

"Well, in the television debate, Berlusconi really let Prodi have it."

"Oh well, if you say so!"

"I'm just sorry that Mariano the communist isn't here with us, just for the sheer pleasure of seeing him suffer."

"Who told you he's not going to be with us? He gets in on the last ferry. I invited him, too."

"You see? The communists . . . they talk and talk, yet they can't wait to live the good life on Capri."

"Don't be such a demagogue now. . . . He's my guest. He's a delightful person in his own way. He might be one of the few people who lives in the same system that he has the courage to criticize. . . . By the way, you know what he told me this morning on the phone?"

"More of his usual gobbledygook."

"He claims that Berlusconi, Fini, and Casini concluded their election campaigns in Naples, not because the city has been on the top of their list of concerns over the past five years but because they know that the Neapolitans will be charmed into subjugation by a populist caudillo."

"You accuse me of demagoguery, but this is the same old hackneyed ideology: Berlusconi is the new Bourbon king and the Neapolitans are the low-class rabble who just want their bread and circus and gallows. . . ."

"You know there's some truth in that. Which is fine by me, but don't forget that corrupt populism, Achille Lauro–style, was born in Naples, and you know that it depended on a skillful and unscrupulous use of people's passions for soccer in order to obtain popular consensus."

"So I guess we should prepare for De Laurentiis to get into politics, seeing how he's bought the Napoli soccer club."

"I wouldn't be surprised if he did. . . . Anyway, all jokes aside, the fact is, in Naples there is an overabundance of popular voters who cannot wait to be duped by some campaign promise and by some charismatic leader. . . . And, as we know, Berlusconi, Il Cavaliere, is a master at it. A true illusionist. And the city is disaffected, disgruntled, and disconcerted. Just look at the increasingly intolerant criticism of Bassolino and the disappointment with which Jervolino's candidacy for a second term as mayor of Naples was accepted. In my opinion, a protest vote, a vote out of spite, might be in the works. . . . But we'll see this evening."

"God willing," De Nittis had replied, with his hands clasped and his eyes looking to the sky, not forgetting about the plates of local cuisine that Marisa was placing on the table.

After a long, cold winter, that spring seemed determined to drive the dark clouds out of my head, once and for all. I liked to breathe in the salty sea air, driven by the wind, and even the chatter around me wasn't bothersome. In fact, it would reach my ears like background music: not too pleasant but not overly unpleasant either. I could have listened for days and never even noticed when it had stopped playing. Tethered to its anchor, the listing boat emitted the rhythmic echo of lapping water, while the sun languished me into a satisfying torpor. I had fixed my sights on the verdant gorges of the Capri coastline in front of me. The fruit trees were almost all in bloom and the delightful scent of jasmine and orange blossoms wafted toward me in gentle surges. In the meantime, Costanza had come over to sit beside me. She was sitting quietly, staring at the sparkling sea, and from time to time she would grace me with a smile. She had also wrapped her arm around my shoulders, and perhaps it was in that moment that I surrendered. Because everything was starting to seem deceptively more agreeable.

Acknowledgments
by the Original Author

First of all, I wish to thank my brother Gianni. He took me lovingly by the hand and guided me through the stories of day-to-day suffering in those places in which his dedication to his work brings him as a speech therapist. I am grateful to him for his countless suggestions, which allowed me to tell this story.

I am grateful for the support of Annabella d'Avino, Maria Teresa Carbone, Massimo Loiacono, and Giuseppe Merlino.

A special word of thanks to Patrizia Antignani and Francesco Improta: with great affection, they endeavored to navigate the labyrinths of pain found in this story. Thanks to Iaia Caputo as well for stemming, controlling, and directing the flow of my magmatic words into a manageable reservoir.

I also wish to thank Benedetta Centovalli for believing in this project.

Last, thanks to Jay Parini for the foreword, and for his love and friendship over the years. Thanks to my dear old friend Mimmo Jodice for providing one of his artworks for the cover photo. I am also very grateful to my friend Gregory Pell for his wonderful work on this novel.

Notes on Contributors

ANGELO CANNAVACCIUOLO was born in Acerra, in the province of Naples, in 1956. He studied literature, with a specialization in Arabic, at the Istituto Orientale di Napoli. After a number of experiences in small local theater companies, he started out as a screen actor in 1981 in Salvatore Piscicelli's splendid film *Le occasioni di Rosa* (*The Occasions of Rosa*) in which Marina Suma—later his partner for almost a decade—would also debut. The following year, he switched to lighthearted comedy by acting in the Vanzina brothers *Sapore di mare* (*A Time for Loving*), often considered the Italian *American Graffiti*, and in the sequel, *Sapore di mare 2*. After extensive acting experiences, in 1993, he decided to get behind the camera to direct his first feature film, *Malesh*. After working on news pieces and documentaries, in 1999 he made his way to novel writing with *Guardiani delle nuvole* (*Guardians of the Clouds*), a Viareggio Prize finalist, which was transposed to the silver screen by Luciano Odorisio in 2004 and featured a soundtrack by Ennio Morricone. His second novel, *Il soffio delle fate* (*Fog Is Just Fairy Breath*), which came out in 2002, was a finalist for the Elsa Morante Prize. This novel dealt with the war in Bosnia and was later turned into an opera with music by Maestro Filippo Zigante and the libretto written by

Cannavacciuolo. In 2005, the writer turned to the milieu of hard-boiled noir with his *Acque basse* (*In the Shallows*), a story partially inspired by the life and death of journalist Giancarlo Siani. His fourth novel is the 2008 semiautobiographical *Le cose accadono* (*When Things Happen*), which won both the Domenico Rea Prize and the Viadana Prize in 2009. After a break of roughly ten years, Cannavacciuolo released his most ambitious and demanding novel, *Sacramerica* (2018), which was set in California, Mexico, and Italy, and won the Premio Letterario Letizia Isaia 2019, along with accolades throughout Italy and even in the United States from such authors as Jay Parini, whose 2002 novel, *The Apprentice Lover*, Cannavacciuolo translated to Italian as *L'apprendista amante* (2019). His latest novel, *Una romantica agonia* (*A Romantic Agony*), is forthcoming in 2023.

GREGORY PELL is a professor in the Department of Romance Languages and Literatures at Hofstra University where he teaches courses on language, cinema, literature, and translation theory. His critical articles examine such poets as Dante, Paolo Ruffilli, Mario Luzi, Davide Rondoni, Tommaso Lisa, Mario Tobino, and Eugenio Montale, the last of which is the subject of his full-length monograph, *Eugenio Montale: Memorial Space, Poetic Time*. On cinema, he has published pieces on Mihaileanu, Benigni, Kore-Eda, Sergio Rubini, Vicenzo Marra, Mohsen Melliti, Paolo Sorrentino, and Matteo Garrone. His latest monograph, *Davide Rondoni: Art in the Movement of Creation*, explores the "non-ekphrastic" relationship between art and poetry in the works of Davide Rondoni, John Ashbery, Charles Wright, Mario Luzi, Gjertrud Schnackenberg, Patrizia Fazzi, et al. Aside from continuing to translate poetry and commentary for Davide Rondoni, his ongoing research projects focus on Vitaliano Trevisan and the Italian northeast, the prose and poetry of Goffredo Parise, and Italian dialects in poetry and narrative, as well as the social issues portrayed in films and novels of the Campania region.

JAY PARINI is the Axinn Professor of English at Middlebury College in Vermont. He is a poet, novelist, biographer, and author of *The Last Station* and *Borges and Me*, among others. His biographical subjects include Robert Frost and Gore Vidal.